GRAND CREW

CU00823257

Published in 2022 by Hardie Grant Books an imprint of
Hardie Grant Publishing

Hardie Grant Books (Melbourne)
Ground Floor, Building 1, 658 Church Street
Richmond VIC 3121, Australia

Hardie Grant Books (London)
5th and 6th Floors,52–54 Southwark Street
London SE1 1UN, United Kingdom

www.hardiegrant.com.au

Hardie Grant acknowledges the Traditional Owners of the
country on which we work, the Wurundjeri people of the
Kulin nation and the Gadigal people of the Eora nation, and
recognises their continuing connection to the land, waters and
culture. We pay our respects to their Elders past and present.

A catalogue record of this book is available from the
National Library of Australia.
Grand Crew
ISBN 9781743798850

Publication commissioned by Courtney Nicholls
Publication managed by Hannah Louey
Edited by Alison Arnold
Cover design by Vaughan Mossop
Internal design by Megan Ellis
Printed in Australia by Ovato Printing

GRAND CREW

TOM CRAGO

Hardie Grant

BOOKS

Maybe I need to work as a barista to meet the right woman. I'm no more lonely than usual but I won't use dating apps and I continue to need an actual reason for talking to people, which means it's been a lean year in terms of non-friend intimacy.

Not so for this guy. He is handsome, unavoidably bearded, and has just made me a serviceable magic[1] at a pop-up café on Flinders Lane.

I'm here having arrived half an hour early for a nearby lunch meeting with a guy who has professed interest in a business I just started. And by 'just started' I mean I only got around to registering it last week, at the bellicose insistence of my mate Rob, a lawyer, who will also be at lunch but who will definitely not be early.

For now, I pull up a milk crate street-side, close enough to the coffee dude that I can watch the man work in some kind of comfort. I'm not prepared to go on record as saying that he's of those types who lives solely to woo women but, Jesus, he's doing a decent impersonation.

Barista is surely the perfect job for a career Lothario, in that you are never more than a pour-over away from your next prospective lover. Your target audience is three-fold: customers, obviously, but also your workmates, and others in the hospitality industry at large. And you never have to pretend to be anything other than who you are. You're that guy. The guy working in a café, seen by everyone. This is significant because, for one thing, no one will ever expect you to have any money. You will, however, have just enough to fulfil your seduction objectives, provided you're devoted solely to that task and not distracted by, say, studying, saving money, or travelling further than the most proximate surf beaches or music festivals. And because you're in the dating business rather than the relationship business,

---

1 A coffee, usually served in a cappuccino cup, made by pouring a double ristretto then filling the cup to three-quarters with hot milk.

it's not like you'll be expected to fund holidays or probably even buy birthday presents. Doubtless you can get by on very little.

I never really worked in hospitality when I was younger, and looking at this barista, now flirting unpardonably with his pink-haired co-worker, I'm thinking, yeah, looks fun but, nah, not me. Maybe a wine bar or a small restaurant. Possibly a bottle shop. I definitely would have had a tattoo.

I'm walking now, en route to the restaurant Tonka, which is the spot the lawyer guy has chosen for our lunch. Rob and I assume he's a lawyer, based on the use of certain words and phrases in the two emails he sent me to set up the meeting. 'This dude writes the same kind of vague shit you write,' I had said to Rob, who concurred.

I'm still early, but figure I can settle in and get a head start on the wine list, an expansive document with which I have more than a fleeting familiarity. Out of the laneway and in through the sliding door to the restaurant and I'll be a bastard's aunt if Rob himself isn't tucked into a corner table, deep in the stretched, skinny dining room, messing about on his phone and sipping, what in this light and from this aspect, appears to be extremely young riesling.

I go across and shake his hand. It's obvious that I'm surprised he's here on time, let alone early, and he says, 'I thought we were meeting at noon,' meaning that if he's five minutes into a glass of wine, he arrived a quarter of an hour after he believed he was supposed to.

'Twelve thirty,' I reply. 'You're early.'

I go to sit down in the chair across from him and he says, 'Not there, sit next to me.'

'Won't it look like we're ganging up on him?'

'That's the paying seat,' he replies. 'The one facing the wall. This guy knows lunch is on him – it's where he'll be expecting to sit.'

I'm about to interrogate that convention when Rob continues, 'I didn't think it'd be too radical a proposition to order a bottle of wine.'

'Well, we don't know this guy,' I say. 'He could be a Mormon.'

'Very few Mormon lawyers,' Rob says, and I know instantly and with absolute certainty that he has no idea whether that is true. 'Current vintage Grosset Polish Hill Riesling.' Rob is practically chewing on the stuff after a large pull from his glass. 'Basic business etiquette. He'd be offended if we hadn't ordered it.'

The concept of the 'business lunch' is mostly new to me and I'm not sure how far removed it is from what our little crew[2] calls a 'proper lunch' or, if the gathering in question happens to fall on a Friday, just 'lunch'.

'So, what, we get drunk at this thing?' I ask.

'Not like "proper lunch" drunk,' says Rob, 'but a bottle per man probably isn't vastly beyond the pale.'

That's good news for me as I've resolved to leave Rob in charge of everything, except maybe choosing the wine.

'Jude, you look like you're in a prog rock cover band. And not a good one.'

'I washed my hair. Anyway, you're the businessman – I'm just a guy who designed a kick-arse man-bag. I'm an artisan.'

'When did you stop buying clothes? Ten years ago? Longer?'

Rob may own suits that are not navy blue, but I have never seen them. He is wearing a tie, which is unusual for him, as evidenced by the bump in his breast pocket, where the loathsome thing usually resides. Big day for that tie. Ferried around for months, always fit for purpose, and now summoned into action for corporate dealings and fancy hybrid Indian-Italian food.

I've known Rob for a long time and he has always looked both exhausted and ready for his next exertion, provided it comes with booze. I presume he mostly is exhausted. Married to another lawyer,

---

2   We call our gang of eight the Grand Crew, although to keep it a bit pretentious around the edges, we pronounce it 'Grand Cru' as per the wine classification. Rob is a member.

a brace of daughters under three, and a vocational compulsion to measure his time in six-minute increments. When his hairline began its recession he developed this tic of forever touching his head. It's an inquisitive touch, a survey almost. I think his hair looks fine.

A new glass has appeared in front of me, and it's nice to be brought a different, 'more special' glass than the default variety, even when ordering a wine that barely troubles the middle of the list, at least in terms of price. By most measures, though, it is Australia's best riesling and utterly deserving of a better-than-average stem. And it's a sentimental wine for Rob and me, a wine we discovered young and have continued to drink.

We tried it first at the cellar door on the swim-through known as the Clare Valley Gourmet Weekend. It is incomprehensible that we would attend such an event today, but at twenty it was the best thing on earth. The formula is basically the same in every wine region: you drive from winery to winery – with some poor sober sod behind the wheel – tasting, buying a glass for ten bucks or so and occasionally a bottle, while eating from restaurants that have partnered with the wineries for the day.

We'd kick things off at Grosset with bacon and eggs and the 375ml incarnation of their botrytised dessert wine, inevitably slugged straight from the bottle. Quite what we were doing there at 9am, I am not certain. I can only assume we were so determined to make a full day of it, that leaving Adelaide not long after dawn made sense to our still-adolescent brains. Anyway, after the sticky we'd settle into a bottle of Polish Hill.

It was a novelty just being at the Grosset cellar door, as their tendency to sell out of wine mostly kept it closed. The weather was always bright, beckoning us to excess in wine country. And there's something about young rieslings, especially the Polish Hill, that smacks of potential. Whether it's the possibilities of the day, the year, or a lifetime, from the first sip you're optimistic, unpacking the acid and the non-fruit intensity and looking forward with a buoyancy that's childlike. Especially at that hour of the morning.

Rob has said before that it was like smelling fresh-cut grass at the school cricket team's first practice of the season. No one had yet told him that he'd be playing third grade, would be batting number eleven or would be allowed two overs maximum of his wayward left arm off spin. Those disappointments could be shelved until later, at least until the end of that first net session. For now, he could breathe in the grass and contemplate his future and the possibility of someday opening the batting for his country.

High-quality Australian riesling rarely disappoints. I have more of it in my cellar than any other white varietal, and I tend to drink it with at least ten years on the clock. At the Clare Gourmet Weekend you got to experience the genesis of that voyage. The local wine tasting, held simultaneously at the town hall, would always have a selection of unfinished rieslings that had been in the bottle for a matter of days and made from fruit picked only a few months earlier.

We'd check in there for an hour or so – usually right after visiting Grosset. At times the experience was almost comical. Bottles would explode every few minutes on account of the volatility of the still-fermenting juice, and the whole place smelled like an apple orchard. Sometimes you would swear that what you were drinking couldn't possibly be wine.

Another reason we liked Australian riesling was that we felt we could buy 'the very best', even with limited money. There were German and Austrian rieslings that were ten times the price, and they are the stock and extraction of all Australian riesling – its very lineage – but few of those wines were bone-dry and it seemed to us that Clare Valley riesling was an entirely different animal. The best of its breed. And then, as now, you could pick it up for half the price of a mediocre bottle of white burgundy.

Damn it, I'm daydreaming, trying to avoid my reflection in my glass, and five minutes or more have passed, time I could have spent preparing with Rob for this ridiculous meeting.

At that moment, a disarmingly tall, well-dressed gentleman of maybe Chinese appearance approaches our table and offers a sweeping smile, revealing a seemingly abnormal quantity of teeth, each crown suggestive of expensive dental work.

I'm mentally workshopping a scenario that would see me in a position to properly count those teeth, probably with some kind of professional tool, when the guy introduces himself.

'Terry Lee. Thanks for agreeing to meet.'

He and Rob shake hands and exchange business cards. Terry gives me a card too, and it looks like it's been printed that morning. It's absent of even the most perfunctory glance in the direction of a graphic designer, and bears only his name, the title 'Director' and in slightly larger type, 'Neufco Proprietary Limited'.

I don't have cards, but resolve to get some printed should I be called upon to attend more meetings of this nature.

'Bottle of Polish Hill on the go, I see?' says Terry as he sits down. 'Excellent.'

I could do business with this guy, I think, and from there things move pretty rapidly.

Just over two hours later

Terry has paid the bill and we're off into a typically fitful early spring afternoon in Melbourne. I'm pretty sure I just sold my business to the guy for a million bucks. The riesling had gone down like Gatorade on a hangover and Terry, having ordered kingfish for his entrée, was quick to reach for the list and search for something else *blanc* to accompany. He chose a Rockford Semillon, which elicited a raised eyebrow from Rob and a look of near astonishment from me.

This is not to say it isn't an excellent wine. More that it's not especially fashionable – and a borderline miracle that it's on the list at all. Semillon has been grown in the Barossa Valley since the 1850s and is the region's most important white grape, but it seems to disappear mostly down the gullets of those to the immediate west of the Victorian border. I'm wondering if Terry just saw the word 'Rockford' and, being a Melbourne lawyer, jumped instinctively to 'Basket Press Shiraz'. Doubtless, many of Sydney and Melbourne's corporate entertainers would be surprised to learn that Rockford makes more than one wine.

But it wasn't Terry's first dalliance with the varietal and he made the right noises about preferring the Barossa style to its thinner Hunter Valley cousin, even though he was a fan of Tyrrell's Vat 1 and had a bit of McWilliams Mount Pleasant Elizabeth in his cellar.

By the time we got through the semillon the deal was well and truly done, so Rob suggested a bottle of the 2002 Pol Roger Sir Winston Churchill to accompany dessert by way of celebration. We toasted our arrangement and Terry said he'd like to get the whole thing squared away that very afternoon and might we revert to Rob's office for some postprandial contracting.

So, we're on our way towards Collins Street, our collective gait unmistakably betraying a three-bottle lunch. Rob's clutching the empty, souvenired Winston Churchill bottle and yapping away to Terry, and I'm wondering what the fuck just happened.

The guy had said that his company had seen the bag I designed, loved it, and wanted to own the rights to manufacture it themselves. And by 'own', for the avoidance of any doubt, he meant utterly own every aspect of the thing, from its design through to the business itself, through to any and all rights associated with the product. This was, he said, a 'lock stock' offer and, on that basis, what was my price?

At that moment, roughly two-thirds of the way through the bottle of Polish Hill and having just placed our luncheon order with a waitress, Hannah – whose name I had solicited, maybe inspired by coffee dude earlier in the day – Rob asked Terry if we might have a moment to discuss his proposition.

'By all means,' said Terry, who excused himself, first to the bathroom and then back through the restaurant and to an unoccupied table by the entrance.

'Just to be clear,' Rob asked once Terry was out of earshot, 'we're still talking about that bag you designed? The one Bethany sewed the prototype for?'

'That's my only business, Robbie.'

'How many of them have you sold?'

I had sold, at that precise moment in time, exactly twelve of my man-bags. The whole thing (insofar as you could describe a one-week-old company with no bank account, no means of manufacturing, no branding or media presence and no working capital as a 'whole thing') had stemmed from a long-held frustration with various man-bags I had owned over the years. One day I sketched what I thought to be a superior solution, bought a half hide of leather, and asked Bethany if she'd mind knocking up a sample.

It turned out pretty well, so I tweaked the design and found an old Italian dude in Preston who made me twenty of them, twelve of which had sold over the course of the last six weeks in a store on Little Bourke Street, just a few hundred metres from Tonka.

'I've sold most of them,' I replied eventually.

'And what's the point of it again?'

'A discussion for another time perhaps, mate?'[1]

Rob was gnawing on his left-hand index finger while aggressively swirling his wine and staring at the table. I had never seen him properly think before. If this was what he was called upon to do each day for a living then no wonder he always looked exhausted and was so serious about his drinking.

'What does this guy think he's actually buying?'

'You did make me register the design.'

At that moment a mess of previously random particles in Rob's brain rushed together to form a single dollar-shaped composite.

'This guy's no idiot,' Rob said. 'He's obviously acting for some other company, probably a fashion house. They like the bag and feel they can't just rip it off because you registered the drawings.'[2]

'Isn't the name of the business on his card?' I said, as Rob tapped away at his phone.

'The company name is a kind of lawyer in-joke.[3] They're taking the piss.' He showed me his phone. 'And check it out. It was only established yesterday. I mean, you could be selling this to anyone, we have no idea.'

---

1   My man bag is designed to house the various items one may need to call into service during any given outing. For me, these include: mobile phone, sunglasses (with case), wallet, headphones, small notepad, pen, various leads and jacks for music, a USB drive, and (soon) a business card holder with cards.

2   See Appendix 1.

3   Neufco resembling 'New Co', which is a default name given to companies before anyone has gotten around to naming them properly.

'Google Terry then.'

'Just did. He's legit. Been around the traps at firms in Sydney.'

'But if that Neufco company has the cash, and they sign the contract, then –'

'The cash is one thing. They could bring this new company in as a subsidiary to a tax consolidated group, whisk away your asset to the head company, shut down the entity we've contracted with, and then a step or so later the whole thing is offshore.'

I was looking at Rob glassy-eyed, partly confused, but more with an expression well known among my close friends which, translated, means something like, 'And I should give a shit, why?'

Rob got it and moved on. 'So what do you reckon it's worth?' he asked.

'I dunno, twenty grand?'

'Would you sell it for that?'

'Probably not. I'm having fun with it, people like it.'

'So what then? Fifty? Eighty?'

'That's more than I make in a year. Eighty in a heartbeat.'

Rob stopped playing with his wine for long enough to give me that look I often get when people learn my income then try to figure out how I'm always drinking nice wine and eating at good restaurants.

'How do you even –'

'How the fuck do you?'

'Alright,' he said. 'Let's see how we go. Let me handle the negotiation.'

Terry ambled back – Jesus, the size of the man – sat down and went straight for his glass.

'So' – eyeing us up and down, having drained the last of his riesling – 'are you willing to sell?'

'Look, it's a brand new business for Jude,' Rob began. 'He's excited about it. Sees a lot of potential –'

'Guys.' Terry put down his glass. 'Let me make this exceptionally easy. If we do it my way, under the conditions I've outlined, I can offer you an even million.'

Then Hannah brought over the entrées, Terry ordered the semillon and Rob and I sat in numbed silence until fresh glasses were brought and Terry nodded his acquiescence to the wine. Over the course of his spanner crab Rob had asked a few questions, to look the part I guess, and Terry had responded graciously. Shortly after the plates were cleared, Rob folded his arms and looked across to me and said, 'Jude, I think you'd better shake the man's hand. He just bought your business.'

It was mostly small talk from there, save for Terry's insistence that we sign the paperwork that afternoon, and could it possibly be at Rob's office rather than his? Not long after, I was drinking champagne and thinking about catering options for my victory party.

And now we're sidling through the grand marble modernist tomb that serves as the lobby of 101 Collins Street, Melbourne, up the elevator and past the reception area of the law firm where Rob was recently made partner. Terry has a draft contract on a thumb drive in his suit pocket, which he and Rob set about reviewing on Rob's laptop. I sit opposite in what I'm pretty sure is a Featherston B210H Contour chair, or possibly a fiendish knock-off, but either way certainly not standard law-firm issue.

'It's a cute little document,' says Rob, after five or so minutes of sedulous review.

'I hope it mostly gets us there,' Terry replies.

'Look, I think it does,' and then, 'Just two items from our perspective; interrelated.'

'You're referring to the escrow and the restraint.'

'Both seem excessive given what you're buying.'

'Guys, let me know if I can jump in anywhere,' I say in a tone so half-arsed that Rob takes pity and invites me to the grown-ups' table.

'Come around and take a look, Jude. Don't get me wrong – the agreement's great, I'm a fan. But they're saying you don't get the money for a year, and during that time you can't work in the fashion or accessories industries, can't really make or manufacture anything in the broader textile space… I mean, you'll barely be able to get a suit fitted without risk of breaching this clause.'

'I can take a year off,' I say, maybe a little too willingly.

'What do you do for a crust, Jude?' Terry asks, 'Other than this.'

'I sing. Choruses mostly.'

'They have different people for the verses?'

'Sorry. Choirs. And in the chorus for musicals and opera.'

'Always had a soft spot for Rodgers and Hammerstein myself.'

'I toured *South Pacific* a few years ago. Extra sailor number four.'

'Gents, back to the agreement. Our greater concern is the stipulation that the proceeds of the sale are held in trust for twelve months,' Rob, steering the ship back on course.

'I understand where you're coming from,' says Terry, 'but consider our perspective. Naturally our plan is to bring your product to market ourselves. We need some clear air in order to do that. We can't have you working on something similar, or really anywhere near it. We're paying a heavy premium to put you on a desert island for a year. And when you come back you get your money.'

'What about six months?' Rob says.

'I'm afraid our proposal is twelve.'

'How about nine?' I say.

'If only negotiations were that simple.'

This elicits a smile from Rob. 'How about a coin toss?' he says.

'I'd be more amenable to that,' Terry says.

'What about a blind tasting?' I say, and not just because I'm getting thirsty.

'Hmmmm,' from Terry and Rob.

'You'd have a bottle in here somewhere, Rob?'

'If the deal point is twelve months versus six, then I need favourable terms in the tasting,' Terry says, not unreasonably.

'Maybe you just need to correctly identify the varietal?' I suggest.

Rob is clearly straining under the burden of having to recall, half-drunk, what wine he might have stashed in the drawers and filing cabinets of his office, and whether any of them might serve to deceive a man who, at the very least, knows his way around Australian semillon.

'Varietal and country,' says Rob eventually.

'Fine. But only if we're talking a straight varietal. No blends.'

'Champagne and sauternes to one side, I only have one bottle in my office at present,' Rob says, and I realise we are actually doing this. 'Terry, you're happy to settle matters in this way?'

Terry nods and Rob calls in his secretary and takes her over to a set of drawers beneath the window and whispers something to her, and she whisks a well-covered bottle straight back out and the whole thing happens with such speed and precision that I wonder if Terry is asking himself if this a ruse we've planned all along and if he's about to come up against a bottle of room-temperature Lebanese obaideh.

Rob's secretary returns a minute later with three ISO XL5 wine-tasting glasses, the type that should be retired from receptacle duties of any kind on the grounds of their extreme shitness, each half-full of red wine. Terry picks his up and pours the contents into his now empty water tumbler, in a move that I rate extremely highly and that brings to mind the story of Olivier Krug drinking his own cuvée out of a butcher glass[4] in the front bar of the Exeter Hotel in Adelaide several years prior.

I take a sniff at my own juice and my heart's smacking away at my ribs like I've just flopped the absolute nuts[5] in a poker game,

---

4   A 200ml glass used for beer, and something of a South Australian oddity.
5   The strongest possible hand in a given situation in poker.

and then I sink a little because it seems very obvious to me that this wine is cabernet sauvignon.

'This is a Bowen Estate Cab,' says Terry, less than a sip later.

Rob's quiet in that way lawyers are when they're worried or know they're wrong about something, and it's clear Terry has just handed us our arses.

'That's impressive,' Rob says, eventually.

'It's an old friend.' Terry holds his glass at eye-level. 'It's the wine we were drinking when my parents told me they were breaking up.'

'Wow,' I say.

'Dinner at home. I was nineteen. A huge relief to hear them say it.'

'And you can taste that still?' asks Rob.

'I'll never forget it. Hints of it blow off in those first moments of aeration, but it's still there. Albeit on its way to something different.'

We all take a mouthful.

'In fact, I was so determined to maintain my bond with this wine that I put it on the list at Tetsuya's.'[6]

Terry sanctions himself about ten vertical degrees of grin, although only for the left side of his face.

'Right,' says Rob, 'so…'

'Sommelier there for two years. While I was at law school.'

'I was there last week,' says Rob, to no one. And then we're quiet again, staring at the wine.

'Excellent.' Terry returns his glass to Rob's desk. 'Twelve months on the escrow and restraint. Jude, we'll pay the funds into trust and I have no doubt you'll be walking out of a bank a year from today a healthily remunerated man.'

'I can live with that.'

---

6   Beloved and classic restaurant in Sydney.

'My kind of wine options game,' says Rob, gathering himself, 'where you still get a million dollars if you lose.'

And now Terry's smile spreads freely across his face, revealing maybe seventy per cent of that magnificent holding of teeth.

'Dollars? I'm so sorry – I should been clearer. Our offer is in euros.'

Rob exhales, reaches for his phone and punches some numbers into his currency converter app, then hands it to me showing an amount in Australian dollars that is significantly higher than the figure that already got me pregnant.

After that, I sign the agreement, we finish off the Bowen and I'm back on Collins Street, dazed, standing for a moment in the flight path of a plane tree's swirling pollen, watching bankers and shop assistants rush to their cars to get ahead of traffic bound for Caulfield or Ringwood, and I think maybe I'll call my friend and see if she wants to come and drink champagne with me at the Supper Club.

That evening

It doesn't taste Australian. But I'm drunk on Krug and what's in my glass is cold and sparkling and that feels like enough.

'I gotta take a slash,' I say to Bethany, and she raises an eyebrow like she can't believe I haven't been already. We are two bottles deep, and she knows I was here at least an hour before cajoling her into joining me to celebrate my outrageous success.

I don't even need to go, just feel like I could do with a moment with a mirror and my drunkenness to sense-check whether I should leave or, at the very least, eat something.

The mirror offers little by way of encouragement. 'You should go home,' I tell it, and then decide that since I'm in the bathroom anyway I may as well urinate and, Jesus, sign of my age and inebriation, I take the cubicle option and sit down and luxuriate over what must be the longest and most satisfying piss undertaken by anyone that day, at least in this part of Melbourne.

'How'd you go?' asks Bethany as I pour myself back into my chair.

'I made it,' I say. 'Mostly because of you. When did all these people get here?'

Bethany has refilled the flutes, which sit shining on the table like a couple of gold coins in a fountain. Tantalising.

'Do you ever take coins from fountains?' I ask her.

'I don't go out of my way, but if I come across one – sure.'

'How many coins would you have swiped, over the years?'

'Hundreds. Easily.'

I'm staring at one of the flutes, more than staring – practically gaping like I'm hypnotised, but in an oddly mindful way, isolating individual bubbles and tracking their passage from the base of the glass up into space. Connecting with the bead somehow, occupying its checked cosmos, its fleeting plane of immanence.

I know this room so well I could probably traverse it blindfolded, relying only on vibrations. We have the best seats: two oversized armchairs adjacent to a red sofa that backs up against my favourite window in the city. It is tempting to choose a spot right in front of it, but Bethany and I prefer to watch everyone else jostling for the view out of its grand arches.

All wood and leather, this place feels of another era, and I think maybe I'll impress Bethany with my bit about how champagne is the secret to time travel. Wondering what it must have been like to be in a speakeasy in Chicago in the 1920s or at the Salon in Paris in the 1860s? Pour yourself a glass of high-quality fizz and close your eyes.

I like to travel back to cabaret halls with big bands and chorus girls. America between the world wars. The kinds of places where you dressed up and took a date and sat in a booth beside the stage or at a table right in front and started with a cocktail like a Sazerac or a Manhattan and, after that, called the jacketed waiter over to order a bottle of champagne, which he'd bring in a silver bucket with Josephine-style glasses, ice-cold. And with some ceremony he'd open it, have you try it, and then pour all the way to the rim and… that first sip, with the music, the dancers, your date (herself the most beautiful woman in the room). You can imagine closing your eyes then, like now, and drinking. Drinking.

'Ever notice how people gush bullshit about champagne way more than any other wine?' Bethany asks.

'That's because it's romantic.'

'I think riesling is romantic. I think grenache is romantic.'

We don't even know for sure this is champagne, as our bottle is concealed by foil – a swine act attributable to our smart-arse friend Hayden, who is the sommelier.

I am presently so slumped in this chair that my own arse is entirely off the seat cushion, my head pressed against the middle of the chair, and the mere act of swallowing is more challenging than it needs to be.

I'm wearing this jacket for the first time since our friend Heidi's husband insisted their newborn be subjected to baptism. I know this because the order of service is still in the pocket and, now that I think of it, there was Krug that day too. Just one bottle, shared by our close crew of friends while the rest of the throng drank King Valley prosecco – not that there's anything at all wrong with that.

Bethany's job demands corporate attire, but she circumvents the worst of that by coaxing her long limbs into suits modified from menswear and sewn by her own hand.

She writes investor relations copy for a bank but is crafty as fuck, her craftiness precipitating my improbable windfall. Hence tonight's Krug. Hence tonight.

Whenever I describe Bethany to someone who has not met her, say to the squash court attendant when I am first to arrive for our game, I'll usually say she has fair hair and looks a bit like a newborn giraffe. That description overstates her number of legs while understating the grace with which she is possessed, at least while sitting down.

Another thing about Bethany is that she is partial to pairing men with wine. Not in a 'lining them up and tasting them' kind of way, but she's been known to come home of an evening, have a glass or two of something while getting changed, just to get a feel for it, then trot out to a bar or club to find a guy to match.

I asked her once whether her wine selection might subconsciously be informed by the kind of guy she'd already decided she wanted. I mean, if you get home and reach for a balls-out bottle of nebbiolo it surely speaks a little to the type of night you have in mind?

It's nuanced, though, she says. 'Big' doesn't always translate to 'big' and sometimes it's a matter of a note on the mid-palate, or something curious structurally, and that element alone will drive the pursuit.

And besides, it is about matching. You don't necessarily want a guy 'the same' as the wine, you want someone who will complement it, who'll heighten the experience overall and make the whole exercise richer and more pleasurable. It's like pairing wine with food, only more total, more carnal. Bethany found that men could have a similarly intoxicating headiness as wine, provided she chose carefully.

A psychology student at some party once told her that, enneagramatically speaking, her personality type was 'glutton' and that a lot of her life choices were informed by a reflex fear of deprivation of any kind. They didn't sleep together, but she did tie him up for several hours, firmly beating him with a rolled-up issue of *Wine Spectator*. He was a more than willing participant, having introduced the notion of deprivation in the first place.[1]

When they get into the whole wine and men thing with Bethany, most guys ask, 'So what's my wine, Bethany? Come smell me and tell me my match.' This misses the point, but it's one of those dull, obvious enquiries, so sodden in well-intentioned social lubricant that Bethany tends to smile and offer a stock response from a mental file she maintains titled 'stock responses', which usually involves references to pinot grigio and a 'good time not a long time'.

My eyes must be rolling back into my head at this point because she reaches over and puts a hand on my leg and says, 'You okay?' and I think, fuck it, now's as good a time as any, so I say, 'This whole wine matching thing...'

---

1   The night was notable for the fact that not a single drop of wine had passed Bethany's lips. It felt more like a whisky kind of night, and there's no point fighting that. She told me later that she did share a half-bottle of De Bortoli Noble One Botrytis Semillon with him as part of the 'aftercare' component of the encounter.

'Don't be boring, Jude.'

'It's my birthday – surely that gives me some latitude?'

'It's nowhere near your birthday.'

She's right, but the misdirection and maybe the fact that I look ashen elicits a sympathetic grin and she takes my wrist, gently, and I'm thinking, that's nice, then I realise she's just stopping me from reaching for my glass.

I sit back in my chair and say something about how the patina of the leather reminds me of a baseball mitt I had as a kid, but how mitt leather always looks better than chair leather, and that's probably because mitts spend a lot of time outside in the sunshine, where they can really get their patina on.

'It's okay, Jude, we can talk about it. I just don't want weirdness with you, I won't have it. I have enough shit going on at work and with my parents. With life in general. I need us like we are now.'

'Oh God, absolutely…'

I'm glad she's saying it, because I'm an idiot and I'd probably try a clumsy move at some point, even though I know it would likely rankle.

'What's happening at work?'

'My boss is making me write a list of things I need to work on. Can't even write the list himself. Then he's going to set pay increases for each item. Like I'm a fucking shopping list, or a restaurant menu.'

'That's actually quite funny…'

'It's killing me. I should just quit, but I'm paralysed. I have bills. I have wine orders.'

'Can we drink this?' I ask, jumping on the wine segue and pointing at my glass.

'Not yet. I'll tell you when.'

I go back to watching the bubbles.

'You want to know your wine,' she says, 'the wine I'd match with you?'

'Definitely curious.'

'You know I don't do this just to feel superior, right?'

'I know it's not a gimmick. But why do you do it?'

She frowns slightly, in a way I find desperately cute even on a best friend, then says, 'Wine's just always been about sex for me.'

'I felt that when I met you.'

'What, when I was fourteen?'

'I don't count that whole period. You were like a different species to me then. I'm talking about your twenties.'

'It was before that. I was seventeen and I hadn't drunk at all, like not even a drop. Then the guy I lost my virginity with was from a wine family, and my first glass was with him.'

'All at the same time?'

'The wine came first, third date maybe, but I was so fixated on sex by then that I was going crazy. I just wanted to do it – not to get it over with or because most of my friends had, but because I wanted to move to that next stage of my life where I was a person who did that, who could do that if she wanted to. Who knew how to do it.'

'And you were into the guy?' I ask, hating myself for the squat shot of jealousy that follows.

'I really was. He was older, seemed much older, and he was shy but he'd had girlfriends and he'd been with girls before. Different to the deadshit guys I was going to school with.'

'Where did it happen, your first sip?'

'At Joe's,' she says, referring to a restaurant, long since closed, on Rundle Street in the middle of Adelaide, which was run by a guy we kind of knew and where another friend of ours would work much later as a waiter. The restaurant was not called Joe's – Joe was the guy who ran it – but after trying for a few seconds to recall its actual name I realise I can't, and I know Bethany is thinking the same thing and can't either.

'We sat down' – nostalgic now, rare for her – 'and it's not for dinner or anything, it's four thirty on a Friday, and he says, "What can I get you to drink?" and I say, "A glass of wine, please."'

'Smooth.'

'I'd pictured myself in that situation a thousand times. I'm out with a boy and he offers me a drink, and I look at him and smile, and I say, "A glass of wine, please."'

'And the line came out okay?'

'Yeah' – looking at me like I'm an idiot – 'I'd been rehearsing it for more than a year. It was perfect. Then he says, "Red or white?"'

'And you wonder what etiquette might dictate?' Despite her unconventional table manners, occasional slurred speech, and, well, frequent nudity and sporadic unsolicited karaoke, Bethany is actually (in a very Adelaide sense) rather concerned with social graces.

'There's two things here,' she says. 'Firstly, all of my brain is occupied by sex. Sitting here now it seems far-fetched, but I remember at the time making a grandiose pledge to myself that I'd never forget that feeling. That I'd always recognise it as valid.'

'Well, same.'

'Jude, the baseline arousal level of your average post-pubescent teenage girl striving to become sexually active is way off any kind of chart of your imagining. You think you were a horny little bastard as a kid? I was fanatical.'

'I had no idea,' I say, wishing I'd had some idea. Not that I properly knew Bethany until she was at university, but I did know girls and I figured they were mostly into horses and studying.

'I see these girls today, walking around the city, waiting for trams, tapping on their phones, and I know exactly the brand of smut-laced fog that's clouding their brains.'

'I was never told.'

'Boys that age are hopeless. Almost literally useless. And Barratt was twenty, which now of course seems infantile, but was a big deal back then. He was at uni, lived away from home, even had a car...'

'You mentioned two things...'

'I knew his family owned a winery but, like I say, I knew nothing about wine. Couldn't have named a single varietal.'

'You knew champagne?' I look at my glass, outcast on the table.

'I knew champagne had bubbles.'

I'm guessing she chooses white at this point, maybe because it comes first in the stock vinous syntax or because it seems more feminine, but Bethany says she asked for red.

'And he smiled – I would say approvingly. He didn't say anything, just went to the bar. Came back with a bottle and two good stems. Proper glasses. So many times since I've drunk good wine out of shit glasses and thought back to that day and how that guy, that restaurant, gifted me my first wine experience out of crystal Riedels, and how everyone deserves that for their first time.'

'And the wine?'

'Thicker than I was expecting. Viscous and ripe.'

'Shiraz, maybe? What did it smell like?'

'It smelled like sex – that's what I'm saying. It smelled like everything I wanted, and it was right there in a glass in front of me.'

'Did you tell him it was your first time?' I'm in that room myself now, with those stems, and the quality of the light late in the afternoon. Even acoustically – the sound the glasses made when you touched them accidently with the bottle while pouring, and the chink and reverberation of each toast.

'He didn't need to know.'

'Do you remember your first sip?'

'Yes.' She stops. Around us at the Supper Club people stare out the window, lost in the view and in their glasses, and we are nowhere near them. 'It was a call to action for the first gulp. I sipped, then honestly I lost control of the muscles between my brain and my fingers and I went straight back in.'

'Familiar.' My head's tilted and I can't stop grinning, and Beth's making the exact same face. 'My face exploded. Everything tingled. It went down my throat and that felt lush, but at the same time it went up. Up into my brain and suddenly everything was about what was in the glass. At that point I'm gulping back giggles and I think, Bethany, just put the glass down, at least do that. Next I tell myself to stop smiling, but that never works, and Barratt laughs too, and I start to get my shit together. But, Jude, you have to believe me – I'm being drawn into that glass. I'm looking at it and it's calling me, and I have to restrain myself from reaching out and gorging myself.'

'God, I've been there…' I'm interrupting, and not even because I need attention. 'Sorry to hijack, but –'

She nods.

'A housewarming,' I begin. 'Guy from my school.'

'I know you didn't lose your virginity with a guy.'

'This is a wine story. We're in our early twenties and he's actually bought this place, which is a big deal because none of us had any money, and I come early to the party and he has a bottle of Grange decanted and sitting on the sideboard.'

'Yikes.'

'Yep. Grandmother had died. He gets a house and some Grange. I eye it up right away, never tried it before, and there are only a few of us there, and my mate says, "How about a glass of Grange?" Actually asks the question.'

'Definition of rhetorical.'

'Pours me a generous glass, and we toast the new house…'

'His grandma too maybe?'

'I try the wine.'

'Older Grange, or a baby?'

'Old. 1972, I think. First taste was magical, and I have that "I'm drinking Grange for the first time" moment, but my point is that right after that sip, my friend says, "Let me take you on a tour." And for reasons unknown I put my glass down on the table before trotting off after him.'

'Schoolboy error,' says Bethany, who's been known to take drinks into toilet cubicles.

'The tour takes less than five minutes, but that glass of wine screamed at me the whole time. Maybe not screamed. Summoned. The lure was biological.'

'And people think drinking stops after you've swallowed.' Bethany smirks.

'People are idiots. Could you have been drinking Grange as well? I mean, that would be something.'

'You know, I don't remember.'

When I'm drunk and people tell stories I teleport from place to place, and now I feel like I've just arrived back at the Supper Club after an afternoon at Joe's. It's like a shelter up here. Warm and safe and full of wine and Bethany.

I reach for my glass, thinking that surely now we can drink. This time Bethany sits up, takes her glass and says, 'Push over.' No problem there, at least not with the sentiment, and I slide over so I'm occupying maybe two-thirds of the available armchair real estate, which pound for pound is an equitable enough division between us.

She sits down in a disarmingly wonderful way, mostly beside me, but with her entire right leg and part of her waist pressed against me. I bring my arm around her shoulder, our heads nearly touching. We're holding the champagne flutes and I'm trying to think of something witty to contribute when she says, 'Close your eyes,' which I do.

She's silent, and I want to open my eyes because I'm sure she's looking at me, but I do what I'm told and I feel a kind of serenity that I can't ascribe entirely to inebriation.

'Take a mouthful,' she says. 'As much as you want.'

Finally. With my eyes still closed, I find the rim of the flute and pour a rude quantity of juice over my tongue. I'm halfway through swallowing when I feel Bethany's lips against mine. I can taste the wine on her. She's not kissing me so much as letting me savour her. We come together with the wine still popping and fizzing, making its way down.

I open my eyes as she pulls away, her head at an angle, half-smiling as she regards me. I'm beaming like a dope and swaying slightly, tracking the reflection of a ceiling light across our glass-topped table.

Sometimes, a kiss like that can be passed off the next day as a goodbye embrace gone slightly awry on account of drunkenness and incidental follow-through. That's a harder sell when you're both single. And you're not saying goodbye.

But surely not. Surely it's just another one between friends?

'Talk to me,' she says, still sitting more or less on my lap. 'What did that taste like?'

'I don't think *taste* gets us there.'

'How did it feel?'

'Like celebration. And relief.'

'Keep going.'

'The wine reminds me of a bottle I had when I was eighteen.'

'Yes…'

'It lived on a bookshelf at home and my parents always said it was mine, even when I was little. "Look at Jude, trying to get his bottle." That kind of thing. Then I was chosen to go to America and sing in this ensemble.'

'I remember.'

'It was a big deal, totally out of the blue and my first trip overseas. I got the news and straight away grabbed the bottle and put it on ice. My parents came home from work and I popped the cork right as they walked in. You know, "Surprise!"'

'They were proud?'

'They were surprised, shocked even. I figured it was because they were worried about how much the trip would cost. I find out later, years later, that my uncle had brought that wine to the wake after my brother died.'

'Fuck.'

'I was four years old; I don't remember any of it. But when Mum told me about the wine, she said it had been awkward, surreal even – like who brings champagne to a funeral?'

'I'm sorry, Jude.'

'She and Dad decided that actually it was meant for me when I was ready, but really I think it reminded them of Kai. They'd got rid of his stuff. All those memories. I had to ask if I even wanted to see old photos.'

'What happened after you drank the wine?'

'They put the empty bottle out with the recycling. And then later on they put a picture of the two of us playing onto that spot on the bookshelf.'

'They let go of something.'

'It felt like they found something. I was ecstatic, sharing that wine with them. It tasted like someone telling me I was good at this thing I'd been trying so hard to be good at.'

'Does all champagne taste like that?'

'No.'

Bethany returns to her chair, then starts to pull away the foil from around the bottle.

'Guesses?' Her eyebrows are raised.

'No idea.' I exhale. 'It's good, though. Maybe Ruinart?' But the bottle is the wrong shape and I doubt even Hayden would bother double-decanting champagne.

She removes the foil.

'Well, I'll be fucked!' I say. 'It is Australian.'

It is, in fact, a recent vintage blanc de blancs from Domaine Chandon in the Yarra Valley.

Hayden comes over to survey the scene and my first reaction is to think, damn, he probably saw that kiss. I doubt he'd care, or even be surprised, but anxiety sometimes make me snarl and I'm nervous from Bethany's touch.

'Be nice to Hayden,' she says, still soft from my story.

'Hayden owes me a case of pinot noir,' I say, in an attempt at deflection.

This is true, and the consequence of a bet on the composition of the blend in a certain Super Tuscan.[2] Hayden acknowledges he lost but, for reasons unknown, is yet to make good.

'Actually, you should sort out that out,' Bethany says to Hayden, thank you very much.

I'd told Hayden about selling my bag design somewhere in between his shift commencing and the arrival of the first bottle of Krug. He said he'd only heard about the bag in passing, and that he thought Bethany had come up with the idea.

'How's the wine?' he asks, filling our glasses and offering his best impression of a man doing his job.

'Your handiwork, I presume?'

'I wrapped it.' A nod at Bethany. 'She chose it.'

---

2   Castello di Romitorio, Romito di Romitorio Sant'Antimo Rosso 2004: sixty per cent sangiovese, twenty per cent cabernet sauvignon and twenty per cent canaiolo nero. How we ended up wagering for pinot I don't recall.

'But the bottle was on the table before I even asked you about my wine match?!'

'Interpret that any way you want,' Bethany says.

Damn it, I hate being predictable. I'd almost rather be rude.

'I was just trying to be cute.'

'You're too old for cute,' says Beth. 'Try for distinguished. Don't fret about being predictable either – you're not. I can join your dots, though. I know where you come from.'

'I come from Adelaide.'

'I mean the way you're put together. Structurally. Part of you is from a different time, ancient almost. The rest of you reimagines and rearranges that imprint, tries to put a modern filter on it. And in the end it sparkles.'

'What were you saying about champagne and bullshit?'

'This isn't champagne.'

I still have a half-full glass of the blanc de blancs, which I drain while standing up.

'Fuck this, Bethany. Let's go downstairs for dinner.'

Two weeks later

Rob sends back corked wines at restaurants almost as a matter of sport, but I'm more cautious, having been caught out a couple of times with bottles that appeared faulty at first blush but were actually displaying other unsavoury notes that soon blew off. Our friend Antoine, who is meeting me in Paris and whose palate and overall wine knowledge are incalculably more impressive than that of the rest of us, sometimes doesn't send back corked wine at all, believing that taint can contribute to the narrative of the wine in a manner that, if not always entirely pleasant, is at least worthy and sincere.[1]

I tend to let a suspect wine sit in the glass for a minute or two, swirling it like a matinee nutcase, before awkwardly conferring with the sommelier. That is unless it smells just utterly like dank cardboard, which is precisely how this Chartron et Trébuchet Meursault has presented, albeit at 40,000 feet and as a kind of luxe chaser to the gin and tonic I drained immediately after departure.

Watching the flight attendant mix that drink brought into shocking focus the obsceneness of the G&Ts I make for myself. Hers was a double, with Tanqueray No. 10 and fresh lime, but in a tiny tumbler with only a few cubes of ice. Serviceable, but disconsolately small. At home I like to take a Riedel H2O Highball Glass, fill it a quarter full with ice, pour in a stubby bottle of tonic water, rub a wedge of lime around the rim of the glass and then throw that in along with an additional wedge, before filling the vessel

---

1   Antoine has also pointed out 'corked people' at restaurants and wineries, namely, actual human individuals who have come into recent contact with the chemical compound TCA and who as a consequence emit faint traces of its aroma. He treats them no differently to non-corked people.

near-as-dammit to the brim with gin. Given the capacity of those glasses is more than 650 ml, you find yourself quickly in the realm of a fairly serious drink.

Anyway, the aeroplane version went down before I'd even finished my pretzels and I'm here now with the chardonnay and an attendant who, based on her appearance and the region of origin of this airline, may well have never tried alcohol, let alone come up against a corked bottle of white burgundy.

'I might have to ask you to open another bottle of this,' I say, attempting a gently disappointed expression.

'Ah. Was it not cold enough?' comes the unanticipated reply.

'No, no, just a little problem with the cork.'

I wonder if we're going to have to navigate the 'corked wine' minefield at large and if this might be what my friends with children call a 'teachable moment'. But I'm not a parent, the attendant knows what she's doing, and moments later she returns from the galley with news that the problem bottle is sadly the last aboard. There's a different chardonnay, though, not on the list, which she has arranged to be brought to the bar where she herself is about to begin a shift and, if I'd care to follow, she'll make a point of pouring me a glass as her first order of business.

I travel pretty regularly but this is the first time I've ever turned left upon entering a plane. And I'm not sure quite when it happened, but the concept of an onboard bar rates as a welcome and significant milestone in the history of aviation.

My bag bonanza was massive and this trip to Europe is both a reward and a chance to clear my head, so it seemed reasonable to fly business class. Even if that meant hastily applying for a new credit card with enough of a limit to fund, for a few months, a lifestyle to which I am entirely not accustomed. And now aeroplanes have bars and so off I amble, down the aisle and past a rank of mostly middle-aged men who all look kind of the same, and who are all drinking thick red wine, wearing headphones and gaping at action films that I guess they're not allowed to watch at home.

The bar itself manages to look both old-fashioned and like something out of *Star Trek: The Next Generation*, which is a mean achievement in interior design and presumably exactly what they were aiming for. Two dozen red roses sit in faux-gold vases, along with a couple of high-grade ice buckets against the backdrop of a fully stocked bar. There are seats for fifteen, but it's just me and Nadya, who it turns out is actually from Bulgaria and does rather enjoy a drink despite living in a sort of compound where no alcohol is allowed, presumably at the behest of the airline.

I ask to look at the wine list, even though she's already pouring me a glass of Grand Cru chablis from a domain I am not familiar with from the Vaudésir climat, and I'm surprised to see a handful of Australian options, including the Clonakilla Shiraz Viognier, which is a hell of a wine and one, I would wager, that would stand up well in these conditions.

Wine does taste different in aeroplanes, mostly because altitude dulls our senses. The dry air numbs our tastebuds and dries out our noses, meaning we miss notes and flavours we would experience when drinking the same wine on land. Acid and tannin stand out impudently, and I'm convinced the noise and pressure have an impact as well.[2]

And yet the experience of drinking wine in the sky is so often immensely pleasing. Why? In my case, I suspect it's related to three other aeroplane-specific phenomena:

1. I cry watching movies, even when they're not all that sentimental.

---

2   We experience wine above our palate as well as below, and when our inner ears are stressed or disorientated I reckon our brains process the sensation differently.

2. I tend to be more creative and have better ideas.
3. I'm even more inclined than usual to get drunk.

'How's the chablis?' asks Nadya.

'Delightful.' Which it is. 'Have you tried it?'

'We try them in training sometimes, but I don't know this one.'

It's still just me and her at the bar, and she's setting up a selection of snacks – olives and roasted almonds – and I'm wondering what the etiquette is for chatting up stewardesses in business class. A friend of Heidi's worked as an international hostie for a few years and she was all about meeting dudes on planes, so I'm conscious of there being something of a precedent. I'm not sure where Nadya's at, though, and I'm determined to avoid the usual pitfalls of this kind of engagement: asking the same questions that everyone asks, being boring, being a dick, or morphing into a pseudo-bodyguard, charged in my own mind with protecting her from sleazy passengers, of which I suspect there are many.

Right on cue three guys saunter in, presumably having finished their Hollywood explosion-fests, looking pretty jagged already from all that Clonakilla, and it's clear from the way they carry themselves that they're frequent travellers and have possibly even met Nadya before at one aeroplane bar or another.

Nadya ignores them. She offers me a faintly intimate roll of the eyes and then finishes skewering the olives. The guys are doing the whole 'Don't you remember us?' and 'Is this guy bothering you?' routine, falling into the pit of every trap I'd already contemplated in less than five seconds.

She is not amused, but hey, she's got a job to do so she gets them their cognacs and offers them snacks, setting them up over the other side of the bar as far away as possible from me. I'm hoping she'll return, and she does. She refills my glass and seems keen for a chat.

'My friends always say that it's easy to tell when I don't like someone,' I begin, ambitiously, 'because my face gives the game away.'

She laughs. 'My God, I'm supposed to be a professional' – with another winsome eye roll – 'you can really tell?'

'Nothing to worry about.' And then it's desperately hard not to say something like 'I bet you get hit on all the time up here,' but mercifully I shut my mouth, and she says, 'Where do you live?'

'Melbourne,' and then unnecessarily, 'in Australia.'

'Love it. It's on my roster every month.'

'We're doing what we can down there. What's it like where you live?'

'There are parties,' she says, almost remorsefully, 'but, you know, it's the Middle East, everything is so new, and alcohol is banned in a lot of places. I don't even drink at home, only when I travel.'

'What do you like to drink?'

'Champagne and sweet stuff.'

That makes sense so we talk for a while about what she tends to find herself pulling the cork out of (Moët, of course), and about how in Paris I plan on drinking my share of bubbles along with burgundy of both persuasions.

'You're going to Paris for work?' she asks.

'I'm going to Paris in a vacuum of work.'

She's trying to figure out what I mean, so I say, 'I'm taking some time out, meeting up with friends. I just sold my company. Thinking about what to do next.'

'What is it that you do now?'

'Mostly I'm a musician. A singer really. A classical singer.'

'Like for opera?'

'Well, sometimes. Not the crazy stuff. I'm one of the guys in the background.'

'Huh. And you sold a singing business?' She grins.

'Difficult to scale a singing business.' I smile back, deploying some low-level business jargon I presume I acquired from Rob. 'No, my company was pretty random. It was in the fashion space.'

'Who did you sell it to?'

'Actually, I don't know. They worked pretty hard to keep it a secret. It was a good deal, though.'

'Did you have a massive celebration?' Smiling again, checking her lip gloss with her tongue.

I'm wondering if this kind of temperate flirting is par for all business class courses, when my mouth suddenly starts moving and I hear myself say, 'Do you ever go out with guys you meet when you're working?' Damn it, I was doing so well.

'Oh, I would,' she answers, not even remotely put out, 'but I have a boyfriend. A lot of girls working up here are on the lookout, though.'

'I would have thought most of the men at this end of the plane would be married, kids and all that?'

'Hmmm – not a deterrent for most of my friends. If anything it's a positive. Means they've been trained.'

Definitely not the response I was expecting. And beyond that I wonder – Jesus, I'm not married, but am I trained?

'Kids even?' I ask eventually.

'Makes them even more desirable. Shows they can do it.'

'Huh.'

'What about you?'

'Long way from married. I pass my days getting crushes on my friends.'

'Is that because you know they'll never go anywhere?'

I take a second to try to figure out if she means my friends or the crushes, then realise the answer is the same anyway.

'It's more that I fall in love with them. Not crazy once-in-a-lifetime-love but –'

'I know what you mean. How old are you?'

'Let's say early-to-mid-thirties.'

'I'm early-to-mid-twenties. Every boyfriend I've ever had was a close friend first. That's how we do it.'

Trust a bartender to make me feel like less of a weirdo.

'Tell me about the party. Your crush came?'

'For a while. The last couple of weeks have been funny with her.'

'Because of selling your business?'

'I don't know, maybe? We kissed as well. Just for a few seconds.'

'I'm not sure we can measure the intensity of a kiss by how long it lasts…'

'Good, 'cause this one felt pretty significant.'

'You talked about it after?'

'I was drunk. We went to dinner. Then I was getting ready for this trip. She works a lot, she's stressed – there hasn't been the moment.'

'Moments are made. Why not at the party?'

'The party took on its own life. Started on Friday afternoon, ended Sunday night. That wasn't in the plan.'

'I never found a bar in Melbourne that stayed open so long.'

'It was at my house. At the house I share with a couple of my friends. Actually, I live in a wine cellar.'[3]

'So you drank at home for more than two days?' asks Nadya.

---

3   This is not technically true, but it's true enough and people seem to find it romantic or at least quixotic. It also sounds better than saying I live in a basement in a falling-down share house with three other people, no heating and a single bathroom renovated at the moment the 1970s receded to make way for the '80s, thereby encapsulating the worst of both decades. For a long time I rented bedrooms like a normal person and paid wine storage fees I couldn't afford at climate-controlled facilities, but then this place came up and it was three times the size of a regular room, and having my wine there saved me money which, naturally, I put to vinous ends. I can record music down there too.

'People came and went. Slept and woke. Drank and sobered up. I was out of action for a few hours but I was conscious for most of it.'

'What about your friend?'

'Her name's Bethany. She was there. She slept in my bed the first night.'

'While you were partying?'

'Yeah.'

'Sounds like a moment.'

'It was...' I can't find the words, so I change tack. 'Everyone who came brought a bottle, which I matched with a bottle of my own. Then we drank them both side by side. That was part of the reason it got so messy... everyone always had two glasses on the go at once.'

'Must have been some wild matches.'

'It was as much about the person as the wine.'

'What if I'd come with a bottle of this chablis?' Nadya asks, 'stolen from my employer. Let's say an excellent vintage, since it's such a special occasion.'

'That depends,' I say, wheels spinning. 'With that and for you I would probably reach for my last bottle of Château d'Yquem Sauternes.'

She gets it. She beams.

This is my sixth time in Paris, but my French is still so abysmal that I struggle not just with grammar and vocabulary, but with rudimentary pronunciation. When Antoine messaged me saying he'd made a reservation at Le Cinq, I spent the ensuing days saying I'd be going to 'Le Sink,' despite knowing very well that *cinq* (or 'sank') is the French word for five, and that the restaurant was located within the Four Seasons Hotel George V.

I can remember most of the wine I have drunk in my life, an inordinate number of song lyrics and, oddly, the precise manner in which hundreds of poker hands have played out, but I can say a French word ten times out loud only to forget it a moment later. This is because memory is not simply a blank page. And why wine memories are fluid.

I'm staying at the Hotel Banke, which isn't quite the Four Seasons but is still a serious step up from the kinds of places I usually occupy in Paris or elsewhere, and which is exceedingly comfortable and housed, spectacularly if obviously, within a building that used to be a bank. It's in the 9th arrondissement, not far from Place Vendôme, on rue La Fayette, just a shanked drop-punt from the most celebrated shopping mall in the city.

I suppose I've come to Galeries Lafayette every time I've visited Paris. I don't know why, originally – maybe someone put it on a must-see list or maybe a girlfriend wanted a scarf as a gift – and I'm here now mostly because it's close. Making my way through the ground floor concessions, I'm mindful for the first time of what a maddening clusterfuck the place has become.

Was it always this way? Certainly I feel like there were fewer people ten years ago. Ahead of me is a tour group, complete with diminutive guide waving a wooden stick with a plastic goldfish glued to it. She's dressed quasi-corporate, although wears trainers and, Jesus, she looks tired.

How anyone can function as a tour guide for more than a month or so is baffling to me and I get a sense that this woman's tenure will be measured in days rather than weeks. And tour groups in Galeries Lafayette? What if someone in the assemblage wants to stop and actually buy something? Meanwhile, those of us on our way to the escalators have to shimmy through a huddle of oversized cameras and Gucci loafers.

And then I see Antoine, looking forlorn, at the designated meeting spot by the macaron stand. He's eating a macaron – its quality evidently not sufficient to counter his displeasure at the state of affairs within Galeries Lafayette.

'Can we get out of here?' he asks once the hugs and handshakes are done, and we do hug a lot in our crew, especially after absence.

'Can I have a macaron?'

Antoine's jacket is corduroy but with flared sleeves, as though cut originally as trouser legs, and I'm already wondering how he's going to keep those things out of his wine come lunchtime.

He hands me the bag and I fish out a beige macaron, as per my standard operating procedure, and it is uncommonly good. Meanwhile we're heading for the doors, Antoine leading the charge, and I want to hug him again and for longer but exiting feels like an escape.

'It's the smell of the place,' he says, once we've reached the relative safety of Boulevard Haussmann. 'It used to be so mixed, heterogeneous, notes flying at you from every direction. Now it smells like a Costco or a car dealership. I had to get the macarons to recalibrate.'

'That nose of yours…'

'Indeed.'

'The scent of a city changes, I guess.'

'You have no idea.'

Antoine can make that kind of proclamation and keep you onside.

'If we were standing on this corner, say two hundred years ago,' he continues, 'obviously Galeries Lafayette wasn't yet built, but a lot of this streetscape would look more or less the same. You'd know exactly where you were; it would feel familiar. But the second you took air into your nostrils? A different planet.'

'Sewage?'

'Death and shit. From all manner of species. Indiscriminate and overbearing. You'd gag. We both would. It would be impossible for us to live in Paris. Yet just a short time later, in relative terms, we can stand here and smell... nearly nothing. Faint petrol fumes, your aftershave, whatever aldehydes they're pumping through the ventilation systems in the stores around here. It's fumigation on a massive scale.'

'Let's go and smell the food at Passage 53,' I say.

We've already crossed rue Drouot on approach to what, in terms of Michelin-star experiences, is probably my favourite restaurant in Paris. The chef is Japanese and ex-Astrance, and the place does feel a bit like Tokyo – maybe some slick gastronomical bolthole in Ginza or Aoyama.

To get inside you need to walk through the Passage des Panoramas, which is the oldest covered walkway in all of Paris.[4] Antoine hasn't been here before, and I know he'd be interested in its pedigree, but I'm reticent to bring it up lest I be assaulted with an olfactory bricolage involving rotting fish and the rank, noxious effluvium of an ancient tannery. I mean, we're about to have lunch.

The waiters at Passage 53 look like they've just stepped off a Tom Ford catwalk. Combined with the bijou character of the room itself, this makes for a smooth welcome – a foil to the antediluvian passageway you've taken to get there. We're seated by the window, fronting onto the passage, and obviously I'm paying so I figure I can take the initiative with the first bottle of wine, and for whatever reason I feel like starting with sancerre.

It's unthinkable that I could already be suffering from chardonnay fatigue, but you do get through a vast quantity of it during a decent stint over here so when the opportunity presents

---

4   Originally constructed in 1799.

itself (and when you're not drinking champagne), it's prudent to look at another white varietal. I like my sancerre to taste as little like antipodean sauvignon blanc as practicable, and on the list I spy the Silex Dagueneau from Didier Dagueneau which, while not in fact sancerre, fits that bill precisely.[5]

The wine is now made by Didier's son Benjamin,[6] and the vintage on offer here may well be the first that saw Dagueneau Junior at the helm. I invite Antoine to try it, but he just looks at his glass and nods his consent to the waiter. I know that Antoine has had the good fortune to have tried the Dagueneau Astéroïde, a far rarer pouilly-fumé than the Silex and available only at the winery and in 500 ml flasks. Very much one for the wish list, and it's probably a good thing they don't have it here insofar as it would nudge a thousand euros a bottle and I'd probably want to drink it.

A little over a hundred years ago, not too far from here, the Austrian poet Rainer Maria Rilke stood before an ancient sculpture of the torso of Apollo and responded, in verse: 'You must change your life.'[7] A bottle of Silex might not move you to poetry, but the first time you try it you know you're in the presence of something original.

Antoine is getting into it in a big way, and looking at him across the table, his cheeks blushed and swollen with wine, I feel like our time together began that second, the moment he took his first sip.

'How are you?' I ask him.

'The year has been awful. I'm lost.'

This takes me by surprise, not because Antoine is known for his happy-go-lucky disposition, but because he moved from Melbourne to Spain only eight months ago to teach an undergraduate course he

---

5   It is pouilly-fumé.

6   Didier having died in an ultralight plane crash in 2008.

7   In the original German, 'Du mußt dein Leben ändern.'

had designed called 'The Phenomenology of Wine' at the University of Deusto.[8]

'But… the course?'

He looks at me as though he actually is lost, like a kid approaching a stranger at a shopping centre because he can't find his mother, and he says, 'It's not what I was hoping it would be.'

Antoine is maybe ten years older than the rest of our little gang and he looks older still today. A lot of Italians like sunscreen as much as they like seatbelts, and Antoine[9] spent his summers in Capri or Sardinia where if anything you'd slap on a bit of olive oil early in the season to get your annual basting off to a swift start.

With wine he has been a mentor to our crew, and all he's ever wanted to do is teach this course to students who are into winemaking or maybe philosophy or, at a pinch, art, but to do it in such a way that he controlled it and could more or less indoctrinate kids into a way of thinking about wine that is unconventional.

He left Rome as a teenager to study at Oxford, where he represented the university at its annual Varsity Blind Wine Tasting Match. This thing is real and, in defeating the team from Cambridge, Antoine and his colleagues earned the right to travel to France to take on the best student tasters from across the Channel.[10]

'Are they messing with your syllabus?' I ask.

'It's not the university; they let me do what I want. It's the kids.'

'Well, kids…'

'This Silex…' he says. 'Any one of my eighty students could be sitting with me at this table now, just hanging out, and I'd pour them a glass of this and ask what they thought about it, and what do you think they'd say?'

'Yum?'

---

8   His dream job.

9   Who is Italian.

10   They literally 'drank for Oxford'.

'I would love a yum. A yum from someone and I would award them a perfect score for the whole semester, on the spot, no further assessment necessary. No, they would not say yum. They would say it tastes flinty. Because "silex", of course, means "flint" and because that is how wineworld tells them this wine should taste. And their entire relationship with wine is built on this process of "tasting" – on this crazy, learned, referential vocabulary.'

I nod, as a waiter refills his glass.

'But the story of this wine,' Antoine continues, 'the experience of ingesting it, has nothing whatsoever to do with flint. Don't tell me it tastes like flint. Don't talk about "minerality". I don't want to hear it.'

He is right. The wine is not flinty. Actually, it's like snorkelling in a reef, submerged but breathing through rubber, dulled to the outside world but acutely conscious of the life below. Calm and yet invigorated.

'Antoine, it will take time,' I say. 'You will become a part of this story. This year's kids tell next year's kids, and eventually they'll start to get it. And, besides, what can we do about it?'

'We can get drunk.'

'I've already started'

'Thank you. I'm glad you're here.'

Now more hugs, although this time with chests pressed closer together, a truer energy and the restaurant's gaze upon us.

'When the bag thing happened, this was all I could think about,' I say. 'You and Paris. And to finally being able to pick up the bill myself'

They tend to feed you sans menu at Passage 53, although at this time of year you do get the option of the truffle supplement, said truffles being of the white variety and fresh off the plane from Alba. Today they are shaved atop a bed of ravioli, the dough sealed by hand.

'I hear the party was pretty wild,' says Antoine, referring to my going-away soirée. 'I like the double bottle idea. We should try it with magnums.'

'Adrian showed up with one. So did Erica.'

'Those two.'[11] Antoine smiles.

'Erica made it through the whole catastrophe. Last one standing.'

'You matched their wine with your own magnums?'

'Felt I had to. Adrian went Rhône so I played like-for-like with a Charles Melton Nine Popes.'

'And Bethany?'

Astoundingly I have to think for a second. 'She came with one of those Langi Gs we used to annihilate.[12] Her last bottle.'

'How was it looking?'

'Exactly as we'd left it. And a delight beside the 2006, which was within grabbing distance.'

Antoine was the only member of the Grand Crew unable to attend the party. I could have left it another month and he'd have been back in Australia, but I needed to get the hell out of Melbourne and being able to hang out with him here in Paris for a few days, with the prospect of a road trip to Burgundy later in the week, seemed fair compensation. Plus, Heidi could make it down from Sydney and she needed time away from mothering even more than I needed time in my head.

We're nearly done with the pouilly-fumé when the waiter gently presses a François Mikulski Meursault on us, which doesn't sound like the worst suggestion in the world, and it's open and poured in time for the arrival of the poulet de Bresse.[13]

---

11   Adrian and Erica are brother and sister. They get along fine, but were it not for the Crew we get the impression they'd likely spend less time in one another's company.

12   Specifically, a 1999 Mount Langi Ghiran Langi Shiraz.

13   Chicken.

'Do we have a reservation somewhere tonight?' Antoine asks between chews.

'I was thinking Batard Rouge.'

'Have you let Bruno know?'

'I thought we might sneak up on him.' A swig of meursault sends its nubile horns north and into what feels like my eye socket, and I'm wondering if I'm now actually 'seeing' this wine.

'Not everyone loves surprises, Jude. Although for Bruno I like this plan.'

Starting your day's drinking at lunch with the intention of continuing into the evening sets a distinct scene come mid-afternoon and the second or third bottle. At a quiet dinner, say at a local Italian joint with a friend, you might share a single bottle over your meal and want for nothing more than a whisky at home by way of nightcap. But settling in at lunch, the first bottle comes and goes. And once you're on your way, the rest roll on like wavelets over a reef.

'You can afford vosne-romanée now you're rich,' Bethany said that night at the party, before hiding under the covers of my bed. 'Drink some for me in Paris.'

So that's bottle three, a les suchots premiere cru from Mongeard-Mugneret, and I don't tell Antoine anything about why.

Around twelve hours later

It has started to rain, but fine rain, not the bulbous drops that sometimes tip from Parisian clouds, splattering as violently as bird shit on monuments and washing away the city's mess of grime and cigarette butts. I am smoking, which is bad.

Newly lucrative men's accessories business aside, I mostly make my living from my voice, so it's some kind of drunken indictment that I have a cigarette in my mouth at all, let alone a pack purchased from the cluttered convenience store that runs the full, crossed distance between rue de Richelieu and rue de Montpensier.

You feel like you have to buy something from that place when cutting between those two streets, and it remains the only shortcut option from rue des Petits-Champs all the way to the jutted tangent of rue de Montpensier itself. Cigarettes it was then, as we stumbled from dinner at Batard Rouge to the warm, familiar surrounds of Au Caveau Montpensier.

That was maybe three hours ago, and I'm still clenching the lime-green lighter I inadvertently pocketed from the barmaid at the Caveau. I had to come around the bar to show her how to make an Old Fashioned – not a great sign at a place renowned for its cocktail list.

I guess you'd call Au Caveau Montpensier an American bar in that no one who works there speaks a lot of French and they cater pretty well for expats. Jeb, the owner, is from the States and does a fine line in genial bar talk, expat staff, and spotted dogs. My time there tonight was notable for two reasons:

1. The realisation that I am actually not great at making Old Fashioneds, even when given the run of a fully-stocked commercial bar.
2. Bruno introducing me to Maurice who, along with his mob of friends, is now beside me on rue Jean-Jacques Rousseau on the way to a poker game.

Antoine and I had arrived at 8.30pm at Batard Rouge, having finished lunch around four over a bottle of Jean-Louis Chave St-Joseph[1], which eerily seemed to match our internal constitution. It was as though we were replenishing ourselves with a measure of our own blood. Neither of us said a thing about it, talking instead about cheese and how it's true that dairy fat messes with your palate but, Jesus, you're depriving yourself if you don't pair it with good wine.

After lunch we had mooched around the Passage des Panoramas, stopping for an ordinary coffee very much in the French tradition, and then it was back to the hotel to freshen up and prepare for dinner.

Bethany uses the term 'dregging' to describe the reluctant sensation of sobering up between drinking sessions.[2] It's the feeling you might get an hour or so after your last drink, knowing that it will be an hour or more until your next. The expression is unique to Bethany as far as I know, but certainly the phenomenon is real. It is often, also, unavoidable if you feel that you really do need to give it a rest for a bit, lest you arrive at your second session incapable of speech or forward motion.

The trick is not to fight the onset of dregging with either outright abstinence or by continuing to drink at the same rate. What you want to do is mitigate its eventual coalition. In the same outwardly

---

1   Syrah.
2   The term is also used (although not by us) to describe the act of drinking the last mouthfuls of other people's drinks, at bars or parties.

counterintuitive way that a brunch Bloody Mary can be the ticket to daytime survival, so too can a well-timed mid-dreg pick-me-up.

With this in mind, along with the memory of my underwhelming aeroplane gin and tonic, I had approached the bar at the Hotel Banke at around six thirty and ordered a drink. They make their G&Ts Spanish-style,[3] which I might have deduced given the overall Spanish motif, and anyway I was still working on it when Antoine came down a little after seven having unsuccessfully attempted to nap.

We were into the evening now, we agreed, and so Antoine ordered a bottle of Perrier-Jouët Rosé from the exceptionally well curated list, after lingering for a moment on the Champagne Salon, which at seven hundred euros a bottle we were forced to file in the category of 'right wine, wrong time'.

I remember arriving at Batard Rouge, although that is probably the patchiest section of the evening, then seeing Bruno abandon two guests while in the process of taking their order, to come and greet me and Antoine at the door. There is always a table for us at that place, no matter how rammed it seems and sure enough another couple called for their bill before we'd all finished hugging.

'Boys,' he had said, 'the rumours were true.'

'We come in good spirits' – Antoine, grinning – 'and for that table.'

Bruno doesn't need to wear an apron or badge to be identified unfailingly as the proprietor of Batard Rouge. He's not a tall man either, but in that place he is present like the sun – warming, glowing, searing, showering. The climate changes when he leaves the floor to go out the back for a piss.

Our friends Erica and Adrian once arrived at opening time to try to figure out how long it took for Bruno to develop sweat

---

3   That is, in the largest stemmed glass available, in this case a brandy balloon.

patches in the pits of his painstakingly pressed white shirts. The man never seemed to be actively sweating, and his shirts were always perfectly laundered, yet precipitation spread from the straps of his singlet to the curve of his triceps as though part of the shirt itself. Erica said the sweat was there when they arrived. She went in for a pit-high hug and determined that he smelled of nothing but high-octane supermarket deodorant and high-end French cigarillos.

Batard Rouge translates as 'red bastard' and the name has a particular resonance with Bruno in that he is, biblically speaking, a bastard himself. He also has a deep fondness for the Bâtard-Montrachet appellation in the Côte de Beaune in Burgundy, where there is officially no 'rouge' at all.[4] We've never asked him, but we assume there's a kind of 'misfit' insinuation at play here, especially in light of the medieval legend that saw the commune of Puligny divided up by the local lord, with his illegitimate son the recipient of the patch that now bears the Bâtard moniker.

That particular bastard did well, and so has Bruno with his perfect bistro. The menu runs to just a page, with a wine list on the back that reads exclusively French. He keeps a bottle of Domaine Leflaive Batard-Montrachet Grand Cru[5] in the 'Rouge' section of the wine list, and if you order it you're presented with a couple of those red-stemmed Riedel Sommeliers Montrachet glasses, with black, opaque bowls. And you can eat whatever you want at the restaurant for free.

Speaking of the menu, to begin there is foie gras, along with a pleasingly reimagined French onion soup,[6] charcuterie, and a mushroom dish topped with a poached egg and served with whatever green leaves and herbs are in season. You can have a pork chop, steak

---

4   They don't grow pinot noir or gamay.
5   A chardonnay.
6   Certainly not so violently reimagined as the spectacular interpretation at Le Cinq, across town.

and chips, an ever-changing fish du jour and a take on confit de canard that seldom permits me to order anything else.

There is more, of course, along with a sexy little cheese list and a handful of classic French desserts. It is everything that is good about eating and drinking. It is one of the best places on earth.

We had explained to Bruno that we had come, more or less, from lunch, providing him with a blow-by-blow account of the day's drinking. He nodded, took his leave, and returned with a bottle of beaujolais from Christophe Pacalet.

'Does he think we're dregging?' Antione asked me.

'Let's drink this and then deal with it,' I replied, and so it had begun again.

Predictably we were the last to leave the restaurant, that component of the evening ending with me, Antoine and Bruno drinking calvados at our table. I'd filled Bruno in on the bag thing, although he had heard most of it during a drunken late-night phone call from Rob. Antoine vented some more about what idiots his students were and how he wished he could bring his whole class to Batard Rouge and force every one of them to drink natural beaujolais and scream at the height of their young, drunken voices, 'Wine is a complex living organism. It is no mere thing!'

Bruno is an honorary member of the Grand Crew, having been inducted a few years ago when the majority of our gang came to Paris to celebrate Erica's thirtieth birthday. The ceremony, such as it was, took place in the restaurant, and Bruno cried actual tears. We were all utterly hammered, to the point where Adrian had to restrain Erica from liberating the bâtard-montrachet and the red-stemmed Riedels.

That night was also notorious for Bethany's creation of the official crew anthem. There was no consultation, just the presentation of a receipt from the restaurant Les Climats with lyrics scrawled on the back. She told me to lead the chorus. It went like this:

From Mornington to Meursault

(We go!) Glasses out we roam about

(To show!) A life in vine is twice as fine

We came, we ate, we drank your wine

This Grand old Crew of mine (Grand Crew!)

Antoine had thought it sounded too much like a football song, but there was no arguing with Bethany and it was adopted unanimously. It must now be performed en masse any time a crew member calls for a rendition.[7]

Bruno was festive over the calvados and talking about how much he missed Australia and wished he could visit more regularly.

'You should open a restaurant in Melbourne, just like this,' Antoine said.

'Ah, what a joy that would be.'

'Jude could run it for you.'

'I don't know anything about restaurants,' I replied.

'You didn't know anything about bags.'

The conversation shifted again, but as Bruno was turning off the lights on our way out he said to me, 'What do you think, could this work in Melbourne?'

'This works anywhere.'

Then we'd gone to Au Caveau Montpensier, closed that down and, one lime-green lighter to the good, I had set off with Bruno, the newly met Maurice, and his friends for Cafe Rue Jean-Jacques Rousseau, known universally as Nico's on account of its well-loved proprietor.

Antoine headed for the hotel after the Caveau and I was glad to have Bruno with me as I've never managed a successful solo

---

7   Bethany had spent a few weeks in Sweden earlier that month and it's well known the Swedes are mad for drinking songs. This may have inspired her to put pen to receipt.

negotiation of the short distance between there and Nico's. Bruno called for extremely cold champagne upon arrival, which served as a beer-like palate cleanser, and after that I had an actual beer and then Maurice leaned across and asked if I played poker.

At that hour, in this company, the question was titillating.

'Sure, I dabble,' I had replied.

'After this we're gonna go back to my apartment and play. No-limit Texas hold 'em. It's a friendly game, low blinds, but matters have been known to escalate. Bruno tells me you came into some money recently?'

'I can stake myself into a card game.'

'Very good. We leave when Nico kicks us out.'

Bruno had taken off around then, kissing me on both cheeks and saying, 'Be careful. Come back and see me tomorrow.'

Shortly after that we decamped, five of us, into the night, and I've just lit another cigarette and offered to call us an Uber.

'It's very close,' says a guy called Rémy, who I've pegged as Maurice's right-hand man. 'A short walk.'

Rémy is maybe thirty but the other two look the same age as Maurice, early sixties, and they wear sports coats and I was introduced to all of them but I can't remember their names.

'So you play a little?' Rémy asks me.

'We have a social game every month or so.'

This is true. We started eight years ago, a group of ten of us,[8] taking it in turns to host. I did well in these games from the beginning. I guess the mathematical components of poker sat well with my musical training (Western music is maths, in a way), and inevitably as a performer you acquire some flair for acting. A lot of poker is drama.

I started playing online and in casinos a little, never professionally, but I was able to grind out an income of sorts before eventually

---

8   Not the Grand Crew, although Rob has shown up to the occasional game.

scaling back on the grounds of excessive boredom. Online poker in particular really is a drag. The only way to win in the long run is to play a tight system and the relentless monotony of sitting in a room by myself doing the same thing over and over eventually became too much.

So now I only play cash games, like this one, and at best I'm a 'handy' player, certainly no pro. And who knows, maybe these guys are experts. I'll figure that out pretty quickly, though, and if I sense I have an edge I'll get involved. The fact that everyone is utterly soused is a mark in my favour, as in terms of poker that's the only state I know.

We are on rue Berger now, deep in the flash guts of the 1st arrondissement and we hook right down rue Sauval, which is among my most loved little streets in all of Paris. The restaurant yam'Tcha was right there at number four until they moved around the corner onto rue Saint-Honoré, and despite being so close to the shitshow of rue de Rivoli there is a sense here that you are in your own little enclave.

The older guys are a few steps in front of us and they stop at a doorway that Maurice approaches, key out, to interrogate. He is successful eventually and we're in a marbled foyer with – strange for Paris – a brand-new elevator. Only room for four people, though, and Maurice says, 'Rémy, you and Jude take the next one,' as he lumbers in with his buddies.

'This is Maurice's building.' Rémy, unprompted.

'The whole thing?'

A nod.

'What do you guys do for work?'

'We're in the truffle business.'

The elevator returns and I'm ushered in. Rémy hits the button for the fourth floor, and we sway gently in silence, moving through space on our way to the next place.

The door opens onto the most achingly glorious and extravagant apartment I have ever set eyes on. Maurice has commandeered the entire floor, not just of his own building but of the buildings either side, and the section we walk into, which includes an entirely black marble kitchen, is bigger than a tennis court. Various doors and stairwells jut off here and there suggesting more rooms beyond the present expanse, which is set across multiple levels.

'Well, of course apartments tend to be small in this part of Paris,' I say to Rémy.

The friends of Maurice have removed their jackets and now sit before a cut-crystal dining table at one end of this grand, cavernous space, counting out poker chips and shuffling cards. Two other men are in the room, and they look like they've just finished a yacht race, all tanned and Ralph Laurened and fit-looking.

'Jude, we begin with tequila,' says Maurice from behind his golden glass bar, somewhere in the distance.

I don't query his use of the word 'begin', and beyond that I've always had an 'it's Mexico somewhere' philosophy regarding tequila.

Maurice ambles over with a whisky tumbler and a bottle half-full of bright, almost clear spirit, which sheds the gentlest shade of copper. Handwritten on a crooked sticker are the words 'Ocho 98 Casa'.

'First time I've tried the ninety-eight,' I say, hoping my persiflage will play as well with Maurice as it did with Rémy.

'This one he makes just for his friends,' Maurice replies with a grin and a generous pour. 'Soon we'll move back to wine, but for me it is civilised to take a good tequila at this hour.'

Your house, your rules, Maurice and, sweet Lord, this tastes like a chamber orchestra in harmony, pushing and pulling from all sides but powerfully, spectacularly, attuned.

Meanwhile, the table has been prepared for poker and we all sit down, glasses in hand, and Rémy introduces me in French to the two dudes I haven't met. Their names are Etienne and Olivier and I get the impression they also work for Maurice (possibly piloting his yacht). Then Rémy explains the format, which is pretty standard and calls for blinds of ten and twenty euros respectively, capped at that level, with no antes. I have maybe two thousand euros on me, which seems a reasonable kitty, and doubtless there are cash machines within a short stagger should matters intensify.

These guys play fast and they know what they're doing – I get a sense they play as a group pretty regularly. Mostly they're talking in French, which is fine as it means I can concentrate more on the game. I'm pretty sure they're not going to fuck me over as Maurice seems to know Bruno well and besides it's not like they need to fleece a couple of grand from a drunk Australian they met stealing a lighter from a bar around the corner.

I'm in the right zone for poker, the tequila helped, and I bet hard pre-flop with 10 J suited, which is respected, and from the button I take down a pot of a hundred and sixty euros and we're off to a positive start.[9]

The next couple of hands offer nothing and I muck pre-flop but on one of them Rémy and Olivier go toe to toe and all the way to the river before Rémy eventually gives it up at the urging of a five hundred euros raise from Olivier. Poor Rémy. I would have backed him there but it's a big raise and if you only have, say, a thousand behind you I can understand his reluctance to risk it all on only the third or fourth hand of the evening.

This is doubly true given the quality of booze Maurice is producing. He returns to the table with a Grand Vin Château Latour, also 1998, which he pours in its entirety into seven glasses

---

9   The button means you're dealing; 10 J suited means your pocket or 'secret' cards are a ten and a jack of the same suit; oh, and blinds are the chips the two players to the left of the dealer are compelled to put out before any cards are dealt so as to stimulate the betting once the hand commences.

so deftly that I wonder if he hasn't done time as a sommelier at some point in what has undoubtedly been a life well lived.

The arrival of the Latour is gratifying. I had pegged Maurice as a bordeaux guy and it's always nice to see those socio-vinous prophecies realised. It's also the first time I've tried Latour from any vintage, but after this day and the tequila it sits in my mouth like wet chocolate wrapped in a gum leaf.

And now I've been dealt K 10 of hearts, which is an eminently playable hand for a man in my state and I make the minimum raise to try to bring one or two of them along while continuing to cultivate the impression that I'm an aggressive player. All three of the older guys call, and then Maurice re-raises, again the minimum amount. Everyone calls.

The flop comes three hearts, J 9 4 which, happy days, gives me a flush, and I don't want to scare too many away so I make it fifty to go. Unfortunately, everyone folds except Maurice who says 'how about a hundred' and I'm left to decide whether I flat call or raise again. I'm hoping he's hit a set or has a pair and the ace of hearts which he's figuring might earn its keep later in the hand. I call.

Next comes the jack of diamonds, which is a moderate pain in the arse for me as it pairs the board and means that Maurice could well be in full house territory, which beats my flush. I have to bet at this point to see where I am and I throw out two hundred and fifty. Maurice calls, which doesn't give me a great deal of information, but my read is that he has a hand, and probably a big one.

It has to be a full house and I'm guessing he was dealt pocket nines, which would explain his pre-flop raise. The jack on the turn would have made his full house and I resolve to throw it in on the river if he's aggressive with his betting.

Now the river comes. And it's the queen of hearts. Oh my grande dame. I've improved from a flush to a straight flush on the river and now hold the absolute nuts. And the board can't look all that intimidating to Maurice if he's sitting on a full house, although if I go too hard he could be suspicious of a bigger full house, maybe one involving that queen. I have to bet, though, and bet well and so I make it six hundred to go.

Maurice has his poker face on, expressionless, and around the table there's a sense that some shit is going down. Now Maurice reaches into his pocket and pulls out four five-hundred-euro notes, which he pushes forward along with his remaining six hundred or so in chips.

At this point I could probably make a case for disallowing that bet in that there was never any mention of cash playing, especially cash concealed in one's pocket, but obviously I'm not going to because I have the highest-ranking hand possible in poker.

I don't have enough money on me to call Maurice's bet, so I decide to pull an old riverboat move and stick in all my remaining money along with my watch, which is a 1955 Rolex Datejust that I bought in Paris five years ago with inheritance money from my aunt. It's worth maybe forty-five hundred euros, but could probably pass for more than that in this setting.

'Raise,' I say.

The second I put the watch on the table Maurice takes his own timepiece from his wrist and shoves that in.

'Re-raise.'

I'm doing everything I can not to grin like a carnival clown and I don't even need to look at Maurice's watch, having clocked it back at Au Caveau Montpensier. It is a Patek Philippe Nautilus 3700/1A from around 1980, a watch about which I have had waking fantasies.

'Okay, guys, come on,' says Rémy. 'Are we really doing this?'

Silence from me and Maurice.

'Jude, if you want to call and you lose we can take the watches to be valued tomorrow and you pay the difference in cash. *D'accord*?'

I have my bag[10] on the floor by my chair and I lean down and grab it, placing it on my lap and sliding a hand into one of the compartments. The yacht guys both shuffle in their seats and I think, Jesus, maybe they think I have a gun in here, so I grab what I'm looking for without delay.

Now, under the table, I'm holding a key to the rented Audi TT that Antoine and I are planning on driving to Burgundy later in the week. I don't want to look down, but there's a Hertz keyring that needs to be liberated from the key itself. When I've detached it, I bring my right hand back onto the table and over the stack of money and chips and I place the key on top of it all with the Audi symbol facing up, and I say, 'Raise.'

I don't know what the French word is for 'gasp' but that happens. Maurice actually smiles, I would say sympathetically, and then heads back over to his bar.

'You mucking, Maurice?' I ask, and everyone laughs, and he comes back holding a bottle of wine, a big bottle of wine, which he puts on the table, taking care not to crush the watches, and I can't believe what I'm looking at – I reach out to touch it to make sure it's real. A jeroboam[11] of 1978 Domaine de la Romanée-Conti, Romanée-Conti.

'Jude, if you don't mind I'll take my watch back, and I'll use this bottle to call.'

Insofar as that bottle has got to be worth a hundred grand at least, I have no objection whatsoever.

'Let's see 'em, Jude,' says Rémy and I turn over my cards to show the king and ten of hearts.

Maurice looks perplexed, and I know he can't immediately see the hand I've made. He just didn't think there was a straight flush out there. He's slowly figuring it out as he turns over his own cards

---

10   As in, the bag I designed that I now wear.
11   Three litres of wine.

to reveal pocket jacks, meaning he made four of a kind on the turn. Yeah, I certainly didn't put him on that and of course after the jack on the turn that queen of hearts on the river became a literal one-outer[12] for me on my road to victory.

'Well, I'll be fucked,' says Maurice eventually. No one else says a word, although they've all figured out what's happened. 'Nice hand.'

A shrug from Maurice. He drains what remains of his Latour and then stands, surveying the rest of us, each dumbfounded. 'Let's go to a club.'

A limo – I am guessing Maurice's limo – collects us and we are speeding along the Champs-Élysées with the windows down and all of us are smoking and I'm clutching the giant bottle of DRC[13] on my lap like a loved but peccant toddler and if I were forced to describe the music coming from the stereo I would say it falls into the category of anthem trance.

In the ten or so minutes since I turned over my cards we've talked about nothing except that hand. By consensus it was the most astounding thing any of us have seen in poker, while Maurice's was the worst beat to which we have borne witness. One of his mates has already started calling him 'Jacques' in reference to 'Jack' and it's one of those nicknames that with prolonged application could well end up sticking.

Maurice, for his own part, is taking it in remarkably good spirits and I am moved to presume this is not his last big bottle of Grand Cru burgundy, although I'd be surprised if he went much deeper in '78 Romanée-Conti. He had gone into that poker place (and I know

---

12   My only chance of winning.
13   Most people shorten the name of the domain to 'DRC'.

because I've been there) where you are so sure you have the best hand that you become oblivious to the existence of something better. This sensation is amplified when you can easily put the other player on a hand that is strong, but not as strong as yours.[14]

We make a lap of the Arc de Triomphe and then pull up out the front of a building that is obviously a nightclub, unless some other kind of establishment has started hanging up velvet ropes and renting crowds of beautiful youth to line up in packs out the front, smoking dolefully. I've known Maurice for only a few hours but I feel fairly certain that he is not one for queues and, sure enough, once we're out of the limo we're led through a separate entrance and past the main bar to a large cloth-clad table and I'm still holding onto the DRC like it's an extra limb, although no one seems to mind.

The club is called L'Arc, and it's one of those places where the majority of what should be dance-floor real estate is given over to booths and private tables where you have your own waiter and the only way to drink is to order bottles that come with an obscene price tag but are delivered to your table with some ceremony – in the case of L'Arc with a cluster of magnesium-tipped sparklers blazing from the neck.

I give the DRC its own place at the table and Maurice has already ordered more booze –three sparkling magnums of Dom Pérignon, which bizarrely have no vintage designation and come in bottles that look as though they've been designed expressly for nightclubs. These will be the twelfth through fourteenth bottles of wine that I've got meaningfully involved with today, and to that end it's a good job we're sitting down.

Most of the people at the private tables are men and although Maurice and his friends are probably the oldest, they are not profound outliers. A lot of the women by the bar or on the dance

---

14   Maurice would have put me on a big full house or, if he really didn't rate me as a player, an ace high flush.

floor look maybe nineteen and they're all dressed magnificently if minimally; you can see the hours of preparation that have gone into hair, makeup and accoutrements. The majority of dudes at the tables, on the other hand, wear polos or scruffy business shirts.

There's an enormous guy at the entrance to our area serving as security detail and he's stopping people from coming in unless they're at one of the tables or are just too preposterously attractive to turn away.

A guy at the table next to us gets up, goes over to the security guy and points at a couple of girls dancing. The big fellow leaves his post and walks over to them, actually taps one of them on her bare shoulder, gestures to where polo shirt guy is standing, looking, if I'm honest, like a cowed phallus, and a few words are exchanged and the girls nod and over they come, escorted all the way. Introductions are made and the guy's buddy has already poured them a couple of glasses from their magnum of Cristal and just like that they're sitting at the table, smiling and knocking back fizz at something like fifty euros a sip.

I'm wondering if Maurice is likely to initiate a similar sortie – my flesh outwardly creeping at the prospect – when one of the girls who has made it into the tabled area under her own steam comes over and says something in French that I don't understand.

'Rémy!' I shout across the table, and he comes over. 'Translation, *s'il vous plaît?*'

'Funny,' he says after a second or so with his ear at her mouth. 'She wants to know if she can take a selfie with the bottle.'

Well, why not? I give my best appropriation of the Gallic shrug and smile and hand her the thing and she squeals delightedly and grabs it by the punt,[15] its neck to her left breast, and then deftly whips out her phone and bangs off a few snaps before handing it back, kissing me on the cheek and heading off on her way.

---

15   The dimple at the base of most wine bottles.

And now the girls drinking Cristal come over, holding their glasses, and I catch the look they give polo shirt guy and his mate as they leave. It's a look that says, 'You are old and pathetic, go and fuck yourself,' and the two guys look like they've been kicked directly in the nuts. Hero to zero, and I wonder if it's ever worth it.

The girls are at our table now and gesturing towards me, and I guess Rémy tells them they should talk to me in English because they do and sure enough they want a picture with the DRC too. They take their time with it, and Maurice works their phones and takes a handful of shots. When they eventually show me the artfully filtered result it looks like the cover of a wine issue of *Vogue* and they've tagged it #thebigboy.

Then there's a rush, with women coming at it from all sections of the club wanting photos. Occasionally they ask me to join but mostly it's just them holding the bottle or kissing it or in some instances putting it between their legs or pretending to drink from it, licking it, dancing with it, and all of them post their pictures online with that same hashtag and I think, fuck me, I'm trending.

Maurice and the rest of our party don't appear to mind the attention and no one seems to think that thirty or so women posing for pictures with a wine bottle is that big a deal. Then the girl who approached me originally comes back and I get a sense that she's taken ownership of the whole *joyeux* happening and she gives me another peck and asks if she can take The Big Boy on a little tour of the club.

By now it's close to four in the morning and I'm riding something of a fresh wave from the Dom, but the waters are starting to get choppy and I've already caught myself saying the same thing to the same person twice in the space of a couple of minutes and I'm beginning to turn my mind to the logistics of leaving. I resolve to drink an entire bottle of Evian while this girl has some fun with my wine.

She gives me a smile as dirty as the Seine, presses the neck of the DRC to her shoulder like a gendarmerie's rifle then gives me a salute, another kiss, and takes off back to the dance floor. The revellers part, and she's making a parade circuit of the place, marching in time to the music and stopping to pose for pictures upon request.

The guy in the lighting booth puts a spotlight on the bottle and the DJ plucks The Jackson 5 track 'Big Boy' from somewhere and he drops that to near hysteria, and then I see the main girl is encouraging others to leave lipstick kisses on the bottle, but not on the label, and those hues run from hot pink through the gamut of rouge with one proud instance of iridescent yellow.

'They love The Big Boy,' says Maurice, and it's clear this excursion to L'Arc has served as a salve to the savage bite sustained on the poker table. 'Perhaps we should get you and your prize back to your hotel. How many of these girls do you want?'

I turn my head in time to see him give an 'only joking' grin, thank God, and I stand up the moment my bottle is returned, daubed with lipstick, glitter and victory.

Even though he missed the evening's final hours, Antoine was still too hungover or tired or self-pitying to be roused and I left the hotel early afternoon having slid a note under his door that read '#thebigboy'. When I last checked, the hashtag had appeared online more than a thousand times, including re-posts, with every image featuring the bottle and several featuring *moi*. I was confident Antoine would be able to put the pieces together, insofar as they could arranged to resemble a comprehensible whole.

I was in pain, my throat squealing from cigarettes and a lack of non-wine fluids. To say it was desert-esque understates the scorched moistureless severity of the situation, and it's a good job there wasn't mouthwash or worse sitting on my beside table because anything wet was going straight down my gullet.

Having near-instantly emptied the half-litre of bottled water that actually was there, I noticed its fifteen-euro price tag. The vessel itself was perfectly cylindrical, made of glass and resembled an expensive minimalist vase. Perhaps this dual function was factored into the pricing model. And maybe it was a product of my nouveau riche status, but fifteen euros actually seemed reasonable value, insofar as I was unable to move and the journey from bed to bathroom looked a hopeless folly. You could probably even charge fifty euros.[16]

When I awoke The Big Boy was in bed beside me, making its own indent, like a new lover staying until morning for the first time. None of the lipstick had so much as smudged, which I suppose speaks to the robust constitution of the stuff, although actually I shouldn't be surprised given the myriad hours I've spent scrubbing Bethany's Chanel off my stemware.

This prompted me to recall the ten or so text messages I'd sent her at various stages of the night. Which is to say I recalled the act of pressing sending, not what I'd written. Fuck. Anyway this was something that could be attended to later or not at all.

It was half past twelve by the time I was dressed, having had to sit on the bed to dry myself from the shower,[17] and then I thought I might as well go back to Batard Rouge for lunch. I made it almost out the door clutching The Big Boy by the neck, before realising I could probably stop lugging him around now he'd been transported securely to my suite. I called reception to ask if they had a bigger safe.

---

16   A textbook illustration of the economic theory of elasticity of demand.
17   On account of lacking the equilibrium to execute that task while standing up.

Now I'm at the restaurant eating pork sausages with potato gratin and asparagus and I have just finished explaining to Bruno what happened after he left me with his mate Maurice at Nico's earlier that morning.

'Unexpected,' says Bruno. 'I mean, he loves his poker, but such a large bet?'

'It was a perfect storm. We were drunk, it was late, and he never for a second thought he was behind.'

'There's no way he would have taken your car...'

'Well, it was on the table; it was his if he'd won.'

'Crazy.'

'Best night of my life.'

'So,' says Bruno, piercing an orb of burrata, 'what are you going to do with it?'

'I'd like to think we'll drink it.'

Cue eyebrow-raise and, fair enough. A jeroboam of 1978 Domaine de la Romanée-Conti, Romanée-Conti, is acutely liquid, as far as assets go. I could sell it to a wine broker here or in Australia or just hand it over to Sotheby's who would probably build an entire sale around it. But I have never parted with a bottle of wine on the secondary market and, while this has not been an ardent or even pre-meditated strategy, the prospect of selling a bottle I could otherwise be drinking has always seemed unsavoury.

'A thousand euros says you sell it.'

'Not a bet I'd want to make.' Although I do consider it. 'I know at least I'll take it back to Melbourne with me.'

'Hmmph,' from Bruno, and then, 'A drink?'

I do feel as though I could manage a glass or two, but given my condition I can only contemplate a narrow band and so I say, 'Sure, but it'll have to be hermitage.'

Bruno grunts and summons a waiter.

'Why syrah?' he asks when the wine arrives.

'Familiarity,' I reply, 'I'm feeling sensitive.'

The link between Australia and France, between Australia and all of the old world, is conspicuous in most wine we produce, but it's maybe most pronounced in the case of shiraz. We really did take that one and run with it. Whether it was a consequence of our climate or just that people liked the taste of the stuff, we ended up with a wine style that is at once 'our own' and a literal and characteristic offshoot of the syrah from the appellation near the town of Tain-l'Hermitage.

Vitis vinifera[18] is not native to Australia,[19] and so every varietal planted in our fair land came from somewhere else. The original vine stock for a lot of it was gathered by a guy named James Busby and brought to the colony in 1833.[20] There were vineyards before that, from not long after the arrival of the First Fleet, but Busby assembled a collection of six hundred and fifty varietals. This made him both a pioneer of the Australian wine industry, and a man about whom the phrase 'that guy doesn't fuck around' could safely have been uttered.

I've given up arguing with Bruno[21] about the relative virtues of Australian wine. It's enough that they see it as a curio, that they mostly enjoy it, and that I can surprise them periodically in blind tastings and point to the ever-increasing number of antipodeans working in their vineyards and wineries.

For Bruno and his ilk, we simply lack tradition. We have no pedigree. We're too new to the game. I used to delight in pointing out that many of our vines in Australia are older than the vines in the

---

18   The vine species that gives us grapes for wine.
19   There is a native berry that's a bit like a grape, which Indigenous Australians cultivated and continue to grow, but I wouldn't want to make wine out of it.
20   Including the famous pinot noir clone MV6, from Burgundy's Clos Vougeot, fondly referred to as the 'Mother Vine'.
21   With most French people, actually.

best vineyards in France.[22] This is factually accurate, but the French mostly roll their eyes as though you've tried to pass off soft cheese from King Island as camembert.

We have mostly copied the old world in an attempt to replicate what we perceive to be the essence, the credible core, of each varietal introduced. This is our link to Burgundy, to Barolo, and beyond. A form of faithful reimagining. And even though we've branched out on our own at times[23] and even though we've been at the vanguard of modern winemaking best practice,[24] to the French we're still imposters, and every wine we produce will be perceived and evaluated through the lens of *l'original*: of the thing it's striving to imitate.

'Jude… are you there?' Bruno is tapping the side of my glass with his fingernail.

'Jesus, sorry. My mind slipped into the glass.'

'I want to know if you were serious? About last night.'

'About the restaurant? About Batard Rouge in Melbourne?'

A nod.

'Of course, why not, people would lap it up. I could talk to Adrian,[25] see if he's interested.'

'I don't know Adrian as well as I know you. And always he has a hundred things on his plate. You don't really have anything on your plate. In fact, from what Rob tells me people are paying you not to work at all this next twelve months.'

'Rob is in on this?'

---

22 This is a consequence of the phylloxera blight that saw many old-world vineyards pulled. Australia was affected, but not to anywhere near the same extent.

23 Sparkling shiraz is one example.

24 A lot of which has been adopted in the old world to the great benefit of their wines.

25 Adrian, also a restaurateur, always has four or five places on the go at any point in time. Right now this includes two rustic Italian joints, a Malaysian hawker cafe, a high-end 'modern Australian' bistro, and a tempura bar in South Yarra.

'I ran it by him.' Bruno shrugs. 'Every business needs a lawyer.'

'I was going to use the time for my music. Get a new agent, do some recording.'

'Jude, I've known you how many years and you've spent five minutes talking about music and five hundred hours talking about wine and restaurants. I'm missing something here?'

'I don't have words for music. Wine's much easier. I don't know shit about restaurants, though. Never understood how any of them made money.'

'Surely you see Adrian making money?'

'I see Adrian making "some" money "some" of the time… I also see the places that fail.'

'Jude, I'm offering to back you into this business. As a partner. We take the model from Paris and we replicate. The menu, the systems, the whole show. We build the same restaurant in Melbourne.'

'Come on, Bruno… why?'

'You said it yourself – this should work anywhere.'

'No – why me? Why now?'

'The now part is easy. Look at me. If it's not now, it's not happening. And like everything in this industry it's more about the pleasure dividend than anything financial. I want to come to Australia every year. Twice a year, if possible. To see your crew and… well, mostly that.'

The sentimental part I get. Naturally. 'It'd be a dream to have you there more often – Jesus, the tastings we would arrange… But, come on, I'm not a restaurant guy.'

'You're in restaurants half your life, and on a McDonald's income. No one knows how you do it but the way you eat and drink and entertain your friends is the essence of hospitality. It's what restaurants are meant for. And it's who you are.'

'I just don't spend a lot on other stuff.'

'And I don't care about this bag money. Buy a house with that. Buy wine. You have potential, Jude. You're a weapon that no one has figured out how to use. I want to point you at this and see what happens.'

'I do feel primed.'

'So, let's blow something up.'

'Is this because you don't have children?'

'Jude… this is more about you than about me.'

'What about the wine list?'

'What about it?' Bruno looks at me as though I've accused his dad of being a Nazi sympathiser during the occupation.

'I think we need to make it Australian.'

I expect Bruno to spray his syrah across the table, or glare at me or just clock me with a crisp uppercut. But he says nothing. Instead, he pokes his fork into a piece of melon, nudges that around for a while, then brings it to his mouth, consummating the procedure with a long swill from his glass of Domaine des Lises Crozes-Hermitage.

'If we make the wine list Australian we can go ahead?'

Now I feel like I'm in some weird negotiation where you ask for something you never expected to get, in a deal you're not hugely invested in, only to have that ambit claim accepted without so much as a counteroffer.

'Jesus, Bruno… you really want to do this?'

'Jude, I've turned seventy, the bottle is short of half-empty. Now I start doing the things I want, without worrying so much about whether they're smart.'

'I get it.'

'So,' earnestly now, 'let's make it happen.'

I am silent, but I smile, which signifies acquiescence to Bruno, and he reaches into the breast pocket of his scruffy aubergine-coloured blazer and pulls out a wine-blotched Batard Rouge napkin on which he has made a series of markings with his fountain pen.

'I started to write it down last night after Nico's,' he says, relocating my glass and laying the piece of cloth out before me. 'Of course we can remove this section now,' and he draws a line through a table headed 'Vin'. 'You'll need to make those calculations based on the wine list you devise.'

As he continues, I lean back in my chair and look around the room at the twenty or so other diners, mostly locals, eating and talking; at the cases of wine stacked by the walls; at the bad art and the corkboard of photos of Bruno and various patrons, including me and my friends; and finally at Bruno himself, making napkin notes around the blood-red stain of last night's châteauneuf-du-pape.

'You know I won a jeroboam of Romanée-Conti in a poker game this morning.'

Bruno casts his eyes up from his work, such that his eyelashes meet his brow.

'And you know someone just paid me a million euros for a bag design.'

'Jude, I know this.'

'Those were acts of extreme serendipity and, in the case of the DRC at least, of obscene luck.'

'I don't know which is crazier,' says Bruno.

'Just slightly different shades of insane.'

'The restaurant, though…'

'The most far-fetched of the three. But I say let's round out the trilogy.'

Bruno raises his glass. 'To *folie*.'

'Maybe this wine list completes my oeuvre.'

'You're a strange cat, Jude,' and then, 'Astrid, champagne!'

An ice bucket arrives, already housing a bottle of Geoffroy Pureté Brut Nature. Bruno yanks out the cork and fills two clean glasses to halfway.

'You may yet regret this,' I tell him.

'No matter what, I trust you. Take your time, do it right, make it work.'

We drink to that, and then Bruno slides me the napkin. He has drawn up a rough budget for opening and running the place, with line entries across a range of categories for the first two years of operation.

'I make guesses at some things,' he says. 'The rent, I don't know. The cost of the chef, I make an approximation.'

I'm interrogating the particulars as thoroughly as my hangover will sanction. What he's produced is a concise blueprint for setting up and running a restaurant: a business plan without the bullshit.

'Makes sense,' I say, scanning the numbers and adding a note or two of my own, like increasing the budget for art from a thousand to ten thousand. Nothing easier than adding a zero. Now Bruno retrieves a chequebook, which has its own tan leather case, and it's been maybe five years since I last even saw a chequebook and if I'd designed my bag, say, twenty years ago I would have had to allow for one. And then I think, well, I do have a space for a corkscrew and maybe twenty years from now that will seem as much an anachronism as a chequebook.

It suits Bruno, though, the worn leather and the Mont Blanc pen, and with a flourish he writes something on a cheque, gently tears it from the book and hands it to me with proper ceremony. It is made out to me in the sum of two hundred and fifty thousand euros.

'Should be enough to get started,' he says. 'Hopefully for the first two years. If we're not making money by then, we're doing something wrong. Run all this by Adrian, but, Jude, this is our thing. And in Melbourne it's your thing.'

'I can do it, Bruno.'

He hands me the napkin too. 'Come back tomorrow, there's a lot to do.'

'Of course. And you'll need to plan your trip across for the opening.'

A smile from Bruno, warm as risen soufflé. Then more champagne.

Six days later

I've retrieved the tuba case from the stowage locker and placed it, seatbelted, beside me, as there's obviously no soul ticketed 3B on this night-time flight from Doha to Melbourne. Coming out of Paris, in this same seat, I was hitched at the arm to a spectacular dame from Lyon who was dripping money but absent of discernible pomp or pretention.

As soon as she'd sat down, the inflight manager had come over and apologised in French for there being no first-class cabin on this service but – if my appalling grasp of the language served me even slightly – they had arranged for a bottle of champagne to be brought onboard for her as some small conciliatory token.

The woman had nodded in a 'well, it is what it is' kind of way and then made a slight gesture with her left hand in my direction. I was thinking I'm about to be relocated, or worse, thrown off this aeroplane, when the hostie regarded me briefly, smiled and then said in English, 'Of course, madame.'

Then the woman's phone had come out and it was one of those gold-cased things that isn't even a smartphone, just something you use for actual phone calls and text messages, and she'd tapped away at that for a minute or so, and still I'm wondering what's going on, like is she calling security? And then the hostess returned with the bottle and two glasses and the wine was Taittinger Comtes de Champagne Blanc de Blancs.

My mind by then had tasked itself with a back-of-the-envelope-type calculation as regards the volume of champagne I had consumed during the preceding week in Paris. Well north of a litre a day, I had concluded, and on some days a good deal more.

'For you, monsieur,' said the hostess, handing me a spuming flute of the Comtes, and bowing ever so slightly to my row-mate while wiping the lip of the bottle with her serviette and taking her leave. I had clutched the glass, made a daft half-toast to nobody, and then said, 'Merci madame, je m'appelle Jude.'

'You are welcome. My name is Isabelle Le Roux.'

You could have at least said that bit in French, I thought, but instead I repeated my awkward toast.

I've seen women with this aura before at recitals, although never in such close quarters or for such a protracted period. They are a singular breed. Madame must have been sixty, but with impeccable skin that had surely met the surgeon's knife in the decade past. No doubt her hair had been attended to professionally that morning and her clothes were chic and striking. Her jacket was a kind of patchwork affair, with wool and sections of leather and a hem, of sorts, that was satin or silk. She wore jewels, but not to excess. There was no engagement ring.

Then there's me beside her. Gangly without being particularly tall; unkempt although groomed; well-dressed while scruffy; and anxious and inadequate despite feeling better and wealthier than at any point in my memory. A lot of things, but still not enough.

It puzzles me when women say they like men who are confident. I've never understood what that meant or whether I passed muster, and there has always seemed to me to be a perilously thin line between being confident and being a dick. Ordering for a woman in a restaurant is obviously a dick move this millennium, but maybe taking charge of the post-dinner arrangements, which bar to go to, what wine to order and so on, can be a sign of assuredness and therefore attractive?

My own relationship with self-confidence has been fraught for as long as I can remember, leading me to behave inauthentically from time to time, with Bethany or with other women I've been attracted to. I think they want strength, so I'll try for a version of strong. I think they like power, so I'll shoot for a more potent form of Judeness. But it's like that bad patch we had in the Barossa a while back when a lot of the reds were over-extracted and alcohol-driven in the belief that this kind of power would make for something great in the bottle. It rarely did.

Don't over-extract is the lesson here, and while Bethany has never called me out for it, she observes this trait in other men all the time. Some version of trying too hard or trying to impress. She hates it. She spent six months with a guy who wasn't interested in wine at all but feigned expertise to impress her and us and every second of it was like cork taint.

It's all the more incongruous for me, because honestly I don't give that much of a fuck for the whole charade, and literally zero fucks about stuff like social status or reputation or what car I drive or the damned property ladder. There's not a lot I'm chasing and I realised in my twenties that the only things I wanted that required money were: wine, books, restaurants and travel.

Yet even with life simplified to this extent, even with so much junk and envy and anxiety stripped away, I still don't know how I'm supposed to act so as to transmit that aura of assuredness. All I know is that in my own variegated relationship history I get it wrong, regularly. I once did indoor rock climbing for a year, for fuck's sake, and that girl didn't really like wine either.

In the six-and-a-half hours it took us to fly from Paris to Doha I received a masterclass in self-confidence, imparted with nonchalance by Madame La Roux. And it's not like I haven't been around strong women before; God knows, Bethany herself wants for little when it comes to boldness and our friend Erica is sangfroid on steroids.

For Isabelle,[1] though, the extent to which she was at ease with herself, the extent to which she knew exactly who she was… was captivating and disarming. It was also, unavoidably, incredibly

---

1   I was invited to address her by her first name around two hours into the flight.

sexy, which I guess does play into the whole 'confidence equals attractiveness' thing.

I wasn't lusting after her, or even contemplating any liaison beyond our conversation; it's just that her energy was so potent and amatory. She took what she wanted wherever she went.

We had gotten drunk together. I told her a lot more about me than she revealed of herself, except that she is from Lyon and still lives there, and comes from a wealthy local family but married into an even wealthier one tangentially connected to the wine industry. That marriage failed and now she was mostly focused on a suite of businesses that I sensed were agricultural in nature but that certainly did not necessitate Madame getting her hands dirty or even coming within cork-popping distance of actual soil.

She knew Paul Bocuse pretty well and had some stories about decadent episodes at his restaurant, L'Auberge du Pont de Collonges, and the handful of private parties he had deigned to cater, including one of her own 'milestone birthdays', where Madame's guests were only served champagne and – in fact – only Taittinger Comtes de Champagne Blanc de Blancs.

'Why this champagne?' I had asked her, as the hostess poured out the last of the bottle.

'It suits me,' she said, and of that there could be little doubt.

I told her about the bag thing, which genuinely intrigued her, and in relating the anecdote to a near stranger I was struck by just how improbable the whole arrangement sounded. We'd seen the money, though, escrowed at Citibank and needing my signature and Terry's to secure its release.

'Jude, you have been bought by someone very, very big,' was Madame's take, and I had no reason to doubt her.

One thing I learned about women recently is that the notion they have a diminished capacity for alcohol compared to men is an utter fallacy. On average men drink more than women but when a woman gets into the right zone, when those planets align, it can be like watching dawn break on a hillside. Striking and unrelenting.

I doubt it's hormonal, but it does seem to be highly variable. Erica, for example, who like most of us does drink a little too much overall, can on occasion be merry and content and satiated after three glasses, yet at other times will exhaust multiple bottles, make a decent dent in your whisky collection, and seem less inebriated at the end of it all than when you shared that bottle with her at dinner the previous week.

It's a frame of mind thing, I guess, and it's surely connected to the parts of the brain that moderate appetite and desire. But when those neurons spark, the female drinking unit becomes every bit as puissant as the male.

Isabelle and I didn't set out to get stewed but one bottle led to the next, and the next bottle was also champagne. Vintage Pol Roger Rosé, as it turned out, which might not have suited Isabelle as well as the Comtes but still put in a solid enough shift. We were halfway through the bottle, having already discussed wine, the man-bag and Lyon, when I decided to tell her about the DRC.

I excused myself to retrieve my vintage leather tuba case from the stowage compartment. I'd purchased it the previous day at the markets at Puces de Montreuil for three hundred euros, having been on the lookout all week for something like it but never expecting to find so perfect an example. I'd talked the guy down from four hundred euros, which obviously I would have paid if it came to that, and then trotted victoriously through the rain to the metro station. It's always raining when I go to flea markets in Paris; I don't know why.

The case, which must be a hundred years old, has a hard metal frame, a ratty upholstered fabric lining and a green leather exterior, almost like crocodile skin although surely not, and it's well worn: you can see parts of the rough reinforced under-fabric. The thing is sturdy, though, and the handle is attached with reassuringly dense stitching.

The bottle had fit snugly inside and I'd taken some delight in showing it off to Maurice that evening when he came up to my room at the Banke to enjoy a farewell drink along with Bruno and Antoine. Maurice was touched at the effort I'd gone to and made a phone call there and then. I couldn't decipher it, but Bruno cringed, and twenty minutes later there was a knock at the door from Maurice's tailor, bearing his full kit and paraphernalia who, after the briefest of exchanges, set to work sewing the words 'The Big Boy' in gold thread onto the case.

After that, the fellow just walked out and I had to admit I liked the needlework, and even Antoine (who still found the whole story incredulous) thought it looked sharp.

In the hours leading up to the rendezvous my main dilemma was the wine I'd serve my guests. Bear in mind the pedigree:

1. My new partner in a wine-focused restaurant.
2. The previous owner of a jeroboam of 1978 Domaine de la Romanée-Conti, Romanée-Conti, inarguably one of the world's great wines.
3. A rising star in the burgeoning field of the philosophy and aesthetics of wine.[2]

A bottle of Mumm NV from the Nicolas on rue Cadet probably wasn't going to cut it and so I had set out for Saint-Germain with a view to perusing the selection at La Dernière Goutte. And after a brisk glass of chablis at Freddy's wine bar around the corner, I had done exactly that.

---

2   Influenced certainly by the Italian philosopher Nicola Perullo but nevertheless charting his own course.

The shop had been left in the care of a young English guy, perhaps in Paris on his gap year or university holidays and surely a family friend to have landed such a plum internship. He spoke in flawless French to the customer before me and then, unprompted, switched to English.

I explained my dilemma without going further into specifics than was necessary,[3] and he straightaway suggested sherry. My sherry knowledge is limited, although I did learn a little over the course of a long weekend in Madrid with Rob a few years ago. There are entire bars there devoted to the stuff, and during those few days we'd start early evening with a sherry or two[4] before switching to martinis[5] with only the occasional glass of wine. It seemed civilised, right up to the moment the hard, enervating weight of the gin took hold.

Absolutely I was open to sherry, provided something suitable could be located, and the guy set about retrieving bottles from the wood-panelled cabinets that line the walls at La Dernière Goutte. Then he introduced himself, and to my surprise his name was Jude.

I have never actually met another Jude. Telling him I was called Jude too felt like being five years old and finding another kid in the playground who agreed that Batman would kick Superman's arse in a fistfight. I guess being English he'd met a few others and so wasn't as affected, but still it pointed towards an agreeable purchase.

A quick scan of the bottles he had produced yielded only one word that bore any vestige of familiarity. That word was Масандра[6], and in most articles you read about 'expensive wines bought at auction' you'll find a reference to this place in Ukraine, and to a

---

3   I did toy with asking him whether he'd heard of The Big Boy.
4   Usually at La Venencia on Calle Echegaray.
5   Always at Bar Cock, and then often at the bar at the Hotel Fénix Gran Meliá.
6   In English, 'Massandra', and very different in style from what I'd been drinking in Madrid. They can't even call Massandra 'sherry' any more, after the Spanish tightened the labelling rules in the mid-1990s.

bottle of Sherry de la Frontera 1775, which sold at Sotheby's in 2001 for twenty-five thousand pounds.

Jude the Younger's bottle was from 1945, and he translated the rest of the text as 'South Coast Red Krymwein'. There was a bit going on in Europe in 1945 and I thought the distinction of the date might resonate with my guests insofar as all three were born on that continent. It was expensive, but I bought it without even an allusion to a second thought. Extremely cool-looking bottle too, all Soviet and serious, and the ullage[7] was acceptable for its age. You'd like to think it had been lying in a cold Ukrainian cellar for a lot of its life before making its way to Paris, probably via a merchant or at auction.

I had served it with some formality into glasses procured by the concierge at the Banke, who seemed to know a bit about sherry and suggested avoiding those traditional port-style glasses with rims of small circumference. He'd come back with more like what I'd call a riesling glass. We drank it slowly, so I didn't need to call on the bottle of Massolino Barolo I had bought as a contingency, and it was impossible not to think of the year of its origin and what flashes would spark thereafter to fetch that part of the world, and the rest of us, into the next spell of our collective humanity.

Anyway, that all happened on my last night in Paris and late the next morning I'd Ubered to Charles de Gaulle to be seated, inflight, next to Madame Isabelle Le Roux and had drunk champagne with her and decided to show off my jeroboam of 1978 Domaine de la Romanée-Conti, Romanée-Conti in its salubrious new lodgings.

'Oh my,' she said, when I opened the case on my lap to reveal The Big Boy in all its lipsticked glory. 'But, Jude, there is a problem. How did you get this on the plane?'

---

7   The amount by which a bottle falls short of being full. Often referred to as the 'level', meaning the gap between the top of the wine and the bottom of the seal (the cork, in this case). A big gap can mean juice has evaporated or diffused or been absorbed into the cork.

'I put it through the scanner with my carry-on.'

'But –'

'I didn't want to check it. In case it got stolen, or maybe the temperature in the hold or on the tarmac is volatile.'

'You must see the issue?'

I was displaying early signs of panic. We were talking about my most prized possession here.[8]

'Isabelle, you are giving me cause for concern.'

'You need to go through security again in Doha. They won't let you take liquids onboard and I promise you the staff will not be as lax as in Paris. If you try to board with this, they will take it away.'

Fuck. Over many hours of plotting and planning, including calling the airline to enquire whether or not it was possible to buy a seat for The Big Boy,[9] this scenario never entered my mind.

'What do I do?' Like asking advice from my mother after accidently scratching one of Dad's records.

'Well,' she said, then paused for a sip of champagne, 'it may very well be that we need to drink it now.'

While it was gratifying that Madame's wit had not deserted her in a crisis, the prospect of consuming three litres of DRC between now and re-boarding for Melbourne did not appeal. I'd imagined us sitting in the lounge or, better yet, in some terminal café, The Big Boy perched on a rickety table and Isabelle and I pouring measure after measure into coffee cups or tumblers or whatever we could muster as the PA system shouted 'last call'.

I pressed the button on my armrest and a hostess appeared.

---

8   Bruno's cheque for two hundred and fifty grand is prized too, of course, and it is folded and tucked into my copy of René Daumal's *A Night of Serious Drinking* in my checked luggage.

9   Absolutely possible, they had said, for the same fare as standard, and with no mention of clearing security again in transit.

'This is a long shot,' I said to her, 'but on my flight to Paris I was served by an attendant named Nadya. I don't suppose you've come across her in your travels?'

'Of course!' the girl practically sang. 'Everyone knows Nadya. She's working in economy right now.'

'You're kidding me?'

'Want me to go grab her?'

I nodded, Isabelle sent an approving eyebrow-raise in my direction, and in seconds there was Nadya, bubbling still, and dropping to her knees in the aisle to take my hand in greeting.

'Jude, no way!' she began, in the manner of her generation. 'How was Paris?'

'Eventful,' I replied, and then she noticed The Big Boy, now resting on Isabelle's lap, with Madame caressing the case's recent embroidery in an admiring fashion.

'Lord, what is that?' from Nadya.

But, first, introductions.

'Allow me to introduce you to Madame Isabelle Le Roux,' I said, which elicited a 'How do you do,' from Isabelle and an 'Enchanté' from Nadya.

'I have a problem,' I said, 'and I see it has caught your eye already.'

'How is this even here, Jude?' Aghast, Nadya reached over me, running a finger over the glass, carefully touching one of the lipstick imprints, all the while running her tongue over her own heavily glossed lips giving me cause for optimism that a plan of some sort may already be brewing in her sharp, fetchingly housed brain.

But then she said, 'You realise they're going to take this off you in Doha.'

'We were hoping,' said Isabelle, 'that you might have some idea how that could be avoided.'

Nothing seemed to spring immediately to mind and after a while I said, 'Do you know if this aircraft continues on to Melbourne?'

'It does,' said Nadya, and then, 'You think we could leave it onboard?'

I was heartened by her use of 'we,' and the inference of co-conspiracy.

'The cleaners don't usually check the crew locker,' Nadya said. 'Sometimes we leave little gifts for the girls on the next sector. We could stash him there?'

'Seems risky,' from Isabelle. 'Surely if they see him it's game over?'

'A girlfriend is the inflight manager on the Melbourne leg. I can message her as soon as we touch down. Actually, I think this is going to be okay. I'll tell her you're a musician and that this is your instrument. She won't be too bothered.'

'Well,' said Isabelle, 'maybe we have a solution.' And then, smiling at Nadya, 'Thank you. Allow me to arrange a small gift to show our gratitude.'

'Really, Madame, that's not...'

'It's nothing. A fragrance I can access from Yves Saint Laurent. Something along the lines of your Black Opium but – how to say – a little more exclusive.'

Nadya actually tried to smell herself at this point, flummoxed, and I thought, good trick, Isabelle, but then she found a way to top it when Nadya said, 'That would be incredible! Let me write down my address,' and Madame said, 'No need for that, darling. I'm friendly with the man who owns the airline.'

So there I was in business class, drinking off-menu champagne, engaged in warm flirtation with the most winsome stewardess in the skies while showing off a jeroboam of DRC and I wasn't even the coolest person in my row, let alone the flight. And I didn't care, not for a second, and surveying Isabelle and Nadya affectionately as they germinated a mini maternal girl crush, I thought maybe I love women more than wine, and isn't it fortunate that the two don't seem to be mutually exclusive.

Nadya returned to the economy cabin and Isabelle and I returned to our drinks, then she said, 'You are very well mannered, Jude.' I was excited at having secured The Big Boy's ongoing passage, humming at the sweet exchange with Nadya and more than a little buzzed from all the wine, but for whatever reason that faint compliment from Isabelle, that most trifling *bonne bouche* of flattery, made me blush like a schoolboy kissed in the hollowed-out tree in the playground at recess.

I used to have a thing about 'social standing' and 'class'. It's boring to talk about it now in my thirties, but among my friends I'm one of the few who didn't go to a private school, and my parents never had much money, but I was friends with rich kids[10] and I used to stay over at their places and go on holidays with them sometimes, and in that way I was exposed to their world.

I remember being eleven and invited to dinner at a friend's house, and after the meal there was a cheese plate and the father cut me a slice of something – a gruyère, I think – and it nearly blew my face off it tasted so good. The guy noticed I was having a bit of a moment with it and took it upon himself to run through all the cheeses on the board, telling me where they were from and how they were made and how they were different from one another. That night I went home and told my mum all about it – how there was this incredible world of cheese out there that was, well, superior to the honest Aussie cheddar we usually ate – and the next morning she took me to a cheese shop at the Central Market[11] and told the proprietor that I was interested, and he gave me twenty different tastes and a bit of instruction, and then Mum said I could choose a piece of any cheese I wanted to take home.

After that I borrowed a book from the school library, and maybe all of this sparked my love for wine, in the same way that people

---

10   I mostly met them through music and through performing.
11   In Adelaide.

\

who are interested in art sometimes become interested in furniture, because there's a good deal of common ground. It helped that my parents liked wine, not to excess, but they would drink McLaren Vale shiraz, and some sweeter-style wines, and when I was thirteen they started giving me a glass of sparkling burgundy[12] on Christmas Day. Mum liked port so there was always a bit of that around too.

Throughout this nascent obsession I'm jockeying for opportunities to stay over with friends or go with them to their parents' beach houses, and I'm fascinated by the protocol surrounding food and wine, by the order in which things happen and the manner in which the various objects and implements are used and arranged. The discovery that there was such a thing as a fish knife gave me an inordinate amount of joy.

As I got a bit older I realised I could use this newly acquired knowledge to impress girls – quite the revelation – and all the while my parents watched on unflappably, doubtless amused by my odd catalogue of interests but always supportive and never pushing me in any particular direction, certainly not academically or towards any profession.

I had my eighteenth birthday party the week after the final exam results were released and I invited all my friends, kids from school along with the wealthier kids, and I'd busted my arse at my casual job teaching guitar[13] so that I could afford to serve real champagne to everyone. All the kids got along fine, as you'd expect since all of them were dear to me in some way. But as the night progressed and everyone started to talk about what they were doing the following year, this chasm started to form. Every one of the rich kids was going to study law or medicine or (in an isolated instance) architecture, and very few of the kids from my school, myself included, had scored

12   Not really burgundy, most often it was Australian shiraz.
13   Hilarious, in hindsight.

well enough to be admitted into those courses, nor had we ever considered them as options.

I got appropriately drunk that night and everyone had a blast and friendships were formed that endure to this day,[14] but at one point, as dawn approached, I remember looking around and thinking to myself, Jude, that club you thought you were in, you're actually not in it at all. And it wasn't all sadness or 'woe is me'; it was more a timely salutation from the grown-up world.

I'd find out later than I had failed my audition to the Conservatorium of Music in Adelaide.[15] I stumbled into a Bachelor of Arts, then made it into law where I somehow completed a semester. Only after that did I finally make the grade at The Con. That's where I spent the next four years, studying music and concentrating on that and wine and not a great deal else.[16]

All of which is a roundabout way of saying that I had cultivated an interest in etiquette, so when Madame Le Roux said I had good manners – she who would scoff at the notion of a 'club' insofar as she could buy and sell every member of most – it was pointed and germane and generous.

Isabelle was spending a few days in Doha so we'd said our goodbyes, careful to avoid those airport farewells where you bid adieu once on the plane, and then five times more as you run into each other on the passenger conveyer, in the elevator, and at baggage claim or in the transit queue. I said she should look me up if she ever came to Melbourne and she let out a kind of chortle. I wasn't sure if that was because she'd never contemplate travelling so far, or

14 For example, between Bethany and Rob, who met that night and may or may not have had a cheeky pash in my dad's tool shed. I hadn't yet met the other members of our crew.
15 Well, it's not like you 'fail' per se – they just don't let you in.
16 Around then I started travelling more regularly to Melbourne, and met Adrian and Erica, and then Hayden and Antoine. It was a cross-state blur of practice, performance and partying.

whether Australia just didn't have the requisite allure. Anyway, she'd told me she was always good for dinner in Lyon.

I had sweated, sitting in the lounge, wondering if some cleaner was trousering The Big Boy while I was recalibrating over a Bloody Mary, but Nadya had caught me on my way off the plane and said she'd heard back from her friend and that everything was sorted.

As soon as I'd boarded the plane again I felt a tug at my elbow and turned to find a tall, blonde stewardess wearing a lippy grin; I thought she might have been Australian but it turned out she was from Vancouver and that her name was Sophie.

'Your instrument is safely onboard, sir.'

Then I'd sat down and actually declined a glass of champagne. I was long overdue for an alcohol-free day or two and started the clock knowing that everyone back at home would be wanting to share drinks and stories, especially in relation to The Big Boy and Bruno and our plans for a Melbourne outpost of Batard Rouge.

Not long after my lunch with Bruno it had become clear to Antoine that I could focus on little else than the restaurant. We had already kicked off an exchange of ideas in relation to the wine list and it was Antoine in the end who suggested we skip the trip to Burgundy so that I could return, earlier than planned, to Melbourne. We'd then spent the next few days in Paris doing our usual Paris things[17] while meeting daily with Bruno and eating our way through the entire menu at Batard Rouge.

That proved illuminating because, despite having been there fifteen or more times, I came to realise that I had mostly ordered the same things over and over. The fish dishes had been overlooked entirely, along with the beef tartare, and to that end Bruno and

---

17   That means restaurants, although this time on an unusual budget. We did Le Cinq and Ledoyen in the same day; Pierre Gagnaire for an à la carte dinner; and yam'Tcha and Spring for lunch and dinner on a day spent entirely in the 1st arrondissement.

I spent nearly an hour arguing over whether or not it would be acceptable to substitute kangaroo in the Melbourne rendering of that dish.[18]

I did some walking around, hitting up Macéo and a couple of other joints on rue des Petits-Champs, while Antoine spent time in bookstores looking for old volumes about wine and the history of French cider. Then we went to Hôtel Costes, where we spent the better part of seven hours smoking cigars and drinking Negronis.

And now, right now, I sit reclined and sober in the pale counterfeit light of this comfortable cabin as the plane loops the suburbs of Melbourne waiting for permission to land. Sophie has taken The Big Boy back to the stowage locker, and if you were to ask me now what I'm going to do with that bottle I couldn't give you an answer. Even if the answer is 'drink it', there is still the 'when, where and with whom' to contemplate.

Antoine will need to be there, and he's coming to Melbourne soon so there'll be a window, but really the wine should rest for a while after this voyage, ideally for several months at least. Maybe I'll need to insure it? So much value in a flagon of grape juice, in a thing you could pour anonymously at a party and drink in minutes, without most people even realising.

Bethany is everywhere in my brain. I'm stressed about talking to her but all I want is to share her orbit. A quiet glass of wine maybe. One of those hugs. Another bar and another try at a kiss. God, I'm sober and thinking like this. I wish at least she'd return my messages.

Meanwhile, Batard Rouge Melbourne feels like a strong new crush. I think about it every hour too, my stomach turning and twisting. I've scrawled notes about lighting, about butter, about cutlery, and already I have a list of close to a hundred Australian wines that can make a case for inclusion on a list that I am even now treating as a love letter.

---

18   It would not.

I want to be able to do this. And that's huge for me, especially since so much of it seems alien. Why not launch myself into the unknown, now more than ever? Jude in space. I close my eyes and see my brother, or a photo of him. I want to ring my dad.

It's just after 10pm as our wheels strike the tarmac and I'm thinking I could sleep, probably for eight hours or so, which is optimal for a late-evening arrival, and idly, aimlessly, I turn on my phone like all the men seated around me, all desperate to check email or football scores or message loved ones to broadcast their safe arrival. My phone powers up, locates a network then vibrates staccato on the armrest, and it's a message from Antoine to say that Bruno has died.

The next evening

If an alcohol-free day can be defined as any period of time lasting twenty-four hours during which no alcohol is consumed, then I technically chalked one up immediately prior to lunch with Rob and Bethany earlier today. It's Friday, but this wasn't 'lunch' in our customary sense. This was regrouping. This was planning our wake for Bruno, which we'd decided to hold that evening. Bethany ordered a bottle of Charles Melton Rose of Virginia Rosé.

I'd called Antoine as soon as I cleared customs, and he was struggling, having not taken the news well. He was still in Paris when he had found out. He'd called by Batard Rouge on his way to the airport to return to Spain, had told the taxi to wait while he ran in to say goodbye to Bruno, and there, in the tangle of early afternoon, when the restaurant would otherwise be buzzing, was met by a locked door and a handwritten note. His translation: 'Batard Rouge is closed today, in mourning'.

That's a hell of a thing to have to process, especially for someone with Antoine's frayed temperament, and he had retrieved his bag from the cab, sent the driver on his way, and stood on the doorstep, wondering what to do next.

He related all this to me over the phone, doing his glum best to convey his fear and dislocation.

'Jude, I didn't know where he lived. I had no phone number, nothing.'

'You were sure it was Bruno?'

'Who else could it be? The staff, they all stay a while, sometimes years, but he would never close the restaurant, not even if one of them was murdered on the street out the front. I knew it was Bruno. And I stood there for an hour and I couldn't do a thing.'

Eventually a waitress arrived – Astrid, weepy-eyed – to deal with a delivery, and she knew Antoine well enough to tell him gently that Bruno had died in his bed in the early hours of that morning, and that his wife had phoned the head chef, Gabriel, putting him in charge of the place until further notice. Gabriel had determined to remain closed that day as a mark of respect and asked all the staff to gather in the evening at Au Caveau Montpensier.

Astrid had said that Antoine could join them there, but that didn't seem quite right, not when the staff would be saddled with the twin burdens of losing Bruno and having to muster the fortitude to open the restaurant again the following day. Antoine did have the forethought to take Astrid's number and the contact details for Bruno's widow. We had never met her, and when Bruno had spoken about her, it was always in that jocular 'ball and chain' kind of way.

After that Antoine had returned to Spain – what else could he do? – telling Astrid he would fly back for the funeral. I thought maybe I should get straight back on a plane, that both of us should be there, but Antoine talked me out of that and suggested we hold a wake in Melbourne to honour our friend instead.

It fell to me to notify the Crew, and those conversations were awful, every one of them. When I flagged the prospect of meeting up, Adrian said we could use a private room at one of his restaurants. Rob and Bethany took the afternoon off work. Bethany said she was planning on having it out with her boss that day, but could attend to that piece of business later.

The discussion at lunch was gloomy and scattered and I was still distressed. Tough to wave goodbye to a man on one continent, to hear of his passing upon landing in another. Eventually Bethany insisted I let the cloud shift a little, at least for long enough to plan our memorial.

'What about wine?' Rob had asked.

'I feel like we'll be wanting some.' I was pissy with Rob for no reason other than a mad sense that his grief was somehow subordinate to mine because I had been in Bruno's company more recently.[1]

'We could do calvados or something,' from Bethany. 'It'd make it memorable at least.'

'Bethany, I'm coming off a near-as-dammit three-week bender. The prospect of getting fucked up on straight calvados holds zero appeal.'

'It has to be wine,' Rob said, cutting short my rant. 'Maybe a champagne theme?'

'Champagne and wakes,' said Bethany, taking my hand from across the table.

'Oh right. Sorry.'

I don't remember telling Rob that story, or anything about my brother's funeral, so it must have come from Bethany. I'm relieved he knows though.

'Has to be French, though,' Bethany, back on point.

'Maybe everyone brings the best French bottle from their collection?' *Moi* at *mon* most half-witted here, in that my newly acquired best French bottle goes by the name The Big Boy.

I hadn't mentioned him to anyone directly, but drunk texts were sent, then the hashtag blew up, and surely Antoine had said a thing or two. It all pointed unequivocally to my ownership of a jeroboam of 1978 Domaine de la Romanée-Conti, Romanée-Conti, even if the means of acquisition remained largely mysterious.

'I presume there's one bottle you'd be looking to exclude from that ordinance?' Rob said.

'Maybe we say the best standard format[2] French bottle?' from Bethany.

---

1   Rob actually met Bruno a year or so before the rest of us and had introduced us all on subsequent trips to Paris.

2   750ml.

'There will be some ball-tearers in amongst that lot,' Rob, doubtless reflecting on his colossal cellar and more than a few bottles of DRC of his own.[3]

'If ever an occasion called for it…' Bethany, glass in hand, held my gaze and kept it with her. That's new. Maybe it's grief or something else – I'm not able to see through the fog.

'It fits,' I said. 'Let's do it.' And with that came my first sip of rosé and a muted toast, with eyes still sunk into Bethany. Then we'd messaged the Crew with the wine arrangements and instructions to meet upstairs at Adrian's new restaurant that night at eight.

After lunch I'd gone home and thought about unpacking but instead sat at my desk holding The Big Boy, still in his case. Bruno's cheque was taped to the wall beside Post-it Notes scrawled with wine specials and song lyrics; a postcard from Bethany from when she was last in Paris; and my copy of the contract, signed with Terry just a couple of weeks earlier and pinned to the wall because I hadn't made a file in my little two-drawer cabinet called 'bag business', or whatever, and there was otherwise no obvious place to store it.

Then I'd turned my mind to what wine I would bring for Bruno. My French collection is mostly burgundy and champagne (and lacking in the 'rock star' department). The Big Boy is the only bottle of DRC I have owned[4] and there's not all that much with Grand Cru

---

3   Rob's cellar is immense and chaotic with no discernible organisational schema. It is, however, far less perilous, and appreciably more functional, than his dad's, which is a shed at his house into which mixed-case pallets of wine are unloaded by forklift, having arrived from a still larger storage facility elsewhere. Geoffrey (Rob's dad) then just reaches into whatever case takes his fancy, grabbing bottles through the cardboard and over time creating a Jenga-type effect as the stacked boxes develop structural weaknesses. More than once, Rob has put down his phone in my company, shaken his head and said, 'Dad's just lost another pallet.'

4   Putting to one side bottles Rob and Bethany and I have gone thirds in, which we drank together not long after acquisition.

on the label. But I do have something in mind: a Domaine Blain-Gagnard Grand Cru from Bâtard-Montrachet.

'Put the bastard in the fridge,' Rob messaged back, when I said maybe I'd found my bottle.

Now I'm holding it at my side, probably a little colder than is ideal but that's okay as surely someone will bring champagne which we'll drink first, and I'm shuffling up the stairs to the private room at the restaurant and I don't feel like someone who's about to share in seven or so bottles of uncommonly good wine. I feel rough, lost, and I guess this is mourning.

Heidi stands in the shadow of the door next to a blonde oak credenza, and I'm glad she's the first person I see. Straightaway she hugs me, her eyelids puffy from crying.

It's ten hours since I told her about Bruno, so she has done well to be here at all, travelling from Sydney with money tight and a new baby. It's Bruno we're talking about, though, and I see she has brought a Domaine Leflaive Bâtard-Montrachet, the very wine Bruno kept on his list at Batard Rouge.

'Best one I had.' She smiles.

'But… from where? They're hard to come by.' I stroke the bottle like it is a fresh kitten.

'Paris. Remember we almost bought one at the restaurant that night and the next day I decided I wanted one to cellar, and I asked Bruno for advice, you know, hoping he could get me a discount somewhere, and later that week he just handed me this bottle, in a brown bag, and said, "This is for you."'

'How did I not know this?'

'Because he told me not to tell anyone,' Heidi says. '"Do what you want with it, but don't tell them it was a gift."'

I'm silent, aghast really, and Heidi says, 'But I guess now I'm telling everyone.'

'Heidi.' I pull her close and her hair actually smells of Sydney: the humidity, perspiration, maybe some product even women with hair as thick and smooth as hers need to combat frizz, and it's calming to rest my chin there.

Adrian and Bethany are at the other end of the room by the window, Bethany twirling the curtain cord around her finger. They are drinking champagne that I presume is ancillary to the evening's official list.

Adrian looks even more wired than usual, maybe from lack of sleep, and certainly riding a forced high of enthusiasm and positivity. He is trying to combat his grief with a head-on assault, trying to cancel it out. When he's manic he looks shorter than he actually is, and I think that's because his head bobs around and he arches his back very slightly, pushing out his stomach. He is magnificent when he's like this, though. Unassailable.

Then Rob arrives with two bottles, and I ask him why and he says, 'One's from Dad,' and Heidi starts crying, and so do I, and Rob says, 'Guys, it's only burgundy.'

Rob is the only one in our crew who is categorically not a hugger – we all know it and mostly respect it. It falls to Heidi initially to wrap Rob in a firm squeeze. The canary survives the coalmine and so I go in as well, chest high, enveloping them both.

Robbie is into it – I mean he's not a robot – but he has a bottle of wine in each hand and can't reciprocate. And the bottles are a 1996 Domaine de la Romanée-Conti La Tâche[5] and a 1999 Domaine Comte Georges de Vogüé Musigny Vieilles Vignes Grand Cru,[6] so I forgive him for not entirely embracing the moment. He hangs in there for an acceptable period and then calls time by grunting at

5   From Rob's cellar.
6   From Geoffrey's cellar. In all the turbulence I'd forgotten that Geoffrey knew Bruno very well, having visited Paris more than any of us. He'll be mourning too.

another bottle in his eyeline that is unopened in an ice bucket. It's a 2002 Champagne Salon and I'm pretty sure that's from Bethany.[7]

Hayden is next up the stairs, lugging a cardboard box, which he hefts onto the credenza millimetres from Rob's La Tâche. The box is dotted with pink 'Sexyland' stickers and printed on it is 'x10 Bunnytron Thruster Vibrator'.

'Brought you that pinot, mate,' he says, after his own round of hugs.

I lift the lid with some hesitation and there's twelve bottles of Hurley Vineyard Garamond Pinot Noir in there, along with a single bottle of 1970 Chateau Haut-Brion Blanc.

'Sorry it took so long. I waited for the new release.'

'Right.' Even by his own high standards he's outdone himself here. The fact that he's removed twelve bottles of wine from what one presumes was a perfectly good container, then re-consigned them in the vibrator box… you have to tip your hat.

Some context. Working as a sommelier, Hayden is constantly carrying wine around, delivering bottles, showing up at tastings or dinners. Whether through boredom or general ratbagerry or who knows what, if he has a bottle for you that he knows you're going to have to tote around for a while, it will always be presented in a wildly inappropriate bag or box. He has a penchant for teen fashion labels, and a seemingly limitless supply of receptacles bearing the logos of male erectile deficiency medication. He saves the best ones for handing over rare or expensive bottles. I've sat on more than one tram, under the amused gaze of strangers, and pulled a bottle out and pretended to inspect the label lest anyone think I was packing a mother lode of Viagra.

Bethany once accused Hayden of not just hoarding the bags, but of going to some lengths to contact the brands and request bags

---

7   She'd called me to say her best French bottle was indeed Champagne and
     was that okay.

be mailed to him. He did not deny this charge, and Rob now brings his own bag whenever there's a chance Hayden might show up with a bottle or two for delivery.[8]

Adrian comes over and pours us champagne from a magnum of Marc Chauvet Special Club, which has been chilling in the corner.

'Just to get us started,' he says.

'What's your contribution to the main event?' Rob asks.

'Château Margaux,' says Adrian, '1947. Antoine sent a bottle too. Guigal La Landonne, 1990.'[9]

'Damn,' says Hayden. 'From storage?'

'Freshly picked this afternoon.'

Now Erica skips in, dressed in what looks like a ball gown, only it's light and probably cotton, and in a West African print. And you just know she bought it at a thrift store in Paris, maybe even at that place on rue de la Verrerie in the 4th arrondissement. Kisses all around, although she's doleful, which for Erica is rare, and when she's sad she wears more makeup than usual and it settles in the cracks and ridges of her skin, in what she describes as a tribute to a life spent smiling.

More than anyone in our crew Erica has pulling power. She's like a fucking planet. She draws people in as a matter of terrestrial instinct, but she's also a conduit for mood and temperament. She regulates all the weather in her atmosphere.

If any of us are sitting around in one of those 'hmmm I feel like doing something but I'm not sure what' states of mind, then Erica is invariably on the receiving end of a text. And from there it is glorious submission. She's maternal even, if your mother was Dionysus raised as a girl.

---

8   Another potential reading is that Hayden is actually sick of people using him as both wholesaler and wine mule.

9   One of the three famous single vineyard wines from Guigal, known collectively and colloquially as 'La Las' and, for what it's worth, the only Robert Parker 100-point wine in the line-up.

The bottle she's brought is cute; it's sauternes, Château Doisy Daëne L'Extravagant de Doisy-Daëne, 2010. And that completes the line-up which, in the order I presume we'll drink them, is:

Wine	From
Champagne Salon, 2002	Bethany
Chateau Haut-Brion Blanc, 1970	Hayden
Domaine Blain-Gagnard Bâtard-Montrachet, 2008	Me
Domaine Leflaive Bâtard-Montrachet, 2005	Heidi
Château Margaux, 1947	Adrian
Domaine de la Romanée-Conti La Tâche, 1996	Rob
Domaine Comte Georges de Vogüé Musigny Vieilles Vignes, 1999	Geoffrey
Guigal Côte-Rôtie La Landonne, 1990	Antoine
Château Doisy Daëne: L'Extravagant de Doisy-Daëne, 2010	Erica

That's an impressive ensemble, and if Bruno were to walk in he'd be moved to enquire what the fuck kind of celebration might call for such an exquisite selection of the Great Wines of France.[10] He may even detect the semblance of a theme, what with the brace of Bâtard, and certainly he'd be as happy as any of us to be within drinking distance of the cork being pulled on a bottle of '96 La Tâche.

We're seated now, entrées are up, and it's impossible for the kitchen to have planned for the wine. We could just as easily have had nine bottles of pinot. But the course of beef tongue on salsa verde with endive is well suited to the Salon, and it gives the fizz some space in which to work.

---

10   Minus Château d'Yquem, so it's serendipitous that Erica brought sauternes at all.

Rob makes a fine toast to Bruno, but we realise as one that none of us have much experience with wakes. Grandparents have died sure enough, my own brother when I was a toddler, but as a group of thirty-somethings we've barely borne witness to death.

It's around us, though, like humidity. Stifling and suffocating. I want to make a joke about how not even this wine or our friendship or our privilege or even Erica can recondition the air, but I don't because this is our state and all we can do is try to breathe.

The entrées are being cleared, and obviously Adrian has told his staff that this is no ordinary dinner. They've put on solemn faces and mostly look at the floor, and it feels weird because any one of them, any other day, would be flush with excitement at the wine, and would be angling for a sip or even a smell.

'Guys, we need an adjustment here,' I say, trying to fracture the melancholia. 'Some music?'

'Of course,' from Heidi, flicking through her phone, summoning a playlist. Adrian plugs her in and then at least we have music and mercifully Heidi has steered away from anything too sombre.

'Matched to the wine or the man?'[11] asks Bethany.

'We already did the matching.' Heidi smiles.

When the restaurant below was a milk bar or cobbler or pet shop, the owner would surely have lived in this room. It's the top half of a terrace, and heavy marks on the ceiling suggest it was once divided into several spaces, maybe for a family. There's a lean-to bathroom and storage room tacked onto the side, and the façade at street level says 1891. All of it is typical for this part of Melbourne.

When Bruno visited this city for the first time the thing that struck him most was the number of old buildings. For him Australia was supposed to be 'new'. He was expecting Kuala Lumpur with

---

11   Heidi experiences wine like music. Not classical music; almost always a
     more modern sound. She writes about music for work, and sometimes a bit
     about wine.

koalas, built in the middle of a desert. When Rob told him that Melbourne was once the richest city in the world, the way Bruno rejected that proposition out of hand was truly cross-cultural in that Rob does the same thing to people, down to the gesture, all the time.

Here upstairs the floorboards are waxy rather than polished, with stains from spilt wine and water. The walls are white like they always are, as though painters have only one colour for rooms like this, and the fresh splotches on the power sockets betray the amateur origins of the job. The furniture appears foraged.

If Adrian were a room, rather than a man, it would be this one. Engineered to bring people together. And looking around, the milieu has altered, lifted, the Haut-Brion is being poured and it's excellent, which is luck of the draw with a bottle that age, and now, for a moment, it feels more like dinner with friends.

'So, babe, something about you opening a restaurant?' Bethany's making light, and that's better than darkness but I'm still in a fog with her. I can't read her at times like these and it's a coin toss as to how to react.

I try laughing it off, but everyone is earnest and nodding and it's like some director at a board meeting just tabled a cost-cutting measure that, while harsh, makes undeniable fiscal sense given current market conditions.

'Wait, what?'

'We heard a cheque was presented,' from Adrian.

'That Batard Melbourne was a goer,' from Erica.

'We heard there was a napkin.'

I brought the napkin with me, and take it now from my bag, and Rob's put his damn glasses on as though he's about to inspect a subpoena. Clearly there's a consensus that he should undertake this initial review.

'Definitely agreed to do it,' I say, downcast. 'Spent all week figuring it out.'

Clinks and sips and the scraping of cutlery and the foil being scrupulously removed by Hayden from the two bottles of chardonnay.

'So what the fuck?' says Bethany. 'What's the issue?'

'Beth, that was then. Everything's changed.'

She's scowling, but through wide eyes so that she's all pupils and untamed eyebrows and then Erica says, 'If I was Bruno's widow I'd probably want some input?'

'How is this even a conversation?!' Bethany's scowl unfurls to a glare.

'The napkin's definitely a contract,' Rob says. 'Bruno's even initialled it.'

'But come on,' I say. 'What about his wife?'

'I don't think he liked his wife,' says Rob. 'Did anyone ever meet her?'

Silence, then Heidi says, 'Just once.'

'Jesus, when?'

'Four years ago. She came to the restaurant. I was alone, the place was only half-full. I could tell it was her. He ushered her in, brought her to the bar, and it was clear he wasn't going to make any introductions, so when he was out the back I went up and introduced myself.'

'She spoke English?' Hayden asks.

'I did it in French.' Heidi grins. 'The briefest of exchanges. Then Bruno came back and we spoke some more with him translating. It was nice. In the end I think he was relieved.'

'What did you think of her?' asks Rob.

'She looked like she was already a widow.'

Adrian gives a kind of commiserative grunt, as though, yeah, that's a hospitality industry thing, and he has form insofar as he's already chalked up his first divorce.

'Antoine will be at the funeral,' I say. 'He can ask her. It all seems too much just now.'

I feel like I need to break this thing down into small chunks, rungs on a ladder maybe, and take one at a time before stopping to check the lay of the land. If it works I move up a notch. And it's easy to step down if it doesn't.

Hayden has poured the two Bâtard-Montrachets side by side, and obviously there is solemnity around Heidi's bottle, which makes it all the more unusual when Bethany stands up and says, 'Grow some fucking balls for once, Jude,' and then walks out.

Heidi and Erica swap glances that say 'should we go after her?' but neither leave their seats.

'She'll be back,' Rob says. And damn right she'll be back given the calibre of wine still to be served. Someone could stick a corkscrew through her hand and she'd come back, but that's not the point and I look around blindsided and in search of sympathy. It comes, but a millisecond or two later than I'd like, and I take stock of the room, find the presence of mind to take a breath, and then ask, 'What's happening here?'

For some reason it's Hayden who speaks first, maybe emboldened by his bet fulfilment or maybe because he'd drawn the short straw earlier.

'It's been a big month, Jude. The bag thing, fine, once-in-a-lifetime kind of deal, then the DRC, which is a miracle unto itself. And *then* the golden ticket to set up Batard Rouge in Melbourne? You hit the jackpot three times in a row.'

'You're a lucky son of a bitch,' Adrian says.

'I don't feel lucky.'

'If you're talking about Bruno, that's exactly the point,' Hayden continues. 'You are lucky, Jude. Right now you're the luckiest guy on earth. And with Bruno dying, aren't you kind of obliged to ride that luck?'

I'm worried about Bethany, thinking maybe I'll go to her, but just then she skulks back to the table, thereby managing to execute a full-blown storm-out and re-entry without missing a single sip of wine.

'Sorry, Jude.' She starts on the Blain-Gagnard.

I want to let her know that whatever she's feeling is okay and that I'm probably the one who doesn't get it, but those words are hard to find, especially now, and in the end Erica jumps in and says, 'To Bruno! The most magnificent bastard of them all.'

I start with Heidi's Batard, staring at it, sounding it out aromatically. Finally, something I can make sense of. It's heroic. A dense vitelline puddle carried by crystal. Drawing it to my lips, blotting it, it's hard to conceive of this wine tasting of anything other than loss.

Everyone is drinking, our gears have shifted, and it's happening noiselessly. Then Adrian, bless him, says, 'Jude, do you remember the time you told Bruno that the geology beneath our vineyards in Australia is millions of years older than anything in France?'

Erica laughs; she was there, along with Adrian and Antoine. The conversation took place not in Paris but at the cellar door at Yarra Yering,[12] and I had mentioned it offhand, half-expecting Bruno to laugh it off or to say he knew it already, but his reaction was one of abject incredulity. He simply did not believe it to be true and, despite the evidence presented then[13] and subsequently,[14] I have no doubt he went to the grave ardent in his view that French soil is the oldest on earth.

'What did he make of The Big Boy?' Hayden asks.

---

12 In the Yarra Valley.
13 A handful of Wikipedia articles on Erica's phone and a fortuitous conversation with the winemaker Sarah Crowe, who walked into the argument on her way to the barrel room.
14 A categorically definitive academic article on the subject that I printed for Bruno and handed him at the airport, saying, 'Here's some reading material for the aeroplane.'

'I did win it off his mate,' I begin, 'and Bruno warned me off gambling with him so there was some initial weirdness. But I won it fair and square and he had no problem.'

'And a regal welcome extended to the queen of hearts on the river.' Rob grins.

'Did I mention we were drinking '98 Latour at the time?'

'You were fucking what?!' says Hayden, slamming down his glass, although carefully enough to avoid any prospect of spillage.

'Back at this dude's apartment in the 1st.'

'When did he whip out the Latour?' Rob asks.

'Right after some crazy, rare tequila he had in this unlabelled bottle fresh from the maker in Mexico.'

Bethany groans in a manner that can only be described as sexual. At the same moment there's a recess in Heidi's playlist, and the conversation breaks. No one fills the space. No waiters are around to fill the glasses. Erica shifts her weight back in her chair. Rob feels briefly for his phone in his jacket pocket, then thinks better of it.

Everybody has the Bâtard either to their lips or in one hand, and the second movement of New World Symphony[15] by Dvorák fills the speakers.

It's not like Dvorák was French, or like Bruno ever mentioned him, but sitting here drinking this wine with this group of people, thinking about Bruno dying and taking in this music, I feel like I understand what people see in churches.

Thank the baby Jesus for Adrian who, a matter of seconds after the movement finishes, and with the overall mood triangulated somewhere between sorrow, catastrophe and existential avowal, says, 'Well, the fucking Margaux is corked.'

And the laughter that follows is the shrill, raucous variety that strikes maybe once a year. We all try the Margaux anyway and it's

---

15   Symphony No. 9 in E Minor, Op.95: 'From the New World'.

shockingly corked, not so much a wine as liquid dank. A stale shell of displeasure.

'Corked from the minute it was bottled, too,' says Hayden. 'Travelled continents, gifted, sold, auctioned probably ten times, even inherited. And always corked. Never a single thing to offer.'

It's too appalling to drink and so we tip it, as we've tipped so many, down the nearest drain and into what I am sure is a well that could run to a river overflowing with The Disappointing Wines of Our Lives.

Mercifully we have two Grand Cru red burgundies up next from a couple of great vintages, and one of them is from Domaine de la Romanée-Conti – pleasing in the context of The Big Boy – and Adrian serves them side by side.

They need some time in the glass to have a think about themselves before they take the final leg of their journeys, and there is some concentrated twirling of stemware.

'Theoretically,' Heidi says, 'which part of town do you think would work best for Melbourne's Batard Rouge?'

'Fitzroy,' I say instinctively. 'Collingwood maybe. Somewhere around here.'

'Not inclined to go for a more moneyed crowd?' Adrian asks. 'Could work well in South Yarra or Armadale.'[16]

'I see it over this side. It's a place for our people. If others want to cross the river, then let them.'

'I know a guy,' says Adrian. 'He owns a few spots that could work. I'll introduce you.'

The La Tâche triggers a kind of hallucination that plays out against the coal-black shutters of my eyelids, closed in meditation as I welcome the gentle funk of the wine. The hallucination is of the

16   Adrian once seriously toyed with the idea of opening an Italian restaurant in the heart of Albert Park called 'Richie Bitchies', figuring he might as well label the tin as truthfully as possible.

open ocean, rippling and rolling, but the waves aren't made of water – they're violets, sprouting from every surface, each bloom folding and gathering the next and swelling fabric-like towards the horizon.

I resolve to stay in this place for a while, eyes still shut, and with the wine yet to pass my lips. I can see now that the water violets are leading me to a flatter, more restful section of their ocean, and then they disappear altogether, replaced by what looks like dirt, only it's twenty or more different types of dirt, each alone and distinct and yet blended somehow to create a patchwork earth that is delicate and protean. I want to eat it.

'Mind-blowing,' says Rob, presumably of the La Tâche. 'You'd like to think you could identify this blind. Maybe not the vintage, but its La Tâche-ness is so exposed. The band it's operating on… that intricate passage.'

'I want every bottle of wine I open to be like this,' says Erica. 'The top of the mountain. Before the cork comes out you're standing there. But you always slip. There's always something with the wine that pushes you off that peak. Not here, though.'

Hayden snorts. 'You really chase perfection in every bottle?'

'I don't chase it. It's just there. Every unopened bottle starts at the summit.'

'That's a bit depressing,' from Heidi. 'Why not start at the bottom and give it the chance to ascend on its own terms?'

'Their terms are their own,' Erica replies. 'That's the point. I don't look at a bottle through the lens of another wine. There is no "other". The thing is the thing, all by itself until it meets me.'

Heidi is about to respond when Bethany says, 'Well, I don't know where you go from a summit but I'm here to tell you the Comte de Vogüé is even better.'

Collectively we startle, then swirl, and I take a big swig before anyone else and the second I splash it around my mouth I know we could argue for years over which wine is superior. They are sisters from different mothers – it seems unnatural to love one more than the other.

'How can you say that these wines don't talk to one another?' Heidi asks Erica.

'Now they can talk.' Erica wears a vinous, festal grin. 'You can compare them if that's what you want. But in essence they're autonomous. As things they're independent.'

'The La Tâche still wins for me,' says Rob, as usual pronouncing his own bottle best in show.

'Jude, the wine list for your restaurant, it's going to be entirely Australian?' Heidi has been speaking with Antoine, and with two glasses of summit-esque burgundy in front of me, along with a plate of sous vide duck breast with green olive and pine mushroom, I'm happy to spill some beans.

'It's true. It was my only condition.'

'And poor Bruno died before he could change his mind.' Rob is joking, but only a little.

'I'm a sommelier and I've never had total carriage of a wine list,' says Hayden, with a fleck of dejection.

'I've owned fifteen restaurants over the years and neither have I,' from Adrian.

'Guys, come on…'

'There are always outside influences,' Hayden continues. 'The owner has shares in some winery, he hates chardonnay, you've inherited stock from the last place, he only wants wines with trophies or high scores – whatever the reason you never get an entirely free run at it. You're always beholden to someone.'

'And I have to deal with the sommelier.' Adrian smirks.

'It's a dream,' says Erica, her eyeshadow glittering.

'There needs to be a process,' Rob jumps in, 'and clearly we all need to be involved. One approach would be for each of us to take a varietal…'

'Dude, it's my fucking wine list.'

Two reactions now from the table. First they are silent, then they smile, closed-mouthed, but eyes sparkling.

'That's better,' says Adrian.

Even putting my bag money and The Big Boy to one side, I do get why this whole restaurant and wine list thing is hard for them to fathom. Out of all of us – out of everyone around this table – I'm the least suitable candidate for the job. This is not because I love wine any less, or because I'm disorganised or unreliable; it's because I'm not the leader of this group or any group. I'm the least leaderly person I've ever met.

'I'll want your help,' I say, finally. 'And yes, we should approach it in a structured way.'

'How many wines in total then?' Erica is straight down to business.

'Has to fit on a page. Like in Paris.'

'So what, forty?'

'In Paris it runs to thirty-two, but that's not to say we have to match that exactly.'

'Could use a smaller font size.'

'What's locked in already?' Heidi asks.

'Basket Press of course.' Adrian, on my behalf.

'Main Ridge Pinot,' says someone.

'The Vat 1.'

'Have to have Block 6.'

'Leo Buring Riesling.'

'Grange, for sure.'

This goes on for a minute, with maybe twenty wines tabled as forgone conclusions and no one disagreeing. I'm on board with most or even all of them, but none of this makes my job easier.

'It'll be the last ten that really mess with you,' says Erica, 'the last five especially.'

'Small price for having the best job in the world,' says Rob, prompting a series of toasts: to Batard Rouge, to me, to Bruno, and to 'the best job in the world'.

The La Landonne has been liberated into a decanter and it's a serious shame that Antoine can't be here for it.

'Surely the right approach is to take a few months and drink your way through every contender,' Erica says. 'There's no time pressure. Why not aim for perfection?'

Bethany is looking at me tersely again, but I'm too soused to take matters up with her in any meaningful way, so I flash her a smile, warmly, or at least that's the intention, and she sticks her tongue out at me. It's coloured just like those violets, and that makes me smile more broadly still.

Then Erica taps a butter knife against her glass and says she'd like to sing for us. This is surprising, but in context not among the ten or so most surprising things Erica has done, even this year, and it makes more sense still when she says she's written a new verse for our Grand Crew song. It goes like this:

To every wine we've ever met
(We cheer!) Forever in your vinous debt
(Hear, hear!) We come to play and have our way
At Batards' Rouge and Montrachet
FOREVER! and this day (Grand Crew!)

I'd probably make a change or two structurally, but it's well received, even by Beth, and is committed to lore. Then Rob leads the charge with a rendition of the original verse, after which all of us do our best to sing along to Erica's addition.

Erica is well pleased by the reception and sets about pouring out her bottle of L'Extravagant[17] while I try to piece together a

---

17   Mercifully in 750ml format, rather than the half bottle.

narrative around the evening, or at least something I can file away for tomorrow. In the end it's the same as before: Batard Rouge and Bethany, and I don't know if that reads like a to-do list or bullet points for a love letter.

Then Heidi puts her music back on, and it's not a song I know but the lyrics are:

> From cinders, fallen mud.
> The Fall that seeps,
> Your sculpture's blood.
> My body though, not for show.
> Ask the crowd for blood.
> They know.

I ask Heidi why she chose that track and she says she's not sure, but that sometimes she thinks that wine is like blood.

Two days later

I'm sitting in the window at Marios on Brunswick Street checking out the menu, having decided to wait until Vincent arrives before ordering a coffee. Vincent is the guy Adrian thought I should talk to about finding a spot for Batard Rouge. Emails were exchanged over the course of yesterday, then I called him last night and he suggested meeting here, which is fine.

I don't know for sure what Vincent looks like, but ninety seconds on the phone with him was sufficient to form a view. Out the window I see a bloke coming out of the bookstore and he's a big man, taller than me, built like a boxer past his prime, and he's wearing black suit pants and a grey, faintly striped jacket that's not quite double-breasted and makes him look broader still around the shoulders.

This is definitely my guy, and sure enough he gives me a little nod through the glass before coming in. He's smiling and shaking hands with a couple at a different table, so I go back to looking out the window, but then he comes over and puts his hand down on the bench right next to me and says, 'Jude, let's go for a walk.'

I almost ask him for permission to grab a coffee for the road, but he's already holding the door open for me so I scamper out and he pats me on the back as I exit and I think, geez, talk about establishing a power dynamic.

It's unusually warm in Melbourne for this time of year and it's hard not to notice that many of Fitzroy's women, local and transient, have dressed lightly for it.

'Nice day for a stroll,' says Vincent as one girl walks by wearing a singlet and a skirt that a more conservative boutique might offer for sale as a belt. 'Heard you blokes drank some good juice the other night. How was the '90 Landonne?'

That's a prescriptive enquiry from a guy I had not pegged as a wine-lover, and Vincent is immediately across my surprise.

'Yeah, I love my wine. It's my biggest hobby, really.'

'Would I be right to guess you have some Italian ancestry going back a generation or two, Vincent?'

'Like all the best bits of Melbourne, mate. Yeah, the folks came from a town about an hour from Palermo, emigrated when I was seven. First word I learned in English was "stop", to try to get the kids in the Altona playground to lay off kicking me.'

'Jesus.'

'Yeah, they didn't keep that up for too long, though. Dad told me no fighting when he dropped me off on my first day. Sort of modified that rule a bit moving forward, if you follow.'

'Not being able to communicate... I can't imagine.'

'You learn quick. No choice really.'

We walk some more in silence, Vincent leading the way, and he's not shy about checking out some of the women walking past. I wouldn't describe him as lecherous but it makes me uncomfortable to the point of shortening my stride to the point of dropping behind him. God forbid I should have the stomach to call him out on it.

'Ever eat at this place?' Vincent asks, stopping in front of a nondescript restaurant frontage, which looks like it might be one of those Japanese/Vietnamese hybrid joints that succeeds only in doing neither well.

'Never even noticed it.'

'Yeah, bit of a shithole.'

We keep walking east for ten minutes or so, and I don't know where we're going – maybe to meet Adrian or perhaps he's going to take me to see some of the buildings he owns – and by now we're in

Collingwood. He stops in front of a three-storey textile factory, fairly typical for the area, and says, 'Well, this is my place.'

'Like to get behind a sewing machine every now and then?'

Vincent chuckles and says, 'Don't know what they make down there actually. Could be shoes for kids.'

Then we're walking through a garage door, which he's hauled up with one hand like he's picking a daisy, and he motions for me to follow him up a set of stairs.

'Jude, I own a lot of land around here,' Vincent says as we trudge up beyond the second-floor landing. 'Rather have my money on the ground than in a bank. Thing is, most of the land I own I don't really use. I keep an eye on it, waiting for the right moment to do something with it.'

'And what do you do with it, eventually?'

'Build apartments, Jude. What the fuck do you think I want to do with it?'

Right. 'So will this place be apartments one day?'

'Not sure. I like this one.'

We're standing in a trashed-looking alcove, with junk mail stacked on a faux Victorian table stand, itself extremely trashed, and Vincent opens its little drawer and extracts a key that unlocks the thick redwood door before us.

The first thing I think when I walk in is that I've somehow ended up in the company of the Australian version of Maurice from Paris, in that this place is vast, incomparable, and seems to speak directly to the persona of its occupier.

Vincent has the whole floor to himself up here and most surfaces are bare and built from dense materials, either concrete, steel or ancient plaster. Most eye-catching are the machines. In the middle of the space is some kind of hauling device, surely built to lift heavy objects from the ground floor all the way to the top, and it's a complex-looking unit, all metal and cables, bigger than a car, and if not actually restored then certainly cleaned and polished so as to appear sculpture-like. Elsewhere are other apparatus in similar states of loving repair. Based on a couple of the conveyer-belt-style pieces, maybe this place was a cannery or something. There are also several huge steel pots stacked against a wall on the northern end of the space.

Even the windows look industrial strength. Triple glazed, maybe – it is utterly soundless up here – and the wooden frames themselves are half a metre thick.

There's not a lot of a furniture: a couch, a dining table and chairs and a shelf stacked with DVDs beside a big-screen television. Sure enough there is also a heavy boxing bag strung from the ceiling, seemingly handpainted with a motif of what looks like ancient Rome.

You could pad up and play a game of cricket here and risk damaging nothing other than the television.

'I want to show you something,' says Vincent, having given me a chance to take it all in. 'Come through here.'

He leads me past what might have been a diesel generator, around a corner and into a corridor with a series of rooms branching off, including a more conventional kitchen and another space that houses five identical glass-fronted wine fridges side by side.

Every time I get to look at another person's wine collection I get a bit giddy, like I'm about to read a newspaper review of a performance I've been in and someone's already told me the critic loved the show. It's as though no bad can come of this. Even if the wine isn't to my precise taste, it's still a fascination, and always revelatory.

'I keep a few hundred here and the rest offsite,' says Vincent. 'Check this out.' He points me to a tablet computer hung like a sad painting on the wall next to the row of wine fridges, and he has some sort of cellar management software running on it and he says, 'That's the full collection.'

I scroll through and it's alphabetical, with a lot of Tim Adams Aberfeldy, and some Adelina Estate,[1] and as far as wine tracking applications go, this one does a fine job.

'Designed that myself,' Vincent says. 'None of the others gave me the flexibility I was looking for.'

'All about discipline, these things,' I say, recalling my own failed attempts at logging wine arriving in the cellar and, far harder, accounting for the bottles going out.

'I've set this up so that when I want something offsite, the software sends a message to the storage place and to a guy who works for me. I can get a bottle here in less than an hour.'

I pull two fingers rapidly down the screen, and I see that the list is long, like thousands and thousands of bottles, and that it seems to be at least eighty per cent shiraz. I'm looking for some way to insert a jibe about Vincent's obvious penchant for the heavy stuff when he says, 'How'd you feel about a blind tasting?'

I don't turn down too many offers of that nature so I say, sure, and then Vincent opens a drawer and pulls out this glass which is exceedingly unusual (I've seen most of what the wonderful world of stemware has to offer, believe me), and I can see it's made by Riedel and it's clear crystal but the stem itself is kind of triangular, climbing from one point by the base to two where it meets the bowl. There's obviously something in there, some piece of technology, although overall it's aesthetically pleasing as an object, and when Vincent hands it to me its weight and proportions are reassuring.

'Had these made up specially too. You'll see why.'

He turns his back to open a bottle of wine, and I look the other way, like the shop assistant when you're punching in your

---

1   Two balls-out wines. Both shiraz and both from the Clare Valley.

pin number, only I actually have something interesting to look at, what with these wine fridges and, Jesus, this guy really does love Aussie shiraz.

I can hear the wine being poured, and it's a generous allocation which I appreciate, so it looks like we'll be drinking rather than tasting. I still don't look around lest I accidently spy the bottle, although having just heard Vincent yank a cork I have one piece of information vis-a-vis the wine's identity.[2]

When I turn around, the glass is enclosed entirely by his gigantic hands.

'Jude, I'm going to send you into my tasting room. You'll go in alone, and when you want to come out just ding the glass with a finger like you're about to make a toast. I've got it set up so that it'll send me a signal out here.' He pauses like he's expecting me to freak out, or at least ask a question, but hardcore as this guy undoubtedly is, I've reached a point this past couple of months where not a lot fazes me.

'The thing about the tasting room,' Vincent continues, 'is that it's entirely free of light. There's a small bulb in your glass that will illuminate the wine, but otherwise you'll be in total darkness.'

Cool, I'm thinking, this is something new, then he says, 'And, Jude, the space is also odourless and soundless. It's what's called an anechoic chamber. Some people freak out at the silence. They can't handle it. If you stay still you can actually hear your blood making its way through your veins.'

'Sounds intense.'

'Just wait.' He's smiling at least when he says this, which is comforting. 'Come on in.'

---

2   And really I have information in addition to the seal in that I reckon this
    guy would have to do some serious rummaging in order to find a bottle that
    wasn't shiraz.

Vincent opens the door at the end of the passage, and maybe a metre further in is another door, not the bank-vault-style hatch I was anticipating, but a bloody thick door nevertheless. Vincent ushers me into what is a cramped space for two men, then gestures for me to close the first door. It's already pitch-black, and Vincent clicks away entering an access code of some kind, and then the big door opens (sounding like a bank vault, which is cool) and it gets darker still, even in our little in-between space. Vincent presses the stem of the glass he's been holding and it illuminates, faintly, a bowl of red liquid suspended in space. I take it from him and Vincent steps around me, gives me a gentle tap on the shoulder and says, 'Sit anywhere you like. See you in a bit.'

I take a couple of steps forward. Right away I'm disorientated, not sure whether I'm going to fall headfirst or on my arse, but fairly certain it'll be one or the other. Thankfully the path is clear, as in there are no obstacles, and the low light from the glass at least gives me a sense of the distance between my hands and my face.

Once I'm in, the door hisses closed behind me and I think, well, they'd probably never find my body. I am standing motionless, only I know I'm swaying because I can see my wine tilting and I think, okay, let's at least try to get comfortable in here. I drop carefully to my knees, and notice pretty quickly that the floor slopes gently upwards to my right. I follow it, on hands and knees, and texturally it's changing, getting softer and more cushioned. After about two metres I reach a wall, also padded, and because of the gradient of the floor and, I guess, by design, I can lean against that wall and take a breath and indulge in a sense of relative safety if not outright comfort.

And the wine. I realise that I'm not sat at the bottom of an actual bottle of wine, drowned in the juice, with the glass and cork barricading me from the outside world – but that's what it smells like. And the glass isn't even in sipping distance of my mouth.

I wonder if I could get drunk just smelling this wine, and I think maybe I am already so I may as well drink some and see how that goes. I take a big hit, briefly drawing it over my palate, more concerned with simply getting this first lot down, and it slams me. The crushing weight of bass.

I liked techno when I was younger, had a few experiences with high-end sound systems, and so have a working knowledge of the capacity of the extreme low-register of a given harmonic series to occupy the dual quarters of mid-chest and inner ear. But this wine, acoustically speaking, has settled itself by my temporal lobe and is seeping, bleeding, like treacle spilt on felt.

It's in my brain, the various cells and fibres of which are wrapped by it, and yet they hum, quiver almost, like a bird agitating for grub. But that's just the tendrils, the strands. As for the carriage of the main body of sap – the mass, I suppose – it's jarring now but pleasantly, weighing my neck and spine and determining, yes, there is a southerly pathway worthy of exploration. I make a tasting note for Vincent: heady and disorientating.

It's impossible to determine how long I've been in here, although surely not long given I've had only one sip from Vincent's magic glass. I guess in the past there must have been circumstances in which I've left a glass of wine unfinished, although none spring to mind, but I'm ready to get off this ride, at least for now, so I tap the nail of my right index finger against the glass, and the sound it makes is ethereal.

Vincent is straight in, cracking the safe, bringing the light with him, and I stand up, so, so slowly, and walk towards it, glass tucked upright in my armpit, and I feel like I've been in space and we've re-entered the earth's atmosphere and now I need to learn how gravity works again.

'How'd you get on, mate?'

'You're a sick bastard, Vince.'

He waits until I'm through that second door, lurching like a toddler off a playground roundabout, then he takes the glass and slaps me hard across the shoulder blade and says, 'You just set a new record.'

'No way. I must have lasted longer than some of them, I can hardly feel my legs. Get fucking Adrian up here, see how he goes.'

'Jude, you lasted longer than anyone on their first time. You also didn't spill any of your wine. That's never happened before.'

'How long was I in there for?'

Vincent takes his time with this one; it's a question he obviously gets a lot when he's entertaining.

'Jude, there are a couple of things I'll never tell you. Even if we become close friends. Even if, somehow, you end up at my deathbed. The first is how long you were in that chamber for just now.'

I nod and shrug. 'And the second?'

A gold-toothed grin from Vincent. 'Which wine you were drinking.'

I've just had what, by any measure, was a life-altering experience, and I'm still re-acclimatising and all that, but what I say next is so unlike me as to make me wonder if I was hypnotised in that chamber and am about to embark upon the rest of my life an entirely different person.

'I'll give you a thousand bucks if you tell me what I drank.'

'Not even in the ballpark, Jude. Last year a Chinese developer offered me fifty grand just to tell him the region.'

'People are always desperate to know?'

'Always. Most offer money' – and he really does look flummoxed – 'which is hard for me to fathom.'

'Do you always serve the same wine?'

'Yep. And I can almost guarantee you've drunk it before.'

I'm starting to like this guy and I'm hoping there's a way we might be able to work together, what with his land banking and borderline-depraved approach to sharing his colossal wine collection. I'm not quite sure what happens next, though, and I notice I'm sitting on the floor, propped up against one of Vincent's wine fridges, which he doesn't seem to think is particularly odd or out of place, but nevertheless extends a hand and pulls me up and shows me to the couch.

'You're a patriot, Vincent. I've never seen a cellar with so much Aussie shiraz.'

'Always been my thing, Jude. Everyone seems to slide towards burgundy. Never happened to me, not that I would have minded. I was open to it. Don't get me wrong – I'm happy to drink pinot. More than happy. We get a lot right with shiraz here, though.'

No doubt, and if one thing can be set relatively firmly in stone it is that the last wine to pass my lips was shiraz, almost certainly from South Australia.

'Jude, I used to have a bit of a problem with violence. For a variety of reasons I was an angry guy. People think wine is refined, I reckon that's bullshit. It's a violent act, making wine.'

'Violent for the berries.'

'Little bit of bloodlust in there, mate, a bit primal.'

'If you're doing most of your drinking in that room I'd say it's brutal.'

'Leonard Cohen used to talk about getting high on Château Latour – did you know that? He said all the great wines of Bordeaux have a very specific high. And I don't take drugs any more. But I still get really fucking high.'

He gets up and leaves, to the bathroom or wherever, and I'm content to sit by myself for a while, and it does feel quite a lot later than when I was perched on a stool at Marios. Mid-afternoon, maybe? I'm thinking about that wine, but also about two more unanswered messages I've sent Bethany in the last forty-eight hours, about Batard Rouge, and about who I'd invite first to drink in Vincent's chamber so that they may be reborn again, in wine.

Vincent comes back carrying a couple of Bloody Marys in cut-crystal tumblers, the ideal receptacle for the job. Here's cheers then, and the drink is perfect, just what the physician prescribed in that I need something but the wine in the chamber left no road before it, nor a fork, nor even a sign saying 'Next pub, three hundred kilometres'.

The drink is so preposterously delicious that I have to ask Vincent how he made it and he says, 'Yeah, the secret is a bit of saffron. I have a farm on Kangaroo Island. Grow a shitload of the stuff.'

A saffron Bloody Mary. I'll be borrowing from that playbook. I say, 'Heard you might be able to help me out with a building?'

'Yeah, no worries.' A pause. 'Now that I can see we get along.'

'How well do you know Adrian?' I ask, thinking let's join a few dots before launching into a full-blown negotiation.

'We're solid acquaintances. I have a bit of a problem with decanters, as in I'm kind of obsessed with them. Adrian gets 'em for me wholesale. In return I help him out with a building or two.'

'Sounds like a good deal for Adrian.'

'Yeah, and I guess I eat for free at all his places too.'

I'm tempted to ask Vincent if he remembers the last time he paid for a meal of any kind, at least in Melbourne, then I think about asking whether I could take a look at his decanter collection, but he's keen to get to business.

'So for your joint I was thinking about that place we stopped by on the way here.'

'The noodle joint?'

'Yeah.'

It seems like it was last week when we were there, but no doubt the location was spot-on and any place I find is likely to require significant fit-out. This building is at least already being used as a restaurant.

'What about the current tenants?'

'They're on a month-to-month. Not doing too well I don't think.'

'And the kitchen?'

'They put it in a couple of years ago. Couple of huge wok burners which I doubt'll be much use to you, but the rest of it's pretty standard, all your usual gear. French-type place you're looking to set up, yeah?'

'A bistro.'

'You'll need new chairs and all that. Shouldn't take much, though.'

'And what are we looking at roughly in terms of rent?'

'Yeah, I've been thinking about that. Current guy's paying seventy grand a year, but I probably stuck the claws into him a little hard. Bloke fell in love with the site. Rent can come down.'

Nothing here so far that will cause serious affront to my napkin budget. There's silence while I crunch numbers in my head and start to frame a question or two around terms and timeframes.

Eventually Vincent says, 'There might be another way we can sort this out.'

'I'm not sure free meals are going to get us there, mate.'

A smile from Vincent, some warmth. 'It gets us some of the way,' and then, 'I hear you recently came into possession of a significant bottle of wine.'

Huh.

'But Vince' – I feign a frown – 'you realise it's not shiraz?'

'I make a few exceptions,' he says. 'DRC is one of them. Plus, I have a daughter born in '78. So you know, sentimental shit.'

'I'm not sure how comfortable I am bringing The Big Boy into this.'

'I understand. And I'm not proposing buying it outright. That building we're talking about, I'm probably going to want to develop it in five years, so I can't give you a long-term lease. And there's a chance I may need to get at it a bit sooner, depending on the neighbours over there. So here's what I'm thinking. Actually I had it drawn up –' He pulls a single A4 page, folded into quarters, out of his jacket pocket and hands it to me.

As regards the lease of the retail and/or commercial property ('the premises') identified by Vincent; Jude and Vincent ('the parties') hereby agree that the initial term shall be for three years. Jude shall place his jeroboam of 1978 Domaine de la Romanée-Conti, Romanée-Conti (hereafter, 'The Big Boy') into secure storage upon the commencement of the lease, with both Jude and Vincent required to sign for its release from said storage. The parties agree that should Vincent, for any reason whatsoever, be unable to offer a three-year extension to the initial three-year term, then The Big Boy shall be returned to Jude at that time and rent paid retrospectively at the agreed rate. In the event that a three-year extension is granted, then ownership of The Big Boy is passed to Vincent by way of full consideration for the six-year lease of the premises.

'So you're looking at one of two scenarios,' says Vincent, and I welcome the summary. 'Either you pay nothing for three years, then fix me up retrospectively while keeping the bottle, or you get six years rent in return for that one double mag.'

'What would you do with the wine, honestly?'

'Mate, I'm going to drink it. Ideally with my daughter.'

'What about if I wanted one glass, in your anechoic chamber.'

'Done.'

Vincent raises his Bloody Mary, and we chink, and I guess I just found a home for Melbourne's Batard Rouge, widow issues notwithstanding.

'I'll have my guy make a few amendments and circle back to you,' I say, refolding the document and thinking Rob is going to absolutely love this.

Vincent grunts his assent and says we should agree on a place to store The Big Boy. I say MW Wines works for me, and he says sure.

'I did mean to ask,' Vincent says, 'how confident you are in relation to its provenance?'

'Mate, I won it in an illegal late-night poker game in Paris, off a black-market truffle dealer I'd met just hours before. I don't know how much more confident I can be.'

Vincent smirks, and I blush, oddly proud that guys like him seem to find me interesting enough to keep around. I stand, shake his hand and thank him for the Bloody Mary and especially for the wine and we resolve to meet later that week to finalise the lease agreement.

As I'm making my way out the door, still a little off-balance, Vincent hands me a compact disc and says, 'Adrian mentioned you were in the music business. I'm in a band, kind of an early Springsteen-type sound. Lemme know what you think of our demo?'

About a week later

Amid planning for the restaurant and trying to decipher Bethany's state of mind and a thousand other things, I have inexplicably agreed to take on work in what remains my actual paid field of employment. So now I'm rehearsing a part for Mozart's Requiem in D minor, which I know already, having performed it on a more or less annual basis for the past twenty years, but it's something you don't want to botch, especially when it's at the Melbourne Recital Centre and you're being paid to get it utterly right, and by that I mean better than note perfect, more like harmonically transcendent.

Despite its grotesque popularity,[1] this piece of music snatches me by the throat whenever I'm near it, inciting a form of paralysis such that even during the performance I need to remind myself to move my head once in a while or at least lift my chin. 'You looked like an emo kid singing along to the Smiths up there,' Bethany once observed. I'd spent the show clad in a black cloak staring at the floor, so the comparison made sense.

In the absence of traditional communication methods, like actually speaking to her, I'm left fidgeting with my phone, conducting daily, forensic reviews of my chat history with Bethany. Most of the action, at least by weight of words, occurred in Paris around the time I acquired The Big Boy. It's mostly me telling her how incredible everything is, and her responding periodically with 'wow' or 'crazy'. If I hadn't been so ceaselessly drunk I might have realised even then that something was awry.

Maybe five years ago I agreed to be a part of an amateur performance of the Requiem because I wanted just once to sing it drunk with a full choir. I chose one of the early rehearsals for the

---

1   The Jacob's Creek of classical compositions.

experiment and by way of warm-up consumed an entire bottle of 1998 Moss Wood Cabernet Sauvignon. The choice of wine had been fervently workshopped by the Crew.

In what passes for gossip in classical music circles, Beethoven apparently once told a friend[2] that he found Mozart's Requiem to be 'too wild and terrible'. The Master probably never said that, but as rumours go it's just sufficiently unchaste as to titillate. And it's the story I chose to tell as I introduced the Crew to the wine-matching challenge.

Remarkably, everyone agreed the wine should be cabernet, except for Heidi who thought sauternes, and after the fact I could see her logic.

It was odd, initially, to be drinking just for this purpose. Kids get drunk before they go out to rid themselves of inhibitions or anxieties, and doubtless some people drink to forget, but wine for me has always existed just for now. Sitting at home drinking aged Moss Wood from a Vinum Extreme cabernet stem with the express purpose of singing drunk in a choir had a distinct and illicit novelty.

I'd decided to open the bottle an hour prior to rehearsal so that full absorption would be in progress as I took the stage. It is absolutely possible to consume three-quarters of a litre of wine in this timeframe, but it is a task best approached methodically and alone.

I had settled on the Moss Wood after narrowing the field to a small handful of Margaret River cabernets. Wines from Cullen and Vasse Felix were shortlisted and duly considered, but the thing about the Moss Wood is that it's always had this propensity to sing to me in the glass and in something like the register occupied by the Requiem.[3]

---

2   The violinist Karl Holz.
3   At the rehearsal I held notes longer than I should and more than once started humming to parts of the arrangement that were not my own. The rest of the time I was anxious about people realising I was drunk.

Most people think it's boring or pretentious when someone says wine speaks to them, or that wine is their life force, or that in one sip they can take a journey up and down a post-tonal scale, or that a wine sings to them from the glass. I don't mind that kind of talk, though, and I prefer it in spades to the bullshit expelled at formal tastings and functions.

I have no special animosity towards garden-variety wine wankers, it's just odd that their rules and lexicon have become the touchstone for wine communication. If you attend a wine-tasting course more or less anywhere in the world, you will be taught to speak about wine in accordance with their syntax, and that means the fucking aroma wheel and hours spent pondering complex notes of white peach, fennel bulb, aniseed and citrus blossom.[4]

Anyway, I'm supposed to be studying the score to the Requiem when Erica calls and says there's an issue at the facility.

'What kind of issue?'

'Jude, if you'd been down here you'd understand the problem. It's a two-cubicle affair, and right now we have cartons stacked higher than the urinal.'

'Jesus, in less than a week?'

'Word spreads.'

'I should probably see it for myself.'

'Get your arse over here.'

As she hangs up my doorbell rings.[5] I'm wearing boxer shorts and a singlet and I've yet to trouble the shower since awakening four hours prior.

I figure it'll either be someone I know or someone I can shoo away, so I climb the stairs and peer into the sunshine and it's Bethany

---

4   Domaine Thomas Morey Chassagne-Montrachet 1er Cru Morgeot 2014.
5   It plays Toccata and Fugue in D minor by J.S. Bach (thanks to Felix Mendelssohn). What is it with D minor?

standing beside her bike wearing yoga pants, which means she's taken the day off work.

'Let's go for a ride,' she says.

'Give me two minutes.' Damn it, I could have gone to her myself today, could have ridden there this morning. It's her, though. Here. As usual. With what I'm hoping is an olive branch.

She leaves her bike on our porch, which is so stereotypically Northcote share house it could feature on the front of a coffee table book on that subject, and follows me downstairs to my room.

'Fuck it's cold.'

'It's a wine cellar, Beth. And it's actually nineteen degrees down here today, borderline too warm. I'm thinking about turning on the air-conditioning.'

I'm fumbling in my wardrobe for a pair of jeans while Bethany pokes around the wine racks, picks up one of my guitars and plays, as always, the first ten or so bars of 'Patience' by Guns N' Roses,[6] then spies the cheque from Bruno taped to the wall at my desk beside the contract Rob and I signed with Terry for my bag business, and she says, 'Wow, actual evidence,' which I find a bit strange so I say, 'What, did you think I made it up?'

'Didn't seem especially real.'

'Is it even real? Look at me.' And I'm into my jeans, stubble scraping the collar of a wrinkled, unbuttoned shirt Rob gave me eight years ago.

'You don't look too different.'

'So far I've got a few bits of paper stuck to my wall.'

'You have The Big Boy, too. Where's he?'

The DRC, which Bethany has never seen, was dispatched yesterday for storage.

'He's gone away for a little while. Sorry.'

---

6   C major.

'You say sorry a lot, Jude.'

It feels like this chat might work better on the road so I grab my shoes from the floor and retrieve my bike. It's out the front, locked up next to a Børge Mogensen sofa that someone on our street had turfed for hard rubbish collection.

'Actually, Beth, can we ride by the facility? Erica says I need to check it out.'

'Sure, I haven't been either.'

We set off, down the smooth slope of my short street, where every house except ours has been renovated or is in the process of being renovated, because now they're undercapitalised and it makes sense to add a new level or a swimming pool. Our place is destined for that same fate once the owners are ready, or maybe they're hoping that in another ten years it'll be so decrepit they can get permission to knock it down and build units.

Bethany is riding slowly and I pull up beside her and say, 'I hate this.'

'Then change it.'

'I'm not holding the reins.'

'That's so weak, Jude.'

Now there's that churning, twisting sickness that reminds me of when I was a kid and in trouble for not coming inside when I was called, or breaking a toy that had belonged to my brother, and it's a feeling of worthlessness, really, a sense of letting someone down or being a disappointment.

'Why are you so pissed off with me?'

'Why are you pissing everywhere?'

'Fuck, Beth.'

'I thought I'd be there,' she says, hunching her shoulders and leaning back on her bike. 'I thought I'd be a part of this, but I'm nowhere. I sewed that bag, dude. I was a *big* part of that. And I feel like a kind of servant, or maybe just someone like everybody else.'

She stops riding right after we cross Merri Creek, and all around it's green and lush but still suburban. We're next to one another when she says, 'Now I don't know what I want.'

I'm trying to find something to say other than sorry, and what comes out is, 'I wanted you there. I want you there.'

'I need some space.'

I nod, like I understand. She takes off and I follow. Again.

We've rolled along in silence all the way down Smith Street, past the eye-candy furniture stores full of mid-century lamps and bookcases that maybe now I can afford, past all the restaurants, any ten of which would make a medium-sized town a culinary destination, right up Gertrude Street and the housing commission flats and the fashion stores. After that it's left onto Nicholson Street, where the Royal Exhibition Building and Melbourne Museum sit in loveless union. A grand, centuries-old courtesan married off to a giant, lame Transformer toy.

On Spring Street, Bethany steers towards a convenient streetlight where we chain our bikes together, then she hugs me, not wholeheartedly, but kindly.

Erica comes out from the restaurant, one of Adrian's, holding a clipboard. She has a pen in her mouth and she's grinning like a shot fox.

'Three hundred bottles so far and we're going to need a bigger room,' she says. 'On average they're sending two bottles per winery but a few have sent multiples of their entire range. And this is only the beginning.'

It was Erica's idea to sensitively disseminate news of Batard Rouge's impending opening among certain segments of the wine trade. Bottles started appearing not long after – mostly from distributors, sometimes from wineries, many mailed, and a few hand-delivered. The great majority have no chance of featuring on a small list that seeks, with undeniable pretension, to serve as a kind of résumé for Australian wine at large.

The facility itself[7] is the staff toilet at Adrian's restaurant and, given the Lilliputian dimensions of the premises as a whole, it had quickly proven unfit for purpose. The staff now have to share, well, facilities, with the punters – an arrangement that by all reports has a limited shelf life.

'Why can't I just keep them at my place?' I ask Erica.

'Happy to arrange that, Jude, but you'll need to catalogue all the arrivals and manage the tasting notes, and you'll have wine reps knocking on your door day and night.'

'Rob's maybe?' says Bethany

'He has the space,' I reply.

'And the secretaries.'

Lunch service is commencing as we edge through the restaurant, twisting by tables being seated and waiters reciting specials, back past the customer bathrooms and through a russet rayon curtain to the kitchen. There are four souls back there, including the dishie, and quarters are close. They are well-drilled in traversing the space, choreographed even, and although the bench tops look chaotic it's clear that every item belongs precisely where it has been placed.

I was half-expecting a glower from the chef for filling his bathroom with wine, but he gives me a sort of knowing nod, as if to say, 'Nice work scoring all that free wine, buddy, keep it up,' and I'm reminded of one of the many times Bethany and Heidi crashed at my place after a night out, and we took a taxi, late, all sitting in the back and laughing and maybe I had my arms around their shoulders, and when we arrived they got out ahead of me and the driver gave me that same look, like, 'Well played, mate, you're going to bed with two chicks tonight,' and it's such a low, premeditated blokey gape

---

7   So named by Erica.

that I wonder how many women have even seen it. Now I give the chef the same look right back and this is why nothing ever changes.

I don't recognise a lot of the labels on the boxes. This is no great shock as new wineries open in Australia at an unrelenting pace. It's disconcerting, though, and brings into focus an aspect of this challenge I've not properly considered: namely, to what extent can I get away with choosing only wines that my friends and I have always liked to drink? I suppose I could. In all likelihood I mostly will. But there needs to be a nod to the new in there somewhere and that probably means more than including something like a primitivo-dominant wine from Massena.[8] Can I risk a wine no one will have heard of? Can I risk, even, a region that's unfashionable?[9]

Surely I can't just turn in a restaurant version of Langton's Classification of Australian Wine – an abiding honour roll that adorns studies and cellar walls all around the country. Although, would that be such a crime? It's certainly appropriately proportioned by region,[10] and its own criteria are well formed.

Now I'm thinking about all those lists that rank restaurants, specifically The World's 50 Best.[11] Antoine is a judge (in the 'well-travelled gourmets' segment of the Academy), although you don't have to be especially well-travelled to form significant annual objections to the eventual rankings. It is hard to fathom, for example, someone eating at Le Châteaubriand in Paris and then later that week at Kadeau in Copenhagen and concluding that

---

8   A young gun label co-founded by a young(ish) gun, Dan Standish, but in
      some ways still 'old Barossa' by virtue of the fruit and Dan's pedigree.
9   I've tasted some genuinely pleasant wines from Queensland's Granite Belt,
      for example.
10   In a recent classification there were seventy-nine wines from South
      Australia, thirty-six from Victoria, twelve from Western Australia, nine from
      New South Wales and two from Tasmania. Then there's Penfolds' high-end
      Yattarna Chardonnay, which can be blended from all over.
11   Probably now the most famous of the lists, rivalling even the Michelin
      Guide in popularity.

Le Châteaubriand was the better of the two restaurants. And yet, by ranking, the Danes tend to straggle far behind.

There is tyranny in objectivity, and even though the voting format is designed to equalise obvious disquiets like geography and outright nepotism, still the thing suffers. And this is despite it being about as good as it could possibly be, given the ball-achingly thorny challenge of asking a thousand people who are obsessed with fine dining to figure out if this restaurant is better than that one. If nothing else, the list urges debate, which then concentrates attention on the list, which in turn aids its consolidation as a register of import.

Langton's wine classification functions along similar lines, albeit with a more scientific underpinning.[12] And standing here now, looking at case upon case stacked urinal-high in a poky Pine O Cleen'd dunny, I'm thinking my list for Batard Rouge mustn't go the way of either Langton's or The World's 50 Best.[13] This list is going to come from me and the Crew, and we'll defend it to anyone interested in having the conversation. And the weight of wine in this room tells me that plenty of people growing grapes want to be at the table while that conversation is happening.

'Jude?' Erica has a hand on my wrist, like she's checking for a pulse.

'Has he slipped into a kind of wine euphoria?' says Bethany.

'Sorry guys, I'm here.' I close a box. 'This is a lot of wine.'

'They're going to keep sending it, Jude,' Erica says. 'Everyone wants to be on this list. I called Rob while you had your anaesthetised face on and he's fine to start taking deliveries.'

'We need to schedule a tasting,' I say.

'Agreed.' Erica grins. 'Let's get onto that after lunch.'

---

12 Determined by formula, based on wines traded in the secondary market.
13 Determined by committee.

Hayden offers to hold the get-together at his place on his night off. For a guy who works in hospitality, he lives pretty well, owing to parents who were moderately wealthy and spotted him the cash for a house deposit back when the notion of home ownership in Melbourne was less ludicrous.

He earns enough to service his mortgage and to buy wine[14] and, despite our many differences in opinion across a commodious array of issues, we have chosen to live our lives in broadly similar ways, the main difference being that Hayden doesn't travel much and isn't such a slut for restaurants.

This means he has more money to spend on wine, and his preferred poison comes from the north of Italy, specifically Piedmont, with occasional nods south to Tuscany. He also drinks his share of Australian gear, mostly cabernet and, insofar as he is a human being comprised of flesh and blood, enjoys the pinot noirs and chardonnays of Burgundy.

Hayden is a sensible drinker, certainly more sensible than me and Bethany and, obviously, Erica. He never drinks before he works, and he starts work at 5pm most days. He can't get smashed on the job working as a sommelier, so most nights he'll have sips of maybe forty different wines and then, when he knocks off, a glass or two of what's left over.

He's still prone to a wholesale blowout, though, and starting late each day means he's able to push on well past the rest of us, even near-as-workless idlers like me. And in his spare time he'll usually see the corks out of a few bottles, with us or with his mates in hospitality.

---

14   Always at mates rates.

What he tends not to do is sit at home and drink simply as a matter of course. Even Rob – he of the alcohol-free Monday – will launch into a second bottle with his wife every other weeknight around the time the plates are cleared from dinner. So that's a bottle a day, at least, before corporate hospitality and weekends are added to the mix.

We all wonder the extent to which our drinking is causing us lasting harm. It seems hard to quantify beyond the health warnings, the scare tactics and the misnomer of the 'standard drink'. Erica has her liver checked every year,[15] is always given the thumbs up, and drinks as much as me and Hayden combined.

What would we do anyway, even if we knew? Say some test could tell me that ten drinks in a week was the limit and every drink I consumed over that would take a day off my life? Seems obvious to say you'd only ever have those ten drinks, but that's not even a bottle and a half. And imagine how resentful you'd be, sitting in a nursing home aged ninety and wanting to die, thinking back to all that wine you passed up so as not to lose a day.

Anyway, we all have a barometer of sorts and keep something of a check on one another. So far no one has fallen too deep into the bottle. Even Bruno, who was surely a two-bottles-a-day man, never displayed outward signs of dysfunction or even drunkenness.[16]

Antoine is back in Melbourne, although I'm yet to see him, and Bethany says he's fussing over which wine to bring to the tasting at Hayden's. Right after my maiden visit to the facility I had put out the call to the Crew to arm themselves with one 'non-obvious' wine for the Batard Rouge list, offering them access to the facility if they wanted to peruse the collection there.

---

15 Through a blood test, which I've been putting off.
16 Antoine says the prevailing view is that he died of some kind of aneurysm unrelated to his lifestyle.

What I'm really saying is, don't bring Grange or Kay's Block 6; bring something more humble or unsung and be prepared to make a case for its inclusion.

So now I'm knocking on Hayden's door, it's a Monday night in Brunswick East, and under my arm I have a bottle of sangiovese rosé from Coriole in the McLaren Vale. Hayden's housemate, Ken, answers,[17] shakes my hand and says he's on his way out. I go in and there's Heidi sitting on Hayden's faux Chesterfield sofa, drinking a beer.

'Hayden's in the shower,' she says as I kiss her on the cheek. 'What did you bring?'

I show her the wine, which I'm expecting to be contentious, although maybe not to Heidi who was there with me at a lot of the music festivals held at Coriole.[18]

'Love it. I thought you'd bring something from Noon.'

'Too obvious,' I say, 'and almost certainly already on the list.'[19]

I go to grab a beer and chill the rosé, and even though I should be used to it by now I still giggle like a pre-schooler when I open the fridge door to reveal Hayden's latest installation.

Because he doesn't ever eat at home, Hayden has transformed his fridge into a kind of art space for an audience comprised, most days, of him alone. Today, and in an obvious nod to the New Zealand

---

17   A couple of years ago we said to Hayden that he should rent out a room because he has a lot of space and is rarely at home. He was resistant at first, but then found out he could earn eight hundred a month, and so now has this young accountant dude living with him and a pledge to spend all rental income, in perpetuity, on barolo.

18   Every year since 1999 Coriole has held a classical music festival at the winery. It usually goes for a couple of days, with a different program for each event.

19   Illuminating that for our crew a wine from Coriole is considered 'less obvious' than a wine from Noon, who remain among the smaller producers by volume in the McLaren Vale, and whose wine is exceedingly difficult to buy.

artist Peter Madden,[20] he has built a sculpture around a hardback of Jancis Robinson's *Oxford Companion to Wine*.[21] I'm guessing he's then done an op-shop run for *National Geographic* magazines from which he has meticulously cut out photographs of all kinds of species of snake.[22] There's roughly three hundred snakes bulging out of every section of the book, evenly distributed throughout the some nine hundred pages. He's put it on the main shelf of the fridge and placed an empty bottle of 2003 Château Pavie from St-Émilion in Bordeaux[23] on top. Truly a work of some refinement.

Elsewhere in the fridge are six identical bottles of Bollinger La Grande Année 2012, a magnum of 2013 Giaconda Chardonnay, and a silver rectangular serving tray housing nineteen corks, arranged in the shape of an erect penis with accompanying testicles.

'The beer's in Ken's fridge,' Heidi calls out, and I recall Hayden's demand that his housemate provide his own fridge while offering exclusive use of the pre-existing freezer. I grab a beer and stick the rosé in there while I'm at it, then join Heidi in the living room.

'Is he taking a swipe at Robinson there, do you think?'

'With the snake thing?'

'Historically he's been a fan,' I say. 'Has put her on a pedestal actually.'

'Biggest wine book he could find, I'm thinking.'

Heidi has made it over again from Sydney and has gone to greater lengths than ever to conceal her weariness. She's not wearing lipstick, or much make-up at all, but lashes thick with mascara mask dry, tired eyes.

---

20   Born Napier, New Zealand, 1966.
21   Fourth edition, Oxford University Press, 2015.
22   On close examination it's clear he's purchased specialised blades in order to properly execute this task, and if we're talking, minimum, ninety seconds per snake then the cutting alone would have taken him close to eight hours.
23   The wine Jancis Robinson and Robert Parker famously went to war over, with Parker scoring it 95/100 and Robinson 12/20.

'You look great,' I say.

'You don't lie very well,' she replies.

We spoke at Bruno's wake, but not for long enough, and I say to her, 'How's motherhood?'

'Hard,' she says.

'Does it get easier?'

'Yeah.' She takes a swig from her bottle and wipes her lips with her thumb. 'I've been leaning on my friends, just most of them aren't in Sydney. It's small stuff. All those care packages you sent, Jude. I actually cried when I opened the box with your note and the bags of FruChocs.'[24]

'And Ruby? I want more photos.'

'She's a delight, a joy. But it's unrelenting. And for me it's not about tasks and chores, or the anxieties or the lack of sleep or anything like that – it's just never getting to be alone any more.'

'Happened overnight, I'm guessing.'

'It did. I used to work in my studio at home eight or ten hours a day and always by myself. Now I'm still at home, still in my studio, but never alone. Not even for ten minutes.'

'You have to get out of there. Rent a workspace somewhere?'

'I have to be with Ruby. Working from home I get that, but I lose what I had.'

'And actual work?'

'I get an hour here or there. When Sam[25] comes home. Occasionally when she's sleeping. And it's crazy, I'm productive, I'm doing good work. And I can just switch it on, like if I know I have a forty-five-minute window I can launch into it.'

'I can't comprehend how you do it.'

'You find a way. Now she's nearly one, and Sam's figuring out what he can do to help, and he's working a bit less… it's progress.

24   An exceptional provincial South Australian chocolate treat.
25   Heidi's husband.

But I need these little adventures. Even one night here, less than twenty-four hours away, it's like two weeks in Paris for me right now.'

'So come more often. Come every month.'

'I'm going to try. I care about the restaurant thing, about the wine list. I think about it all the time and I want to help.'

I want that too, and then there's another knock at the door and I get up, kissing Heidi again on the way out. It's Antoine, looking slim, and holding a bottle of Mayer Chardonnay from the Yarra Valley.

'I have many suggestions for this list, as you know,' Antoine says, 'and I'd love to see something on there from this fellow.'

Timo Mayer is definitely an Antoine kind of guy in that he advocates minimal intervention in the winery and is, by most measures, functionally insane. In fact, he'd be more likely to take issue with the descriptor 'functional' than the word 'insane' in that appraisal.

I take the bottle and gesture for him to come inside, but instead he grips my forearm and says, 'Just a quick word first?'

We're on the porch, one of those grand stoops that adorn weatherboard houses in this area, and the sun's out but in recession and there's enough green space nearby to smother the exhaust fumes from Sydney Road. The neighbour's dog campaigns for his dinner but otherwise it's still and windless.

'Everything okay?' This could be anything. I haven't spoken with him in more than a week and it is a madhouse around here.

'I think so… only I spoke with Bruno's widow at the funeral. It was just for a minute, and in French, but I explained the arrangement you had reached with Bruno.'

'And she knew about it? Had he told her?'

'He had not. But we expected this. I was not at all surprised.'

'And?' I'm not exactly panicking here, mainly because Antoine appears so calm, but a ripple of anxiety has begun its slow spread through my gut.

'It was a lot for her to take in. It was clear at the funeral that there were many things about Bruno's life that were a mystery to his own wife. I said to her that we were pushing on with the restaurant on the basis of our agreement, but that first and foremost our thoughts were with her.'

'Definitely.'

'She said it would take some time to work though the minutiae of the estate. Bruno being Bruno, left no will, so I asked her if she was comfortable with us cashing the cheque.'

'Oh.'

'I guess I gave her the opening, and she didn't know of any cheque. She asked its value, then said she would be grateful if we waited a month or two until some dust had settled.'

'Jesus.'

'We needed to be upfront here, Jude. If what was theirs is now hers – and surely this is the case – then she's your partner in the restaurant.'

'I know. You're right.'

'You'll just need some patience.'

Up walks Bethany, on cue, so bright as to appear sparkling, and Rob and Erica and Adrian are behind her, having climbed from an Uber together. Spirits seem high. Best push this whole widow thing to one side for the evening, and anyway it's not like she said she hated the idea.

'Okay,' I say to Antoine, 'let's check back in with her, what, at the end of the month?'

He nods, then he's off down the path to greet everyone.

Bethany sidles up the stairs, extends both arms while dancing a kind of mock two-step, passes me by and then breezes over to Hayden, who has appeared at the door.

Looks like she's resolved to keep things upbeat, although there's a chance she's just drunk. I do know that she was working until five, and an hour isn't enough to do meaningful damage, even if spent entirely with Erica, who is ebullient. This is not from booze, though, just from seeing Antoine for the first time this year.

'Whole sick crew together again.' Rob grins, shaking my hand while trying to disguise the bottle he's carrying. 'First time since Heidi was pregnant.'

Erica grabs me around the waist and attempts to pick me up, succeeds in lifting me a few centimetres off the ground, and says, 'Well played, buddy, this is perfect.'

'It's not all about me.'

I need a drink, this beer doesn't count, and everyone's inside by now so I figure let's get the party started.

Somehow, but almost certainly not through the traditional method of walking into a shop and handing over legal tender, Hayden has procured an immoderate quantity of charcuterie and about ten kilograms of cheese. He'd asked Heidi to pick up bread on her way from the airport, so we have that too, and it's all piled, still packaged, at one end of his dining table.

Insofar as a conservative estimate of time spent cutting out snakes for his fridge sculpture was eight hours, you might expect Hayden to have mustered ten minutes to rip the wax paper off a couple of rounds of cheese, rustle up a board or two, or at the very least fetch a fucking cheese knife. He has done none of these things, and so Rob and Erica go to work while I attend to the wine.

I hadn't mentioned a blind tasting, but almost everyone has made an effort to conceal the identity of their bottle. There are seven lined up beside the microwave, including Antoine's Mayer. One is in a bag with the telltale Cialis[26] logo, which must be Hayden's selection. I need to figure out a serving order so I liberate them from their cloaks and, yeah, this is an absorbing line-up, with a couple of genuinely oddball choices.

---

26   Erectile dysfunction medication.

'Alright,' I announce, walking back into the living room, 'no formalities tonight. I'll make the identity of each bottle known in turn, then you make your case for why it should be on the list.'

A small cheer and a clinking of stubbies.

'Okay, we begin in the Barossa. The maker is Tscharke, the wine is called Girl Talk, and the varietal is savagnin.'

'This one's from me.' Bethany takes the bottle, opens it, and starts pouring it out, which is fine by me.[27]

'Everyone's tried this before?' I ask, to nods all around.

'Why do I love this?' Bethany begins. 'Even though it's called Girl Talk, and even though Damien says he makes it for his four sisters, for me this an antisocial wine.'

'We're opening a restaurant, Beth. They tend to be social places...' Adrian looks primed to continue but cops a glare from Erica and retreats to his glass.

'Absolutely you can share it,' Bethany says, 'and I sometimes do. But it's usually a journey I take by myself.'

'Where do you go?' asks Heidi.

'To a place I've never been. It feels like it could be real, like it could exist somewhere, but it's only in my mind.'

Most of us look at our glasses as though expecting to see a reflection or some stitch of Bethany's imaginings.

'I guess the place is an orchard, although there are other types of trees. It's autumn, all shades of autumn, and it's sunny but the tree branches form a canopy so only dappled light makes it to the ground. The elms and oaks are taller than the fruit trees, as though they're giving shelter, and when the leaves fall they pass down through all

---

27   One of the main stresses associated with hosting a tasting like this is
      making sure everyone gets the same sized pour from the bottle. It is a finite
      resource, after all, and it can piss people off when they're shortchanged.
      Some wine clubs use measuring beakers to ensure millimetre perfection and
      you can understand why, especially if you've paid a couple of grand for the
      opportunity to share a once-in-a lifetime bottle.

the fruit that's hanging from the branches. There are pears and apples and peaches, so ripe and lush, but they don't fall, they stay fixed, by the tiniest of twigs.'

'You're walking?' I ask.

'My body isn't there at all. I drift. Sometimes I'm still, sometimes I follow a leaf all the way through the understorey to the orchard floor. I try to float past a pear, touch it even, and all the fruit is perfect.'

'Sounds a bit like city-girl escapism,' says Rob.

'Jesus, Robbie…' says Erica.

'Feels like the opposite of where you grew up,' I offer.

'It's the opposite of where I spend my life,' Bethany replies.

That's the Girl Talk on the list, and as people drain their glasses I go to the kitchen and remove the cork from Antoine's offering.

'We need chardonnay on this list,' he begins, in a statement of the dazzlingly obvious. 'We must try to situate Australian chardonnay as its own object, held up against the other.'

Antoine starts pouring, and no one is disconcerted by his selection. Most of us have met Timo Mayer, either at one of the Friday afternoon tastings at Barrique in Healesville or at the winery itself where you sometimes encounter one or two older bottles with corks removed and an invitation to inspect.

'It's a long way from sunshine in a bottle,' says Rob, recalling that less than golden era of Aussie chardonnay.

'It is,' Antoine says, 'but that story is in the bottle too. This wine is a conversation about chardonnay. It begins in Burgundy. It moves to Australia, and that dross from the eighties. It recalls the improvement of the white wines of Burgundy by the introduction of new world techniques, and it returns to Australia and the response of our winemakers to the ever-evolving Australian palate.'

'Shit got pretty lean and minerally there for a while,' says Hayden.

'Shit got whacked with a fair bit of sulphur too,' Erica adds.

'And in your glasses we see that dialogue, that exchange.'

Everyone gawps at their wine, only now a few of us draw our glasses a centimetre or two towards one ear in case the conversation Antoine is describing has taken on aural qualities.

He takes a final long pull from his own glass then concludes the hearing. 'Of course, ultimately it's the story of a man growing grapes by a hill.'

Antoine is paid by a university to lecture on wine, and while I wouldn't accuse him of yanking that line directly from his syllabus there is something about the whole 'object and other' analysis that smacks of the postmodern underpinnings of big chunks of his schema. Seriously good booze, though, and the idea of talking to a wine while you drink it is less crazy than a lot of things I've done with glass in hand.

My turn now, and I don't need to justify or defend my selection,[28] but I'm trepidatious, maybe because of the story I'm about to tell – which nobody knows – or because at the end of the carnival ride it's an Australian rosé we're talking about here.

Given the constraints around the length of the list,[29] it's no lay down misère that we get a rosé at all. Which was partly my reason for bringing one. I like it with French food, particularly foie gras and pâté, and I find it meets you in a different place to other wines, especially when taken as an aperitif. This is doubly true when you've been drinking a lot of champagne, or even chardonnay, and you're looking to step away from tight acid and into more commodious surrounds.

Again, no great consternation as I reveal the wine and crack the Stelvin, and Heidi makes a noise from somewhere in her oesophagus that sounds acclamatory.

'McLaren Vale,' I say, 'via the north of Italy.'

---

28   It had occurred to me to not even enter a horse in tonight's race.
29   One page.

'Hard to argue against including something from Coriole,' says Rob, like he's talking to a jury. 'Sangiovese rosé, though?'

'I get that. But I want rosé on the list. I also like the idea of including less common varietals in Australia, so sangiovese rather than grenache or whatever.'

'From Australia's oldest sangiovese vineyard, in fact,' Hayden says, and I've no reason to doubt him.[30]

'All the better.' I walk around the table, pouring out the wine.[31]

'Pleasing colour,' says Antoine. 'There's so many shades of plastic pink in life that we forget the truly pink segment of the spectrum.'

'Like sunset at their cellar door,' says Beth, ripe with romance for everything but me.

'Does this have to do with the music festival,' Heidi asks.

'Yep – the first one I went to.' I'm waiting for some smartarse to point out that Coriole weren't making a sangiovese rosé then, and as expected that smartarse is Rob.

'Maybe not even the nebbiolo rosé,' Erica says.[32]

'Let him tell the story.' Thank you, Heidi.

'I was at uni, just moved out of home, and my parents said they wanted to take me to this thing.'

---

30   Antoine tells me later that Montrose in Mudgee planted the varietal a few years earlier, but that the vineyard no longer exists.

31   None of us rinse our glasses in transition any more since Adrian and I were schooled on the subject by a particularly irascible cellar door staffer in the Napa Valley who said the impurities and overall chemistry of water were more likely to leave undesirable remnants in the glass than leftovers from the wine before. We brought those learnings back and they were embraced by the Crew, except for Bruno, presumably on the grounds that French water was and remains as pure as the driven snow.

32   Coriole has in fact been making rosé on a more or less continuous basis since the early 1970s, pausing only when they felt its popularity was becoming a distraction to the rest of their line-up. The winemaker Peter Lloyd says that every now and then they stumble upon one of those old bottles in a forgotten carton in their cellar, and that they rarely disappoint.

Around the table the wine is disappearing like, well, rosé on a hot day in a hammock. It's striking how when people drink together the colour of the juice in their glasses forms such a suggestive part of the overall ophthalmic landscape. Things are looking pretty pink right now.

'The night before the festival, the Friday night, I'd met this girl through a friend. She was from Croatia, staying in Adelaide for a while, and I'd actually been introduced to her briefly the previous week. I had liked her, and had thought about her, and on the Friday we sat next to each other at one of those wine dinners upstairs at that place on Leigh Street and we kind of sparked.'

'What was the wine theme?' Hayden asks, even though I know he was one of at least three people around this table who was there that night.

'I have a feeling it was Hugo or Shottesbrooke. One of those places making ridiculously good wine for, like, fifteen bucks a bottle.'

'And selling ninety per cent of it in South Australia,' says Erica.[33]

'So we get a bit merry on the booze – we get smashed actually – and clearly it's on and, Rob, you'd gone to The Planet[34] so I knew I'd have the house to myself for a few hours,[35] and we walked there through the park, and no need for details but it was memorable.'

'Cute.'

'And unexpected,' I continue. 'When I brought her to my bed and pulled off the covers there was a stack of clean, folded washing under my doona. That definitely confused her.'

'It's confusing me,' from Heidi. 'What did you tell her?'

'I told her that's how men do ironing.'

---

33   You only need to look around at the open bottles at any decent Adelaide restaurant to realise that South Australians are parochial about their wine. It is reminiscent of the regional preference observable in parts of France.

34   Adelaide nightclub of yore.

35   Rob and I were sharing a house at the time.

Heidi dissolves into laughter. Hers is the most raucous of any in the Crew, especially when she's laughing at me. Antoine joins in and they sound like kookaburras mating. It's the best thing I've heard all night.

'Then you took her to the music festival?' Hayden asks.

'No ticket. She left just before Rob got home.'

'Never to be seen again,' says Bethany, feigning dramatic effect.

'She told me afterwards that she had a boyfriend and that she was going home on Tuesday.'

'Don't tell me you felt used?' from Beth, with a sprinkle of salt.

'It was only ever about that night. But I was sad when she told me.'

'Would you rather have known beforehand?' Erica asks.

'Wouldn't have changed the outcome. Anyway, she leaves at four, my parents are picking me up at seven – why so early who knows, maybe to get good seats at the recital – and I figure there's no point sleeping just a couple of hours so I stay up, sitting out the back of our place, and I have this moment of realisation, like I've moved from one plateau to the next. Or not moved so much as leapt. An event rather than a transition.'

'What did you feel?' asks Heidi.

'It's a bit teenaged, but it ran the full gamut from tenderness to fear-and-trembling loneliness. It was affirming too, though.'

'It was love,' says Antoine.

'It was.'

'And the car ride with your parents?' Erica asks.

'You can imagine. No sleep, still drunk, variously euphoric and wretched, not even showered, babbling answers to their questions and wanting to tell someone what I was feeling, but just wise enough not to.'

'A fucking wreck basically,' says Adrian.

'A total wreck. Then we arrive, and you know they used to put on a breakfast there? Well I'm hungry but I can't eat.'

'Because of love,' says Heidi.

'Yeah. And I didn't eat or sleep much for the next few weeks. Lost five kilos. Smoked cigarettes, made mix tapes.'

'Any poetry?' asks Bethany, this time without the edge.

'One letter. Mercifully never sent.'

'Who was the composer at Coriole?' asks Heidi.

'Bartók[36] maybe. Utterly unromantic program. Food was good, but I couldn't touch it, didn't even want to drink.'

'Except the rosé?'

I drain the final splattering of my wine and shake my head, looking first at Erica who asked the question, then around the table. 'I don't even know if they were pouring it. It's just what I think about when I drink this wine.'

No one responds for a while, then Rob says, sure, that stacks up, and there are no attempts to mount an argument to the contrary.

'Right,' I say, 'let's have some sparkling shiraz.'[37]

Adrian's selection is contentious, as few outside of South Australia would have heard of the wine let alone tried it. That said, it's one of the best we make in Australia, in a category we probably invented.[38]

'Come on,' Rob begins, 'Not Seppelt? Not Rockford?'

'Guys, let's take a big step back right here.' Erica swigs the last of her rosé. 'We have a page. One page. At a French restaurant. How is there a sparkling red on the list at all?'

'Why not?' asks Antoine. 'The list is Australian and this is about as Australian as it gets.'

---

36   Béla Bartók, 1881–1945.
37   A Primo Estate Joseph Sparkling Red.
38   Possibly in still another failed attempt to copy the French, but it turned out okay in the end.

'But not even Australians get it,' Erica says. 'It's a stupid wine, a joke wine.'

'Erica, what's my favourite day of the year?' Adrian talking to his sister here, and it has to be tough at times having a sibling in the Crew, with all that shared history and with every argument an echo of some childhood dispute.

'Christmas. You never grew up.'

Adrian leaves this suspended for a moment, because we all know sparkling red is a Christmas Day wine. 'Right. I never stopped loving it. And now I have kids I love it even more. And I'm sorry, but this wine tastes like Christmas.'

'Is that because you only ever drink it then?' Antoine asks.

'I drink five or six bottles a year. Mostly this and Peter Rumball,[39] and honestly it's more like a foodstuff. You almost need a glass of wine to go with it.'

'I get the Christmas pudding thing.' Erica, softening her assault.

'Turkey too maybe,' says Rob.

'It's both of those and more,' Adrian says. 'Tell me you can't feel it in your mouths!'

I serve sparkling red at Christmas too, always in time to accompany the first bite of turkey. By then it's usually 3pm and you're starving and drunk, having started with champagne, then riesling with the oysters, and certainly a chardonnay of some description over prawns. There'll be at least one decent pinot to come before you launch into the bigger reds, so what better moment to interpose something like the Joseph or a Rockford Black Shiraz.

'Damn it,' says Bethany. 'It tastes exactly like Christmas.'

'No turkey at Batard Rouge, though,' says Rob.

'There's duck, there's foie gras, there's terrine, there's charcuterie, there are half-a-dozen dishes it can work with.'

'Would you serve it by the glass?' I ask.

---

39   Another legendary Australian sparkling red.

'Yes! And if someone's undecided you offer them a try, especially if they have food in front of them.'

'You could come back to it over cheese,' says Hayden, defacing the wedge from a round of reblochon.[40]

'I still call bullshit,' says Erica.

I fetch Heidi's pinot, which is from a small producer[41] I've never heard her mention.

'Naturally this relates to music,' Heidi says.

It's not like Heidi experiences wine 'as' music per se, or even that it's tonal or harmonic. It's more a synaesthesia kind of thing insofar as the connections and stimulations are neural and involuntary. She's learned to run with it and derives a good deal of joy from whatever clinically fucked up bits of her brain are tugging at those strings.

'Different trip to normal, though. This one's about a song I wrote myself.'

This is not in quite the same fraternity as, say, Adrian announcing he's finished writing an erotic novel set in Enchō-era Japan, or Erica refusing a glass of champagne, but it's a thunderbolt nevertheless.

'When I was a teenager I wanted to be a singer, a pop star. I wrote dozens of songs. I had one that I thought was better than the rest, one I really liked, and I recorded it at a friend's studio, got it sounding the way I wanted, and showed it to some friends who were musicians. They said it was cool, that they liked it...' Heidi smiles. 'But it was clear they didn't think it had a chance.'

'I would have murdered them where they stood,' says Rob.

'I would have ignored them,' from Bethany.

'I wasn't angry,' Heidi says. 'Sad for sure, but more than that I just knew. I went home and drank the best bottle of wine I had. Which at the time was an Ashton Hills Pinot Noir.'

---

40   He has done this deliberately and in search of a reaction, knowing that both Antoine and I have an interest in cheese etiquette. Antoine has published on the subject.

41   Ashton Hills. Although they are now less small and owned by Wirra Wirra.

'I had no idea,' I say.

'Heidi, the music industry's not a meritocracy.' Rob's frowning, like he's rooting out an injustice, which is standard for him if he senses Heidi's been mistreated. 'Maybe you get lucky, you meet the right people, who knows?'

'I knew, Rob. I knew as I was walking home, as I opened the bottle, as I poured the first glass. I had to let it go. So I put the song on repeat and drank the pinot. It was doing that thing I love where all the fragmented bits of the wine bounce around the core, and the core is plush but dense.'

'You got drunk?'

'I did. I drank the whole bottle. Sitting alone with my failure. Feeling like shit. But then I kind of pulled it in. Welcomed it. Drank some more wine and then… let it go. It took one bottle. By the time I'd finished I'd shifted spaces. Left that part of my life behind.'

'How did it feel?' Antoine asks.

'Like relief, at first. After that it was… freedom.'

'Gorgeous,' says Erica, and the wine does look radiant. Albeit beneath harsh fluorescent light, and atop shiny blonde IKEA veneer. It's like Hayden wants his nice stuff to stand out by virtue of all the crap surrounding it.

Erica's wine is next, and it is a modest contribution for a woman with conspicuously expensive tastes. She's floated in and out of the wine business, at other times working in the luxury sector in internal communications or brand orientation or some other bastard business function, and she's had a couple of jobs at the pointy end of wine distribution and now works for herself representing a closely curated crop of winemakers,[42] selling their wares into retail and restaurants.

So this could have been a Hill of Grace or The Laird from Torbreck, or Clarendon Hills Astralis or any of the big guns that fill out that heady upper bracket, but the woman who started her

---

42   Basically, wine she likes to drink.

hospitality career at the Rye fish and chip shop when she was fourteen[43] has gone for Wirra Wirra Church Block, a red blend you can usually pick up for under twenty bucks a bottle.

'Is there anyone here,' Erica asks, 'who could say they've drunk less than a case of this wine in their lifetime?'

'A dozen bottles?' Rob says. 'I would have been a part of fifty at least. None lately, though.'

'It's a gateway wine,' says Hayden.

I'm thinking back to the dinner parties of our early twenties, to winter picnics with prosciutto and oversized reds, and to rummaging around for a third bottle on a Thursday night when things had gotten accidentally messy.[44] We used to drink this a lot.

Erica has poured out the bottle and regards the group with what looks like pride. I remember opening ten bottles of Church Block in a single afternoon after an auction purchase of my birth-year release inspired a ring around and an impromptu vertical tasting.[45] Everyone had at least one bottle in their collection.

'It's a wine we take for granted,' Erica says.

'It's a group wine,' from Hayden. 'You'd never crack a bottle by yourself or on a date. You drink it with a bunch of people.'

'They always did a good deal on magnums, too,' Rob says, and imperials as well, if I'm not mistaken.

'All of this is true,' says Erica, 'and there was one gathering at your old place, Robbie, when we were sitting outside late in the afternoon, and the Church Block was maybe the twentieth bottle...'

'Just five or six of us there?' he asks.

---

43   First jobs: Erica and Adrian, fish and chip shop; Hayden, bottleshop drive-through at the age of sixteen; Bethany made soap, which she sold at a market; Heidi and Rob, supermarkets; Antoine, tutoring schoolkids younger than him; me, teaching guitar. Glorious beginnings.

44   'School night messy' as opposed to proper messy.

45   An event at which you try multiple vintages of the same wine.

'More like fifteen. Sat around three tables roughly pressed together, with tablecloths masking the joins. Everyone in constant fear of capsizing a glass on the edge.'

'Did I cook?'

'There were oysters. Someone did flathead on the barbecue. You slow-cooked a couple of lamb shoulders. Salads and cheese, of course.'

'Fun,' says Bethany.

'Big fun. It was sunny and it was a Saturday, and there was a moment when I'd just finished a warm conversation with you, Jude, and someone filled my glass with this wine. I thought, that's nice, about time for a blend, and I'd been neglecting my food because of all the chatting so I had some of your lamb, Robbie, and it was carnally good.[46] I'm drinking the Church Block and I'm about to start talking to Beth, to get into a long chat about something or other, and, Beth, you've been waiting for ages, you're so excited, like now it's your turn, and your cheeks are raised a fraction in anticipation. And that's the moment. That precise moment is like a time capsule for me.'

'It felt special, even at the time?' Heidi asks.

'Yeah. I stopped and looked around. I still had the wine in my mouth and I was fresh from Jude and primed for Beth and everyone was laughing at a joke someone made, and cutlery was clanking, toasts happening, and I had the most profound sense of "now" that I've ever experienced.'

'I'd call it the moment between being and becoming,' says Antoine, and really only he can get away with that, and even then only after around five bottles.

'Holy fuck, Erica!' Adrian practically shouts. 'I can think of more transcendent wines than Church Block!' As soon as he says it he realises he's missed the point.

---

46   If I have my timeline right, then this lunch happened when Erica was coming off a sustained period of vegetarianism.

A kind of individuation, then, and we're talking here about a wine blended from three varietals,[47] with fruit sourced from all over the McLaren Vale. That's quite cool as most people in wineworld are obsessed with single varietal or single vineyard offerings, and of course with terroir. But it's possible to find virtue in combination.

Glasses are emptying, everyone is humming in that contentedly inebriated way, and Heidi has put on some music.[48] Beyond that a few of us are reckoning we really should eat something.

Bethany is sitting across from me and not even the brutality of Hayden's light fittings can subtract from her. Both are possessed of a certain glare.

Heidi has reclined lavishly and is chatting with Erica. Rob is arguing with Adrian, seemingly about Christmas, but there's probably more to it than that.

Most of us know the story behind this next wine, but then we do forget a lot of stuff and only Rob and Hayden were there when it happened.

Hayden takes the bottle, wrings free its capsule, and says, 'The wine is Samuel's Gorge Grenache.'

Most of us got onto Samuel's Gorge as soon as it opened. Chapel Hill up the road was going through a rocky patch at the time, and a new cellar door[49] was reason enough to make a detour.

'Rob and I were there whenever I came to Adelaide,' Hayden continues, 'and we got to know Justin,[50] and loved what he was doing and wanted to support him, so for the first few years we bought as much as we could afford.'

---

47 Cabernet sauvignon, shiraz and merlot.
48 Possibly in response to Erica's story, although I'm not sure. Anyway, she's playing Frank Ocean.
49 Well, the farm shed that houses the cellar door was actually built in 1853.
50 The proprietor and winemaker.

'I'm still working my way through them.' Rob smiles.

'We were heading to a beach house we'd rented in Aldinga for Rob's bucks weekend. The car's full of beer and groceries and all the stuff we needed for the line-up of humiliating activities we'd arranged for him the next day...'

'And a shitload of wine,' Rob says.

'And a shitload of wine. Anyway we were driving through McLaren Vale late on Friday afternoon, and one of us suggests calling in to see Justin, so we do that, and he's had a few already so we hang out and enjoy a glass or two, someone makes us a coffee I think, and we put a mixed dozen together of tempranillo, shiraz and some grenache, which I guess we figure we'll mostly get through over the course of the weekend, and as we're leaving Justin asks what we're doing this weekend, you know, like what's the occasion? I told him it was Rob's bucks and that a bunch of us had rented this sweet house and that we were going to go down there and just hang for a couple of days, and he says that sounds like his kind of weekend, have a good time and all that, and anyway we're in the car park, almost back to the car, and he comes back out of the winery and he's holding this jeroboam of the first ever bottling of his grenache. And he says, "This is for you guys, for the weekend." He hands it over, and me and Rob are speechless, like this wine was never even offered for sale in this format and here he is just giving us a bottle. Eventually we manage to string a word or two together by way of gratitude, and Justin's smiling, and saying thanks for supporting the winery, and we load the thing into the car and take off down the coast.'

'Where it lasted maybe another three hours,' I recall.

'Didn't you guys steal a barbecue that weekend?' Bethany asks.

'Borrowed, Beth,' Rob replies. 'Returned it to the neighbour the next morning, cleaned and with a case of beer under the hood.'

'What kind of beach house rental doesn't have a barbecue?' says Hayden.[51]

'What a gesture,' says Heidi, pulling focus back to the grenache.

'I felt a sense of family,' says Hayden. 'It was like this industry, these people, they're the best in the whole world.'

'Then you came and joined us,' says Erica.

'I did. Took another year or so, but that was the moment.'

Bethany is crying, and because she is the centre of my world I assume her tears are for me.

'I know,' says Erica, pulling Bethany close, and I think, what do you know? then Hayden says, 'If hospo's a family, Bruno was Dad sitting in the armchair.'

'Except I never saw him sit down,' says Bethany, smiling.

Now I get it, and I want to say something for Bruno too, but my brain slips back into Bethany and my glass.

Some wines move fast, asking you to adjust your itinerary so that you might meet them somewhere agreeable. This grenache has more of a loping kind of gait and you need to submit early lest you get ahead of it. Part of the art of consumption is choosing the right second to swallow.

'You know the Samuel's Gorge story has a footnote.' Rob raises his glass as though it's a conch, lest there be any doubt that it's his turn to talk.

'Your subsequent marriage?' Erica asks.

'About three years later I walk into the Salopian Inn,[52] and there's Justin siting down to lunch with his mum. We acknowledged each other but didn't chat. My table finished first, and, on the way

---

51   We had figured the house next door was unused that weekend, having knocked on the door around 6pm, but just after midnight a fellow named Neville turned up, enquiring as to the whereabouts of his barbecue. When he looked over Rob's shoulder and into the room to see twenty or so drunk young men, he wasn't of a mind to press matters.

52   An excellent McLaren Vale restaurant.

out as I was paying the bill, I took care of the bottle of white burg he'd ordered with their meal.'

'Not tempted to shout the whole lunch?' Adrian asks.

'Thought about it. Didn't want to be a dick.'

Looking around I realise we are all drunk, and I'm moved to share this observation and Erica agrees and says it happened quickly.

'I don't feel like I've eaten much.' Heidi frowns.

'Do you even own water glasses, Hayden?' asks Erica.

'I feel fabulous,' Antoine grins, outwardly revelling in the grenache.

'Where to from here?' Bethany asks.

'I'm glad you asked,' Rob says, as this has played out exactly the way he'd hoped. Every glass is empty and Rob conducts a reconnoitre of the room, tracing its pulse, absorbing its sway and thrum.

'Another one from the nostalgia files,' he says.

'Not a monster shiraz I hope, Robert,' pleads Erica.

'It's not shiraz.' Rob's touching his forehead, the part where his hair used to be.

'I submit,' says Antoine.

'What did we used to do on nights like these?' Rob asks. 'At this exact moment, what would we do?'

'You'd offer me a cigar,' Bethany says.

'Then we'd open a bottle of –' Heidi checks herself almost comically as everyone arrives at the punchline at once.

'Port.' Rob is grinning. 'We always drank port. No matter how trashed, no matter how many bottles, no matter how late.'

'Usually Australian port.' I'm thinking back to those old commemorative bottles, celebrating premierships or Melbourne Cups. I remember bringing a bottle of Liebich Royal Wedding Charles and Diana Commemorative Port 1981[53] to a quiz night in the late

---

53   Made from Barossa fruit, if memory serves.

1990s[54] and being treated like, well, royalty, for having furnished the table with something so fittingly kitsch. I might have paid eight bucks for it at auction a few years before.

The thing about all those old ports is that they were made at a time when people actually drank port, which became significant to the next generation of port consumers in three material ways:

1. A lot was made, meaning plenty survived, and because it was never scarce it was never especially expensive.[55]
2. People seemed to just stop drinking it, which meant the price of those bottles still floating around dropped even further.
3. At the time it was made pretty well – it was a legitimate style and treated with care and respect in the winery.

Rob has excavated the cork and is pouring out the bottle, and Hayden probably has port glasses stashed somewhere but we were never avid users of those bastard little things – far better to treat port like wine[56] and enjoy it from a proper glass.

The port[57] is called Potsorts, from Yarra Yering, and it's problematic immediately as precious little of it is made.

'Along similar lines to Adrian,' Rob says, 'I mostly just want this style represented on the list.'

'You propose this by the bottle?' Antoine asks.

'By the bottle and by the glass. Maybe even carafes. Get a few funky old ship decanters[58] in there.'

---

54 Certainly, it was after Diana died.
55 Save for a few rorts committed upon release where the port was pushed as 'collectible' or 'limited edition'.
56 Which it is.
57 Australian producers have actually agreed to not call it 'port' anymore. It's now 'vintage fortified'.
58 Featuring a wide base, curving in towards a narrow flute. Presumably to provide stability at sea.

'Give the gift of lead poisoning,' Erica says.[59]

'What's the minimum number of people you'd need to knock off a bottle of port?' Adrian asks.

'Two, surely,' Bethany says.

'Anyone ever drink a whole bottle themselves?' This is met by silence, which is shocking, as I know everyone here has worked their way through a magnum unaccompanied at one time or another, and a bottle of port by comparison is akin to taking Sunday morning communion.

'And punters order this when? With cheese at the end of the meal?' Erica asks.

'At the teeming, rollicking end,' Rob says. 'We want people calling the restaurant the next morning to dispute their bill, saying they have no recollection of ordering a bottle of port and couldn't possibly have done so as they haven't drunk the stuff in years.'

'Maybe when someone orders a bottle we take a picture of them with it?' I suggest.

'Actually hilarious.' Bethany grins. 'Photographic evidence.'

'Robbie's bringing back port!' Adrian yells.

'Fucking yes.' Rob downs his glass. 'Excess in a bottle. We don't need it any more than the cigar, but when nudged down that path...'

'Into that abyss,' Erica says.

'A different brand of drunkenness.'

'I feel it even now,' Antoine says.

'Didn't we stop drinking port because we realised it made our hangovers twice as bad?' Bethany asks.

'That and the cigars,' Erica says.

---

59   It turns out the lead from old decanters can indeed poison you, but only if you leave alcohol in there for a prolonged period. One study found that brandy stored in a lead decanter for five years had lead levels of 20,000 micrograms per litre. About 15 micrograms per litre is considered safe for water.

'You're missing the point,' Rob says. 'Or actually that is the point. It's about this moment, this very stage of the evening. We never do it anymore and I want to commemorate it and I want to bring it back.'

'It's past and present in one,' says Heidi. And I can live with that.

Early the next month

You would never suspect it to look at him – long limbs with few discernible muscles – but Hayden is one of those guys who is uncommonly handy, who is able to fix things and make things, has a shed full of tools and could probably knock you up a bookshelf or a wine rack, and is certainly not too proud to level off a few square metres of sand and lay some pavers or even build a recessed deck out the back of your house should circumstances allow for it.

It's Hayden who is standing next to me now, shattered, sweat-soaked and resplendent in the fine-fibred glisten of what is probably asbestos. We ripped the ceilings out first, mainly because I wanted to use the crowbar, and that set the scene for what has been a strenuous, liberating demolition.

Vincent booted out the previous proprietors a week ago and handed us the keys immediately. I got a few quotes from professional demolishers, the cheapest of which came in at more than eight grand. 'Yeah, it's a bit of a funny industry,' Vince had said, giving us his blessing to take the job on ourselves.

Taking stock of my financial affairs, and despite the weirdness of my cashflow situation,[1] I remained in the extraordinary position of having a building for which I did not need to pay rent, a cheque that would cover my initial operating expenses,[2] and well north of a million bucks in escrow.

It wasn't like I needed to skimp on Batard Rouge's fit-out, even if that meant another round of meetings with the blokey crew-cutted adolescent at the bank with the name plaque 'Manager'. I

---

1   That is, pretty much non-existent.
2   As soon as I can cash it.

told him the whole story, which I'm not sure he entirely followed,[3] but the agreement with Terry seemed to count for something and after a long phone conversation with an anonymous superior in Sydney he said I could list The Big Boy on my asset register, thereby increasing my overall net worth to approximately the value of that bottle of wine.

In the end I walked away with an overdraft that gave me the freedom to get properly started on the restaurant.

'Let's tear this place apart,' Hayden said, seconds prior to receiving his first face-full of toxic insulation, and over the past three days we have done just that, with sledgehammers and spades, but where possible with the steel-capped Blundstones we bought for precisely this purpose.

There are few things more satisfying than kicking in a wall with nothing more than the force of your own boot, and once we were done with the ceilings we turned our attention to the seven or so makeshift, seemingly randomly situated partitions that turned a once open, welcoming space into a kind of noodle warren where it was possible to get lost while walking from the counter to your table.

The quality of workmanship was poor – Hayden's first strike smashed the timber framework as though it were balsa wood, and we accounted for the interior walls in less than two hours.

The hard graft came in the details – little tasks like removing the skirting boards so as to preserve the original wooden floorboards[4] and ripping up the faux-tiled linoleum. Both took punctilious hours that Hayden and I would rather have spent putting boots through walls.

The building itself is a narrow-fronted terrace in a row of near-identical buildings, all of them two storeys, and all with two arched windows up top, the vertical sections of which resemble Greek

---

3   In hindsight I might have spared him some details, e.g., the specifics of the poker game in Paris.

4   Or at least not take crowbar-sized chunks out of them.

columns. Because they all look the same, I've never paid more than fleeting attention. It's also hard to look past the hoardings and tacky signage doing their best to turn architecture into an arsehole.

I want to scrub mine down, to reclaim its exterior too. But it's destined to house just another sign, albeit less incandescent.

Initially I'd hoped to use the second storey as a kind of clubhouse for the Crew or maybe as a private dining space, but Vincent said he'd 'probably store some shit up there, don't worry about it,' and so Hayden and I exerted our energies at ground level.

We passed a lot of the time talking menu options. Hayden had visited the Parisian original a couple of times and had welcomed Bruno twice as a houseguest on his regular visits to Melbourne. He'd probably passed as many hours with him as I had, which prompted me to ask, between sledgehammer blows, whether he thought it was strange that Bruno had asked me, rather than him, to set up the restaurant in Melbourne.

'You're perfect for this, Jude,' Hayden said. 'Better than me and definitely better than Adrian. It makes sense. It'll be a vessel. Something you can inhabit.'

'I don't see that. I'm not an inhabitant. I'm more like a transient. And what about all the other stuff in my life?'

'You'll keep your life; it's just a restaurant. And this thing needs spark, grandeur even. Restaurants also need people who worry a lot. You fit the bill really well.'

Hayden has a way of being both sage and kind of a dick at the same time and these last few days have been good for our friendship. Often when I'm travelling I'll spend thirty hours or more with a friend in their city over the course of a long weekend and I find you can get closer in a few days than in a whole year of catching up for coffee. The two of us have chalked up well over thirty hours here on the worksite, have pulled down a barrier or two emotionally, and I'm pretty sure that's not just the asbestos talking.

A lot of men use sport to sound one another out, to check for sensitivities or to ingratiate themselves, but that's a long way from our wheelhouse. Maybe unconsciously we seek to make the same type of progress by talking about wine and food.

As a sommelier, Hayden is a pulpy, fermenting barrel of knowledge who occasionally finds himself taken hostage by wineworld. He doesn't control his own wine list to the extent that he would like, and of course has to talk to his guests about wine in the traditional manner.[5] The Crew offers him a necessary solace. Bethany told me he once said we'd saved him from falling out of love with wine.

His relationship with food is similarly complex. Never as outwardly passionate or verbose about restaurants as the rest of us – and often without trace elements of food of any kind in his house – he nonetheless has strong views about Melbourne's Batard Rouge. By our second morning on the job he was lobbying for a far more modern take on your standard Parisian bistro offering than Bruno or I had contemplated.

The French cooking tradition is rich and multifaceted, at once regionally nuanced and time-honoured. Yet so many tourists spend a week in Paris and come home saying the food was shit. It really is a travesty that most of those corner brasseries serve up such dull fare,[6] and a greater calamity still that visitors don't push on past the first available table and down a side street.

We all love Batard Rouge because its menu draws inspiration from classic bistro dishes while allowing for a daub of artistry from the kitchen, and most importantly insisting upon seasonal, high-quality produce.

You can go to Lyon and eat at Auberge de l'île Barbe or one of the other famous starred places and get a saucy dose of the

---

5   Well, post-Parker traditional.

6   Apparently the food is sometimes frozen, TV-dinner style.

old-school and it's always a good time. Or in Paris go to Septime[7] for an experience that is equally decadent in a culinary sense but more sparse in terms of what you see on the plate and more modern in terms of its handling of ingredients.

While all this cuisine is 'French', it is undeniable that something happened over there, maybe twenty years ago, that prompted a shift away from the traditional style.[8]

As a bistro, Batard Rouge has no starry ambitions and is more traditional than nouveau. The point Hayden has been making, though, is that there's some potentially tasty ground in the middle there, where you might look to invert a classic or two while still delivering on the 'damn, that is a delicious-looking plate of food' imperative so central to the format.

He's talking about flathead flambé, mussels poached and served out of their shells between fine slices of onion and crisp bread, and potentially some kind of micro-gastronomic take on poulet à la Normande. It mostly sounds delectable, but I've got the Parisian legacy to think about along with Bruno's own bidding,[9] plus there's the whole 'if it ain't broke' thing, et cetera.

Yesterday we mostly talked about classical music, and Hayden once again surprised me with the range of his scholarship, which was especially pleasing for me as I'd done the Requiem the week before. On the same bill, with the Melbourne Symphony Orchestra, was Mendelssohn's Violin Concerto in E minor, and the concertmaster asked me to step in at the eleventh hour to play a minor percussion part,[10] and it was totally lustral.

---

7 Or really twenty other restaurants focusing on high-end, modern French cuisine.

8 One theory is that French chefs discovered Japanese cuisine and started to bring those techniques to their restaurants.

9 Both before he died, and my own imagined communiqués from the grave.

10 So minor he could probably have pulled someone from the audience.

I've always been around orchestras, and in many instances right alongside them, but being inside one is inimitable. I met a guy at a bar once who held up Formula One as the epitome of precision – what with all the technology and the danger and the pit stops and the tactics. I didn't quibble, yet to see an orchestra from within – to see instruments and players not just working together but visibly feeding off one another – is pure joy and consonance. The music comes to occupy you, like a kind of epizoism, and you nourish and release and succumb not just with each note but in the spaces in between.

I'm explaining this to Hayden, and he's largely across it, at least conceptually, and another thing I'm trying to articulate is the sanctity with which I've come to view this complicated and arguably fairly minor work.[11] I'm grappling with this, thinking that my connection to it is at best wilful snobbery or at worst a brazen misalignment of priorities, and yet this realisation had come to me so clearly: that if people can't play this piece of music, if we're not performing it regularly and, beyond that, if we're not building spaces in which it can be performed, then what's the point?

Right around then Antoine had called. He'd spoken with Bruno's widow and she was beginning to bring his affairs into some sort of order, and could I possibly travel to Paris to meet with her face to face at some stage during the autumn.[12]

Antoine said she sounded warmer than usual, convivial even, and that his read was that she wanted to give her blessing to our venture in person.

Yep, I could go back to Paris, and I left it with Antoine to consult his teaching schedule and suggest a suitable week for us to rendezvous. Restaurant bookings would come later, although those cogs were already rotating.

---

11   The Mendelssohn.
12   European.

Which brings us to now, this moment, Hayden and I admiring the empty shell of a space that last month doled out noodles at ten bucks a throw.

'Got it done,' says Hayden.

'Smashed it.'

'Did we have a bottle in mind for this moment?'

'Arras Grand Vintage. In the esky under the beers.'

I'm trying to recall where I stashed the champagne flutes when Vincent pokes his head through the doorway to behold his building in its pulverised glory.

'Jesus, nice work, boys,' he says, tapping a pile of rubble with the buffed toe of one of his loafers. 'About to pull the cork out of something?'

'Done all we can, Vince.' I shake his hand and hand him a glass.

Hayden blasts the cork into the ceiling cavity.

'Professional-looking job, fellas. Saved yourselves a few bucks and hopefully got a bit of the old zen glow that comes from doing something with your hands.'

'In spades,' Hayden says.

'How's the rest of it coming along? You got some hotshot lined up to handle the interiors?'

'Going to use a little group Adrian knows.' I raise my glass to them both. 'They did his last place and he reckons they're the business. They'll be in here next week.'

'Well, every new restaurant in Melbourne looks the same so you blokes will have to forgive me when I don't look surprised at the results.'

'It'll be different. More French.'

'And chefs and staff and menus?'

'Not quite as far along as I'd like to be, at least in terms of personnel,' I say, 'but enquiries are ongoing.'

'What about your wine list?'

'Around 800 bottles submitted, and every major growing region represented.'

'Fuck.'

'A lot of that's down to Erica,' says Hayden. 'Once she stared telling people…'

'It's a balls-out piss-up if nothing else.'

'We're getting there.'

'You have to find a way to make this place memorable,' says Vincent, walking around the hollow space, 'and you can't be pricks about it. I remember going to Circa in St Kilda when it first got hot. Three hats, booked out months in advance, all that shit. We arrive on time, ask to be shown to our table, but instead we're herded off to the bar for forty-five minutes. All the while I can see our table in the restaurant, sitting there, fucking empty. No apology, no explanation. Couple of years later I hear that the maître d' used to tell his staff that people should feel privileged to get a chance to experience their bar, that bundling people out there was just what they did. Meanwhile, I want to take that guy out into a laneway and stick the cocktail list up one of his nostrils.'

'That'd be around the same time as the glass incident, right?' Hayden turns to me.

'I'm thinking exactly the same time.'

He's referring to an early Crew experience at Circa when we were barely legal age, and there was a problem with Bethany's wine from the first bottle we'd ordered for the table. It was fine for the rest of us, but close to rancid in her glass. We made the point politely to the sommelier, and it seemed such an open-and-shut case of one glass being tainted with washing detergent or whatever, but this guy just would not accept it. He said they didn't use detergent, that it couldn't possibly be that, that he couldn't smell the difference between the glasses – the whole tortuous ordeal. And you would have to have been dead of palate not to know that something was seriously amiss.

'Lucky we had Rob to deal with that one.' Hayden grins.

Rob had called for quiet as the argument was gathering steam then got up from the table and said, 'Am I going back there to get this woman a new glass of wine or are you?'

Anyway the sommelier did, eventually, and it was a wine they were pouring by the glass so all he needed to do was fetch a clean vessel and make up Bethany's pour from another bottle. When he begrudgingly attended to the task, the contrast between Beth's first glass and her second was glaring. The guy declined our invitation to observe this disparity for himself.

'You don't want to be talked about for that kind of shit,' Vincent says. 'I reckon the best test is if people mourn you when you shut down.'

'Ondine,'[13] Hayden blurts out, like it's a tourniquet for a fresh wound. 'Pearl, obviously.'

'Melbourne Wine Room,' I add. 'Luxe.'

'It was Stephanie's for me,' Vincent says. 'Still think about it. And you guys don't have to be Stephanie's or Loam or any of them, but you want to be a place that people will miss when it's gone.'

'Definitely the goal,' I say, 'but for now we're focused on what happens when a punter walks through the door.'

'Get a glass of wine in their hand within seconds of their arses touching the seat,' Vincent replies. 'That's another thing that pisses me off – waiting around for a drink. And leave the bottles on the tables. Number of times I have to stand up, find my bottle, and pour the bastard thing myself...'

Vincent refreshes his glass from the bottle of Arras, which is as cold as snow on a Pipers River morning,[14] and the big man withdraws his hand upon first contact before going in again more boldly. There's something about obscenely cold champagne,[15] a beer-

---

13   2000-2003. 12 Flinders Lane, Melbourne. RIP.

14   In Tasmania, where the wine is made.

15   Or any high-quality sparkling wine.

like quality almost, which touches you more potently when you're exhausted, when you've exerted yourself. Maybe it's just the sugar, like sucking nectar from a flower. You can see why it's given to sportspeople when they win.

'Vince, I should say I'm heading back to Europe in a couple of weeks. Need to see Annette,[16] Bruno's widow, so I can cash her cheque. And I'm thinking about heading to Piedmont for the truffle festival. Maurice in Paris offered to show me around.'

'Bloke you won The Big Boy from?'

'The very one. He's in the truffle business.'

'How'd you feel about me tagging along, Jude?' asks Vincent. 'Piazza Duomo[17] is top of my restaurant list at present.'

'Well, for sure…'

And for sure indeed, although I never figured Vince as a travel buddy, at least not further than Brae or the Royal Mail Hotel. He's looking down at those loafers of his again, shoulders hunched when he usually stands tall, then he says, 'Yeah, and the other thing, Jude, is that jeroboam.'

'The Big Boy?'

'Yep.' He has his back to me, conducting a faux inspection of one of our skirting boards. 'Turns out it's a fake.'

'It's fucking what?'

'Got in touch with the domaine a couple of weeks ago and spoke to Aubert himself just this morning.[18] It's a good fake, but it's a counterfeit bottle every day of the week. And since I have an interest in it now I reckon I might even have a quiet word with Maurice in between truffles. Assuming that's alright with you.'

---

16   For it is her name.

17   The three-Michelin-star restaurant on Piazza Risorgimento in Alba.

18   Aubert de Villaine, co-owner of Domaine de la Romanée-Conti.

Interlude
Antoine[1]

'Alright, you all have a bottle, unopened at this point, and a glass. The glass doesn't matter; it's whatever I could find in the kitchen. Heidi, you have in fact an olive jar, which I did wash carefully – by all means drink out of the bottle if you'd rather – the point being we're here, all of us, to absorb this wine, and I'll talk about it and about a few other things over the course of that absorption.

'Yes, Hayden, lie down, remove your shoes, find a patch of earth and consider the vista – due south we're facing, looking over the plane to the ocean and beyond that French Island, a hundred kilometres away nearly but because the sky is clear, specked only by cloudlets, we see all the way to the island.

'Take on the sunshine. Meet it. You're drawing it in through every exposed section of skin, through your clothes even. It's changing your composition, subtly, with each ray that licks your body. Lay before it, below it, and take it in.

'Bethany, that's a good-sized glass of wine you've liberated for yourself, and yes of course, everyone, open your bottles, pass around the corkscrew. See if you can throw the corks all the way up to the house – there'll be no resealing required this afternoon.

'Jude, you got the best glass. I don't know why – indicant maybe of your ascent to the helm of the Crew, and very much a subconscious

---

1   About a week later. At which time Antoine holds court at a tasting he arranged for us on the side of a hill at his cousin's weekend house in the Yarra Ranges, overlooking the township of Woori Yallock and a budding vineyarded sliver of the appellation demarked Yarra Valley. He speaks. No one else says a thing.

choice of mine, if a choice at all. It's a pinot noir glass but do enjoy it as a vessel for this gamay.

'This music I'm playing feels like some brand of assault. I can see you're enjoying it, Erica, which raises more questions than it answers. I'll turn it off in a minute but it's playing now not because I like it but because it affected, in some small way, the maker's passage to the vineyard and ultimately to this wine.

'I will be drinking with you. We'll share this experience, but do please imbibe at your own pace. Drink to your own rhythm. Do whatever you want.

'I would ask, though, that you contemplate the colour of this wine, its brightness. Look at it in the sunlight, against the eagerness of spring on the hillside, against all the fledgling colours finding fresh forms around here.

'The vines that produced the grapes that gave us this juice were planted in the mid-1980s, so they're not especially old, and there wasn't a great deal of gamay planted in Australia then, or now for that matter. The vineyard lies in the Piccadilly Valley and after just a couple of years it was grafted to chardonnay, to capitalise on demand for that varietal, and, in fact, berries from these vines ended up in Yattarna for a number of vintages. Rob, as you like to say, "It's a decent bit of dirt."

'Taras from Ochota Barrels knew the guy who owned the vineyard and not so long ago convinced him to head out into that vineyard with a chainsaw and chop off the chardonnay grafts, leaving the original rootstock of gamay. Can you imagine that conversation? Here's someone making, I don't know, three thousand dollars a tonne selling chardonnay to one of the world's biggest wine conglomerates and presumably sipping Yattarna each year with his friends saying "Yes, some of my grapes of went into that," and he's being asked if he wouldn't mind selling no grapes at all for a couple of years, and then selling fucking gamay to *l'enfant terrible* of the Australian wine industry to make what, from its first harvest, was just seventy litres of wine.

'And the wine, The Price of Silence, is named after a straight-edge hardcore band that performed intermittently in Adelaide during the 1990s, including at the University of Adelaide bar and, yes, I'll turn the music off, at least for a while.

'It is fermented by carbonic maceration, just like in Beaujolais, so that the process of fermentation happens intracellularly, within every single intact berry. Those berries are then crushed, in whole bunches, trodden on, one imagines, pressed, and then sent to neutral oak and simply left, although not for long. Then to bottle, and to all of us here.

'Consider what is happening to us now. For me the wine bursts as it enters my mouth. It overruns it, swarms through it. In terms of complexion it is the opposite of round. It's jutted. Almost unfinished. This is because it doesn't finish in the mouth… oh no. That's the start of its trip, the bon voyage. It's still to be absorbed. Still to spread, rhizome-like, across and throughout its many planes and saturated stages.

'And while it spreads, while we drink, can you join me for a moment of reflection? You knew when you arrived that we would be ruminating on the nature of wine, on what wine is, and I hope we all share the view that wine is important. That wine is something worthy of serious attention. Today I want to go further. Today I say that wine is a cultural object, that it is emotional, that it is aesthetic.

'The creation and consumption of wine is an aesthetic project, and while we have not participated directly in the journey of this juice from vineyard to glass, we find ourselves here, at a later moment in that project, but one no less aesthetically charged.

'In interacting with this wine, with this brilliant, fluid entity, we experience it in a way that is intrinsically phenomenological. Is everyone following me here? From a sensory standpoint our connection to the wine is all-enveloping, and nothing is more phenomenological than that. So do please submit to this project. Let us, in fact, declare it a project! An event! And let us contemplate and question the way we approach *all* wine.

'Returning to my glass, making a more urgent approach, I find myself back in the embrace of the wine and it is a *lifted* embrace. Feel the band on which this wine is operating, very different from most, and so very vital, utterly alive.

'You're seeing how it's changing in the glass – or bottle I see for you, Hayden and Erica. Is it becoming greener maybe? Or is that just because we're sitting here and the sun's shining brighter on the grass. What's happening to it? What on earth is happening to this wine? Is it settling? Not at all. It's merely entering a new phase of its life, exposed to oxygen, to this mountain, and to us.

'As it continues that journey, let us reflect on how we have lost our way with wine. I say "we" meaning wine-conscious society. Not just the so-called "connoisseurs" or "aficionados" – although they are surely more misplaced than most – but drinkers of wine, casual consumers, and even those who may identify as wine-curious.

'At some point we started tasting wine and not drinking it. How obscene it sounds to say that sentence out loud but it's true. We objectified wine. And the first step in our project today is to recognise that this wine, that all wine, is more than just an object.

'Look at what's in your glass. If that's an object, then what do you call yourself? The corresponding subject? Does it fall to you to conduct an analysis of the stuff? We are burdened with bent vocabulary around wine, with lexicon. We acquired technique, and it forever changed us.

'This afternoon I'm calling for an abandonment, for a release. Let go of the way you think about wine, give it up! Join me as we take this leap of faith. Let all evaluation cease and let us nurture a new form of relationship. And, please, let us look to build that relationship on ground more steady than mere "taste". Let's stop describing wine as "tasting like something else". Let us recognise that wine is much, much more than that.

'This gamay. This delight. Is there now a fullness to it? Is it now more imbued with flesh of a certain kind? For me it's the flesh of a single stout berry. Not ripe, no, no. Not plump. Ample. Abundant. Is it grounding us at this moment, steering us back to the earth?

'Something is happening. Feel it! All of you, touch your head with your hands. Feel the wine travel. Through our faces, our retronasal passages, our jaws even. Touch your temples with your fingers and feel how the wine has made its way even there. When I pull my hair, I can confirm that the wine has journeyed even there.

'And if you possibly can, contemplate your own brain and how this stuff has pervaded that most vital of organs, from the cerebellum onwards, upwards, and not in any targeted way, more like river water splashed on clay.

'Ask yourself, if you dare, how your brain feels at this moment. Look to remove your body from the examination, forget about your limbs and lungs and so on. Consider your brain as a whole, as a singular article, all its cells and neurons, and whatever other elements sit inside your skull, segregated into lobes and so on and yet networked and entwined.

'My brain is glistening. Like dawn on ancient amber. True, it's in no mood for dense texts, for solving difficult problems, for crosswords even. It doesn't look to be stretched or quickened or overly stimulated. And yet, dashed with this wine, wet by it, I feel a rousing of matter up there.

'Take in some more and then close your eyes. Hold them shut and gently press each eyelid in turn. Don't look at the ground, Rob, keep looking straight ahead. What do you see? You know those shards and fragments but you probably don't know what they're called. You are experiencing a phenomenon called a phosphine. You feel like you're seeing light, but actually there's no light entering the eye. Does it look blotchy? Is it red even? It's different for everyone. But it is shaped and formed, in part, by the wine we're all drinking.

'How long have we been sitting here, drinking on this mountain? An hour? More? Think about the things that have happened, around us and inside of us. How do we make sense of this experience? Is it possible for us to arrange these happenings, these qualities, in any sort of meaningful way?

'We ask that same question of wine, and the word we always fall back on, like a busted crutch, is "structure". But what does that mean? Is it significant or is it more wineworld jargon that we should flush alongside our flavour wheel and scorecards?

'Maybe it's not so important as other elements of our experience up here, but let's ruminate on structure momentarily because it is a real thing that wine possesses – good wine at least. Yet we only become aware of it in the course of engaging with wine and ultimately ingesting it.

'This is problematic for some people. Immanuel Kant himself said that all gustatory objects, wine included, are mere hedonic pleasures that do not invite or even accommodate reflection. So wine can't be art, can't be aesthetic, can't be considered in any sense beyond the immediate.

'But surely the experience of drinking wine, just like our experience sitting here on this mountain… surely we're able to assign properties, virtues, in the course of mulling over what we've absorbed? And those markings we make are temporal, they are "of moments". Of swirling, of swallowing, of the progress this wine has made in our company.

'This is structure. Our engagement with these moments, our active organisation of these inputs… this is what we mean by structure. And not all wine is worthy! Fruit bombs, over-oaked wines, wine that is shot or over the hill – these wines lack the necessary components, the complexity to join conversations around structure.

'This wine, though, this gamay… for me it deserves a seat at the table. From the middle palate it has pounced on my tongue, well and truly. It has taken hold. Somewhere between a grip and an embrace. Everyone, take a large swig and fill the floor of your mouth, fill it like a cup, to the brim. Yes, this is what we need to do… drown your tongue in the liquid sap, don't swallow yet. Press your tongue against the back of your teeth, each one in turn. You're absorbing now, sublingually.

'Closing my eyes again I see the mountain, only it's covered in berries. Berries of all kinds, wild and budding. Not even grapes, but raspberries, gooseberries, currants of varying colours.

'It's a kind of hallucination encouraged by this wine, its very product, and it reminds me that I'm drunk. We all are. Lie down for God's sake. You're not at a restaurant; you're not at your parents' house or even at Hayden's. It's just us, on this mountain. Give yourself over to what's in your glasses. Submit to it. Why not?

'It's left a physical mark now, this wine, a tactile imprint. On your lips, on my beard. If you run your tongue across your teeth you will strip it of a layer of blotted juice. That's the form it takes now. Caked and congealed. A different absorptive track.

'Let's steal a moment to actually look at the wine again, at its appearance in the glass. Is it different? Of course it is. It's been with us nearly an hour. And what's more, so are we, even though you may consider that difference subtle. Over the last hour you have brought new life into your own. The life around us, the life in each of us, and the life force of this wine.

'Because wine is a system. An intricate organism. It's alive and it interacts with humans. The act of consuming wine is a biologically interactive experience. It's not like a work of architecture or, sorry

Heidi, a piece of music. It's more like the ferns in the rainforest down there, or that ivy by the vegetable garden.

'And much of this wine is in your gut. At least half a litre of fluid brooding in your belly and still very much alive. Now interacting, for the first time, with the organisms and bacteria and other vital, thriving matter that reside beyond your lips and mouth and throat. A whole other world. Life meets life.

'How often do you put something in your mouth that is still alive? A freshly shucked oyster maybe? Sometimes in Japan a prawn? Casu Marzu cheese, and yoghurt, with its bacteria and live cultures and so on.

'And wonderful though these experiences may be, they are for the most part nature's bounty alone. This wine from Ochota Barrels, yes, it is "of nature", yes it is "natural", but it's possessed of intentionality, too. It is a product, at least in a sense, of its maker's intent.

'And here I come out to you, my friends, and say that great wines, the only great wines, are those made purposefully, ardently, with guardianship, "raised" almost and yet treated with the gentlest of hands. With very little added, so as to allow the wine to reveal its natural possibilities and to fulfil itself through drinking, through absorption and through digestion.

'I don't say that all natural wines are great – far from it. But in attending to these wines over the past few years, in coming to respect the manner of their cultivation, throughout that process I have grown convinced of their vitality and their value.

'I find most mass-produced wines lifeless. Made with cultivated yeasts, too much oak, lashings of sulphur dioxide, fruit flavours concentred and enhanced by machines, and this whole formulaic pursuit led not by a maker but by a blueprint. Affixed, one presumes, to a glistening steel tank in a spotless winery, where juice flows through thick plastic hoses from reservoir to barrel, at a time and in such quantity as a computer commands.

'That wine is fake. It's artless. But worse than that, it's boring. And increasingly I have found myself looking to my glass, at a dinner or a tasting (and I confess even sometimes in your company), and lamenting that I've fallen out of love with wine.

'And yet… sitting here now I find myself more captivated by wine than ever. Captivated, it's true, by this particular wine, this fantastically complex system assimilating euphorically with my own, but beyond that by the potential of other makers, of other sites, of other vines.

'And now, towards the end of my final glass, the wine is like a storm for me. Only I'm in a bubble, sheltered. It's possible to feel protected in a squall. To feel ravaged but secure, safe in your skin.

'Erica, I see you've finished your bottle. Bear with us, or by all means try to siphon a half-glass from your brother, and do make the attempt because this wine has taken a decidedly generous turn. Is it looking after us, smashed on the side of a mountain? Could it possibly contemplate us as a collective?

'I see you welcoming each sip, each impression. Stalling almost. The final slowly turned pages of a book we don't want to finish. A symphony we hope will find a bonus movement.

'And where does it leave us, this wine? Where in the end do we settle, if at all? Will you indulge me a turn to the emotional? Is that not what this is all about come day's end? Have we not been moved?

'I've moved into the soil, just below the surface, where the roots take form. Where the life of the plant meets victual earth. Where we go underground for the first time. Where the light comes to us not directly, but through a stem connected at once to the firmament of the breathing world, and to the loam and humus in the ground. Where life takes root. Where organisms collide and wax. Where it's lively. But it's silent.'

Three weeks later

Back-end of the plane this time, although Bethany is here and we have a spare seat between us all the way through to Turin, so my relegation to economy class could have been worse.[1]

Vincent turned left upon entering the aircraft, messaging just prior to take-off to advise that he'd been upgraded to first class and was awaiting the arrival of the caviar service. He found the time to send a second message shortly after to tell us he had turned down the offer of Dom Pérignon Vintage Rosé 2003 in deference to a freezing shot of vodka.[2]

Antoine should have been on board as well but had been summoned prematurely to Spain to deal with a spat that had broken out at his university after one of his students played an excerpt from last semester's final lecture to an executive from Bodegas Torres.[3]

Late at night at the restaurant Mugaritz, up in the hills,[4] this kid and his girlfriend, having celebrated a birthday, were waiting for a taxi out the front at the same time as the executive and her husband, and they got chatting (as one does with strangers after an exceptional meal in a shared space), and the woman volunteered that she worked at Torres. The student asked her if she'd ever heard of Antoine Moreno Nicolai, and she had not, and so for a laugh he produced his phone and played for her a section of one of Antoine's lectures where he was less than complimentary about elements of Bodegas

1   Vincent decided we should take care of business with Maurice before heading on to Paris to meet Annette.

2   At The Everleigh with him the night before, he said he felt like a martini and issued the waiter the instruction: 'Grey Goose vodka, obscenely cold, in a martini glass. And you can stick an olive in it.'

3   The Spanish wine conglomerate.

4   Around 20 minutes from San Sebastián.

Torres' overall winemaking philosophy. Ordinarily this wouldn't have been a problem, and Antoine's student had no intention of stitching him up, only Bodegas Torres were patrons of the university and of the Oenology Department in particular. The executive had made her dissatisfaction known to the dean early the following morning.

Antoine told us he couldn't remember what he'd said in that lecture specifically but felt fairly sure it would have been severe. So off he trotted, a week ahead of schedule, to make palliations and generally kiss whatever arses were positioned in front of him.

We planned to rendezvous in Paris to meet with Annette and hopefully resolve the one or two matters left outstanding, in particular the uncashed cheque still stuck to my bedroom wall.

And Beth. I know she'd said she wanted space, but I wanted the opposite of space. I figured I'd only get one chance to ask her and, rather than dicking around, strayed from my standard playbook and phoned her and said, 'Bethany, I'd really like it if you'd come with me to Europe.' She said, 'Sure, I'd love to,' and while it'll need more testing and research, this whole 'just tell people what you want' thing could have legs.

Bethany is in black tights, wrapped and fetching, and lately her body makes me nervous. When I'm nervous I try to be funny and it's lucky there's wine in my mouth to stop me.

'Check out the temper on that bead,' I say instead, looking slant-headed at my second glass of Clover Hill Cuvée.[5] Could be the altitude, but bubbles are positively spewing from the base of the stubby, short-stemmed aeroplane glass.

'Apparently you're supposed to try to taste them,' says Bethany, in between sips.

'I read that somewhere too. But I'd rather think about the bubbles as something different from the wine. A counterpoint.'

---

5   The non-vintage blend, from Tasmania.

'They're virtual,' says Beth. 'They represent potential that is fulfilled in the wine. Not material, but still real.'

'Wow.'

There's a woman with a baby across the aisle, middle seat, and the kid's just launched his bottle a full three rows and now she has to navigate her way to retrieve it, still clutching the child, because what's she going to do with it.

I'd noticed her earlier, or more the way other passengers were regarding her. That sense of dread and displeasure, like 'why would anybody bring a baby on a plane?' Even people with their own kids at home seem to share the disdain, as if aeroplanes are somehow sacred spaces.

I admired her, and liked her more with every angry glance she deflected.

Anyway she's walking right past me now, and the kid is practically in front of my face so I make that gesture I've seen Heidi do, which I've translated as, 'I feel you, do you want me to hold this thing for a second?' And she just passes him to me without a word.

'Suits you,' says Bethany.

'Go fuck yourself,' and then, 'Sorry, little guy.'

The mother's back before I can do any further damage and she looks at our champagne and grins and shakes the baby's bottle as though comparing beverages.

Bethany's brain has returned to her glass as I pass back the baby and she says, 'What we're looking at is a continuous multiplicity of fizz. These bubbles? Only actualised when swallowed. Right now, they're an ideal.'

'Jesus Beth,' I say, as more eyes turn upon the mother clambering to her seat, 'talk to Antoine. I mean for fuck's sake…'

'I loved his sermon on the mountain.'

And here I have to take stock because, while at the time I was as into it as much as the next man,[6] if your thesis is that wine has become a wank then is jerking off into a bottle really the most persuasive way of making your point?

'Wine's never been a sport to me, Jude,' Bethany says. 'Not for Antoine either. In a lot of serious restaurants or wine bars you feel like you're being served by the captain of the footy team from high school. Only his sporting career ended, he got injured or he just wasn't good enough, but he still wants to be able to pick up women, he still wants to "win", and he likes getting shitfaced. So he takes a couple of Ritalin and learns all the appellations of the Languedoc.[7] And at the end of it someone gives him[8] a special award and a gold badge[9] and tells him he's the boss of something.[10]

'And the alternative is the fucking Deleuzian virtual or a Perulloean phenomenology?' I snort. 'At least when you tell people that gewürztraminer tastes a bit like lychee they understand what you're talking about.'

'It looks like a democracy, Jude, but it's not. Wine's like America.'

'I love America.'

'You love Napa and Sonoma – that's not America.'

'Look, fine. I get it. But I'm trying to put a wine list together here. Wine is wine. Seriously…'

'What's The Big Boy then?'

'Touchy subject, Beth.'

'I wonder what's actually in there? I mean, wine presumably. Would the forgers have followed a recipe, had a go at making it seem believable? Do you think your mate Maurice cooked it up himself?'

---

6   Who happened to be Hayden.
7   In Southern France
8   Usually 'him', although the gender imbalance is improving, thank God.
9   It really is a kind of gold medal.
10   Part of the 'wineworld' mindset that Antoine and Nicola Perullo rile against.

'I doubt it. Probably won it in a poker game.'

'Do you remember that Ponsot scam?'[11]

'It was pretty memorable.'

'It came out in the trial that the guy was making fake 1945 Mouton Rothschild by blending 1988 Pichon Melant, crappy oxidised bordeaux, and half-decent Napa cab.'

'Actually that is good.'

'It's like the art world,' Bethany says after actualising another mouthful of the Clover Hill. 'I mean who really knows what's real and what's not? Rich people want rockstar bottles in their cellars just like they want rockstar paintings on their walls.'

'They say with art that the forgeries are sometimes better.'

'Lots of fake paintings hanging in museums.'

'I think it's worse with wine than with art,' I say, 'even if in both cases the majority of people can't spot the fake.'

'You wouldn't back yourself to pick a forged '45 Mouton?' Bethany smiles.

'Breaks my heart thinking about it,' I say. 'You've bought that bottle, it's a special occasion and you're relieved in the first instance that it isn't corked or horribly oxidised, then you try it and you're conscious of something being not quite right. But you're already invested in the romance of it. You've submitted emotionally only to be denied the authenticity of the experience. It's a betrayal.'

'Robbed of your romance, Jude.'

'Denied a real experience. And now every great old bottle wears this veil of trickery. Who knows what's fake?'

---

11   The now-convicted conman Rudy Kurniawan tried to auction a 1929 Ponsot Clos de la Roche from Domaine Ponsot. The head of the estate, Laurence Ponsot, got wind of the sale and was 'immediately alarmed' given his family only started producing wine under their own name in 1934.

'Some ride, though. The club in Paris, the plane trip back,[12] meeting Vincent. The Big Boy's lived a life. Richer maybe than what he'd have offered in the glass.'

I mull on this. 'I wonder what I'm supposed to do with it now?'

'Seems unlikely Mr Truffles will offer a replacement.'

'Vincent can be pretty persuasive…'

'Maybe you auction it? Send it to Sotheby's in London.'

'They'll spot it as a fake. And anyway, I don't need that karma. I can't handle the anxiety.'

Beth grins, not mocking my temperament, it's something warmer, and she catches me gazing at her, taking her in, then says, 'I was just thinking back to those auctions we used to go to in Adelaide.'[13]

She's at my heartstrings, because right after one of those auctions we had a moment back at my place where we almost kissed, almost joined, almost said, fuck it, let's just do this. It was late, on my couch, and if she didn't have a boyfriend everything could have changed. We never talked about it, the couch followed me to Melbourne, and right now I'm not sure she even knows that's where my mind has gone.

'We bought a lot of crap,' Bethany says.

'Made a lot of sangria.'

'Civilised, though. Compared to now.'

'I'll have to get back into auctions if I'm going to put Grange on the list at Batard Rouge.'

'The list is done?' Beth asks.

'It's close.'

'And everything else?'

---

12   Earlier, in the lounge, I had finally gotten around to telling Bethany and Vincent the full story of The Big Boy's trip to Australia, and his encounters with Nadya and Isabelle.

13   Back when you had to physically front up to the auction house, register to bid, and then wave your paddle in the air. The wine was all there and available for inspection, and very often there were bottles open for tasting.

'Kitchen's ready to go and we're almost there with the rest of the fit-out. Shit happens fast when you throw money at it.'

'What about staff?'

'Found a chef. Haven't turned my mind to a sommelier yet.'

The seatbelt sign has been on for more than an hour, but absent any turbulence the cabin crew has decided to push on. This means pinot noir for me and Beth, an entry-level Yarra Valley cuvee from Mac Forbes. At the back of the aeroplane it surpasses all reasonable expectations. The wine looks pale, raspberry coloured, but it's firm on the palate, with greenness and acidity that suits the skies. It has a thrilling quality. Then an unexpected note, something higher in the register. Nothing wrong, more like a jolt, a sense of a wine finding its way with a different set of maps.

'I drank this on a date last week,' says Bethany.

'Where'd you go?'

'Stayed home. I've started using the dating apps alongside my matching system.'

'Wait, what?'

'Turns out a lot of what I want I can do at home, by myself, on the phone.'

'But –'

'The app matches me with a bunch of guys, I sit on the couch, open a bottle, and start messaging. Once I've finished my last glass I can just turn them off or delete them. Don't even have to change the sheets.'

'Who did you pair with the Mac Forbes?'

'Young guy. Sincere. Didn't like finishing his own sentences, but the wine worked well with that.'

I have always tried not to care about Bethany being with other men. My success rate is generally proportionate to how hard I'm crushing on her at any given moment, and right now I'm jealous.

Why though? It's not like I have any claim to her. And even if I did, there's nothing more destructive than possessiveness. Yet I can't stave it off. Always this dull nausea when she talks about sex or the occasional boyfriend or longer-term lover.

And what if we were together? Even then I know I wouldn't be the only one. She'd need other men in her life, and I'd have to find a way to reconcile that – or at least endure it. 'Can't drink just one kind of wine your whole life, Jude,' she's said to me more than once. 'Not even champagne.'

'What was that thing you said about owning every bottle of your favourite wine?' And now I realise I'm talking out loud.

'That it's not something you'd wish for. Even if there were only a thousand bottles made, you wouldn't want to own them all. Enjoy a bottle from time to time, ideally lots of bottles, but the whole production? Never yours to possess.'

'Right.'

'And let's say you have loads of bottles, would you be jealous of someone buying a case for themselves and enjoying it? Course not.'

I doubt she can actually read my mind, but I do wonder at times.

'It's about more than wine, though,' I say.

'It's mostly about my mum,' she says.

'It's what?'

'The whole jealousy thing. My mum's the most jealous person I ever met. She's jealous of what her friends are wearing, jealous of women in the street, even jealous of me. That's why I think about it so much. I don't want to be like her.'

'She does dress very well.'

'She's all dress. Take off the clothes and she's a coathanger.'

'I didn't know it was so bad.'

'It's pretty standard shit, Jude. There's always something.'

'I wasn't told.'

'Ask around,' she smiles.

'I'm asking now.'

'Think about how she looks at you. Always just a fraction flirty. Always some little compliment about your appearance.'

'Beth...'

'It's true. She wants you to want her. Just a little bit. Just so I know I can never have anything to myself.'

'I knew there was tension. I didn't know it was about that.'

She's opened a guidebook now, signifying the end of that little chat, and says, 'Did you know that in Italy, they don't say "have your cake and eat it", they say, "having your wife drunk but the barrel still full"?'

Neither of us has been to the Piedmont region although the whole crew, including Bruno, spent a week in Chianti in Tuscany four years ago. We shared a villa and mostly drank Aperol Spritzes by the pool, not venturing further north than Florence. We'd built the trip very loosely around the Chianti Classico Tuscan Wine Festival held each year in Greve, where fifty or so local producers set up stalls in the main piazza and you bought a glass and a ticket book for ten euros, then wandered around trying what you liked and buying food from the restaurants that lined the square.

The whole thing was close to perfect, and when we weren't on the prosecco back at the villa we were working our way through a motley selection of modestly priced, overwhelmingly agreeable chiantis.

We took it in turns each day going to Il Vinaino di Greve[14] with a budget of around two hundred euros, buying maybe nine or ten bottles at prices ranging from ten to thirty euros. We never knew much about any of them, so we would arrange them on the counter back at the villa according to price, with the cheapest at the back. Then it was a matter of working our way through them

---

14   One of two excellent wine shops in the piazza.

of an evening, and it was rare for even the least expensive bottles to disappoint.

Another thing about having a group of ten or so staying in a villa in high summer is the staggering quantity of beer consumed. On our first visit to the Coop[15] we bought all the beer they had, and thereafter established a run rate of about forty bottles a day. The sheer weight of recycling come week's end elicited a look from our elderly cleaner that Erica placed on the spectrum somewhere between horror and admiration.

That was the week we all really got to know Bruno. I mean, we'd known him for years, but six nights in close quarters in that kind of heat and drinking that quantity of booze will either bring you closer to someone or have you running for higher ground.

Batard Rouge always closed for a few weeks during summer, and we persuaded Bruno to stop in Tuscany[16] en route to his annual pilgrimage to the family home in Corsica. He immediately offered to send several cases of wine from the restaurant over to the villa in advance and took some convincing that this would not be necessary.

The French can be funny like that. You can walk into a wine store in Beaune[17] and ask to buy a bottle of cabernet sauvignon and get a look so blank as to leave you checking you haven't accidently strolled into a laundromat. Some bottle shops in Burgundy don't even sell champagne, and there are few things funnier than seeing Americans trying to order zinfandel at restaurants in France. Their disbelief that the full glorious range of the world's wine offerings would not be available by the glass and bottle at that particular restaurant in Dijon is hilarious. And though they would hate the comparison, on the road the French themselves get similarly nervous.

---

15   Probably the best supermarket chain on earth – Swiss in origin but found throughout Northern Italy.
16   Sans Annette.
17   In Burgundy.

Bruno, however, dealt with his penury with aplomb – we didn't drink even a single glass of pinot noir for the whole week. He went to bed a little earlier than the rest of us and tended to be up first thing conducting experiments on the lardo and different cuts of wild boar that he purchased each day from Antica Macelleria Falorni on the piazza.[18]

We ate salami and prosciutto, along with dry bread and copious amounts of olive oil and tomatoes, and figs from the tree in the garden. Traditional Tuscan peasant food mostly,[19] and Bruno told stories about equivalent French fare and what his grandparents would cook in Corsica and how there hadn't been a single moment in his life where there wasn't a lonzu[20] hanging in his kitchen.

'I'm hot for truffles,' says Bethany, bidding me back to reality. She leans into me with her shoulder, fondly, over the empty seat between us. 'I hope Vincent doesn't attack your mate. At least not before we've eaten.'

'Beth, we'll have truffles with every meal.'

'Fuck yeah.'

Now I could sleep. Maybe twenty hours, maybe longer, but what I'm doing is getting dressed for one of just two meetings scheduled on this ten-day peregrination into Italy and France.

I feel like I'm a tree oozing sap, like my brain is a soaked sponge. Like I'm carrying my limbs rather than them carrying me. I feel soft and everything looks hard.

---

18   Founded in 1806, they claim to be the oldest *macelleria* (butcher) in Italy.
19   Although meat was surely a luxury for Italian peasants in the early modern era and beyond.
20   A Corsican sausage, made from pork loin.

I should have slept between Melbourne and Dubai, but I was chatting and drinking with Bethany and it was a blast, like we were sitting side by side at a bar. Like we were on a date.

My next mistake was nodding off in the first-class lounge during transit. Vincent got us in – 'These two are with me' – and the plan was to have breakfast and a glass of champagne. I made it as far as the first available couch and said, 'Grab me on your way back through to the gate.'

I slept an hour before Vincent's palm met the underside of my chin and Bethany's hand pulled the strap of my bag. Together they yanked me conscious and onto my feet.

Or more like into a stupor. No idea where I was, and pretty pissed off at the prospect of being awake. I stumbled onto the plane, certain that I would fall asleep the second I hit the headrest and longing to slide back inside the gooey crust of long-haul hibernation.

But I couldn't. Bethany was out in minutes and I watched her for a bit, all twitching eyelashes, then tried some meditation exercises, then eventually ordered a glass of red wine and took a couple of melatonin. Then I had another glass of wine and was poised on the very precipice of sleep, awaiting the collapse, but not able to submit.

That started to really irritate me. I blamed the melatonin, then Bethany, then I got angry with her for being asleep, then I thought, I'll watch a movie, maybe that'll work, then more wine, then I heard the guy in the aisle beside me ask a steward what time we landed in Frankfurt and I said to him, 'Frankfurt? We're going to Turin, mate.'

He gave a smartarsed smirk and said, 'I don't know where you're going, but this plane's going to Frankfurt,' and the stewardess confirmed that was true, and my first reaction was, fuck, Vincent and Bethany walked us onto the wrong plane, but when I rustled in my bag and checked the Melbourne-issued boarding pass it said Frankfurt, and in the folder along with all the other bits of paperwork was another boarding pass for the onward journey from Frankfurt to Turin. At that moment we were two and a half hours outside of Germany.

This put me into an internal sleep-deprived rage, which naturally made sleep impossible. We eventually touched down in Frankfurt, the guy across the aisle chiming in with, 'It is a sort of German version of Turin in many ways,' and I feigned laughter and started poking Bethany to wake her up.

No time for the lounge on that stopover, and no more sleep for me until Vincent picked up the rental car in Turin. I lay on the back seat and nodded off for maybe forty minutes to wake again, as though shot, when we pulled up in front of our accommodation at Villa Carita in La Morra. I tried to sleep there too but couldn't get it done, and by the time I went up to the terrace on top of our apartment for an aperitivo it was two hours until our meeting with Maurice in Alba.

Sure enough it was then, gazing upon the lush, felted vineyards of Barolo, looking down towards Langhe and the castles of Serralunga and Castiglione Falletto, only then, seeing Alba itself in the middle distance and taking in the full glory of the Piedmont region at large, did I think, yeah, now I could probably sleep.

But by that point it was impractical and now I'm back in the rental car,[21] half-showered, with Vincent exhorting the thing towards the kerb and saying, 'Alba looks lively.'

It's actually impossible to see Alba at all through the heaving horde of people occupying every cobblestoned surface, and quite how Vincent was able to find this park remains a mystery. That is until I realise that he's actually just found 'a space' and parked there. This has left us not quite in the middle of the road, but absolutely a long way from any conventional rendering of a sanctioned parking spot.

---

21   With a CD from Vincent's band playing loudly on the stereo. Actually decent, although more like late Skyhooks than early Springsteen.

'They don't worry too much about us tourists,' he says, incongruously, but the car is rented in his name so there's that.

I'd heard that Alba was rammed on weekends during the Truffle Festival but it's Thursday night now and still damn near impossible to put one foot in front of the other without colliding with another human. It reminds me of the Royal Adelaide Show when I was a kid or trying to get on a train right after a football game.

And yet… even there amid the fleshy gridlock, by the roadside where car fumes might otherwise steal the senses, it is impossible to miss the manifest inimitable aroma of fresh truffles.

'Yes,' says Bethany, tilting her nose skyward.

'You beauty,' says Vincent.

Now we're walking through the crowd, Vincent with his phone held in front of him like a cattle prod, following the map on his screen and steering us in the direction of Piazza Pietro Rossetti where I've arranged to meet Maurice.

I told him I was bringing a couple of friends, but I didn't mention The Big Boy. Better for Vincent to broach that topic, I figured. I am uneasy enough, especially in my way-worn state. I'm so glad Bethany is here. She's wearing sensible shoes for cobblestones and a slip dress that's a just a piece of fabric with two straps. Vincent, meanwhile, looks like he's on his way to meet his mother at the theatre and is whistling a Dire Straits song as he weaves through the throng.

The cafe Maurice nominated is across from the duomo itself and is packed. There are people milling around the entrance and under the archways on either side, eyes alert and doing their best Italian impersonation of queuing.[22] Maurice's aide Rémy is on the middle balcony on the top floor of the building that houses the cafe. He sees me and then disappears behind the white-curtained double doorway.

---

22   Waiting for the first opportunity to rush ahead of everyone else.

'Let's go inside,' I say to Vincent, and he muscles his way through, a head taller and thirty-plus kilograms heavier than anyone else in the vicinity.

As we walk in I see Maurice coming down the stairs at the rear of the cafe with Rémy in tow. He clocks us, directs the briefest of glances to a waiter, and right away this guy cuts to the closest table and moves along the family sitting there drinking macchiatos and hot chocolates. They look puzzled, but the waiter's having none of it and ushers them out the door and starts clearing the table. Then he turns to Maurice and gives him an apologetic bow. By now we're all standing around the table, Vincent with his arms folded, and Maurice looking him up and down, then he sees Bethany and the next thing he does is take her hand and speak to her in Italian, kiss her on both cheeks and then say to the collective, 'Busy time of year for us, my apologies.'

He shakes my hand, then I shake hands with Rémy, and Maurice says, 'Jude, I was so sorry to hear of Bruno's passing,' and Vincent is still standing there looking a bit mean and not speaking, and eventually Maurice looks at him and says, 'Perhaps we should talk upstairs?' Vincent nods, then he's following Maurice back through the restaurant, Rémy right behind them, with no one so much as glancing back, and when I look down Bethany is seated surveying the wine list.

'Not what I was expecting,' I say to no one, and Bethany is pointing at something on the list and the same waiter nods and trots off to the kitchen. Meanwhile, the other ten thousand people who have been waiting for a table look on mystified as another waiter arrives with an ice bucket and a pair of glasses.

'They'll sort it out, Jude, best leave them to it,' Bethany says and then, 'I'm wondering if we can't order something with a sprinkle of truffle...'

I'm having a minor panic attack and take a moment to focus on breathing, but I'm sitting down at least and there's a carafe of water nearby and Bethany reaches across and puts a hand over my knuckles as I fumble for a glass. She pours it for me and says, 'It'll be okay,' and then, 'Of course if we hear gunshots we get the fuck out of here.'

The waiter arrives with the wine, a prosecco from Sorelle Bronca, and Bethany says something to him in Italian, which he regards with some suspicion but eventually he shrugs and nods then opens the bottle.

I figure I'll focus on Bethany for a while to calm me down, on that dress of hers, and with her sandals slipped off it's just that and her underwear while I'm covered in garments, most of them unnecessary.

'Would you call it champagne-coloured, that dress?' I ask.

'I'd call it golden. Why don't you take off your jacket?'

'Because I'm sweating and I'm nervous.'

The first waiter comes back holding a plate the size of a pizza tray, its surface a yellow mess of scrambled eggs. He places it in the middle of the table, then from his apron plucks a white truffle, as big as a golf ball, which he shaves in its entirety, all over the eggs. A sprinkling of salt and he's gone, leaving a dish that now looks as much truffle as egg, and that smells like sex underground.

'Then there's this.' Bethany grins, reaching for cutlery.

'There's definitely this.'

If there's a better way to consume fresh truffle than over scrambled eggs I am yet to experience it. In an hour or so we'll sit down to twelve courses at one of the best restaurants in the world, but for now there is no vista more perfect.

We're close to finishing, a flurry of forks and gasps,[23] when Vincent's hand reaches down from on high and plucks a single leaf-like sliver of truffle from the remains.

---

23   Two nearby tables have subsequently pointed at our plate and ordered the same.

'You two don't fuck around,' he says, licking his fingers. Maurice and Rémy stand behind him; they can only have been upstairs for twenty minutes at most.

'Mind if we join you, Jude?' Maurice asks.

I look with mild alarm in Vincent's direction and he lets out a low chuckle and says, 'It's fine, mate. What, did you think we were going to shoot each other?'

'It's not a fake?'

'Fake as a porn star's tits,' Vincent says. 'That much we established early on.'

'There was some discussion about the – how would you say? – specificity of the bet,' Maurice says. 'Was the bet not for 'the thing'? I asked, 'For precisely the bottle presented?'

'Or was it precisely for a fucking jeroboam of DRC?' Vincent laughs.

Maurice laughs too, and they're starting to look like a couple of old rugby players catching up to commemorate the anniversary of some past glory.

'What's going on then?'

'Jude, it's okay,' says Vincent. 'We sorted it out.'

Then Maurice turns to Rémy who hands me a wooden box, like a half-sized humidor, and Maurice says, 'A small token, Jude, with my apologies for our original wager going awry.'

I open the box and inside is a white truffle as big as a jam jar.

'No hard feelings,' says Maurice.

'My God,' says Bethany, in a tone that's frankly orgasmic.

I turn to Vincent who nods his assent, and I'm thinking this is maybe ten grand worth of truffle, which leaves me some way short of six years rent back in Melbourne. 'Me and Maurie have done a bit of a deal,' says Vincent. 'It revolves around, let's say, importing and exporting. He does a pretty good line in truffles, as you can see, and he's interested in bringing a bit of my saffron into France and Italy.'

Bethany meanwhile has taken the truffle from its box and is stroking it like a newborn, bringing it directly to her cheek to savour its scent. Then she starts whispering at it and I say, 'Beth, please…' and she says, 'I'm going to call him Il Principe.'[24]

'Always with the names for things,' says Vincent.[25]

'Jude,' Maurice now, 'Vincent told me about the restaurant. We wonder if, in addition to those duties, you might consider running our new produce business?'

'Actually, Maurie, just thinking out loud here,' Vincent says. 'How about we throw some wine into the mix? Say a thousand cases a year from my neck of the woods in return for a thousand from yours? You could stick it on the lists at your restaurants, do whatever you want with it.'

'Yes, yes, trés bien,' Maurice agrees, doing, what, a half-million-dollar deal with barely a nod.

Bethany has disappeared to the kitchen. When she returns, she's sliding euro notes into her pocket and clutching a wood-handled stainless steel truffle plane, the very apparatus employed by our waiter earlier. She's also holding Il Principe, mercifully in his box, as though the rest of us can't be trusted alone with him for even a minute.

I'm expecting her to start shaving there and then, but instead she hands me the utensil and replaces the box gently upon the table. Then she folds her hands and smiles angelically.

'I've invited Maurice and Rémy to dinner tonight,' Vincent says. 'Hope that's alright with you two?'

'Of course,' says Bethany, and with that Maurice points at a waiter, and then at our empty plate, and the guy bows and comes to clear it away, signalling that no payment will be necessary. Then we're

---

24   The Prince.
25   Referring to The Big Boy, I guess.

on our feet and heading for the door, as teams of punters swarm our empty table.

'A stroll through the market?' Rémy suggests, and Beth, Vincent and I are gagging to see it, so off we trot in that direction, and in less than a minute we're standing in the main hall.

It costs, apparently, three euros to enter, but Maurice walks in like he's with the band and no one stops us. It looks a bit like a trade show, with stalls selling not just truffles but cheese and hazelnuts and even wine. The truffle vendors wear white gloves and store their wares beneath hinged, transparent plastic domes, and some of them look a bit eccentric, one or two with Akubra-style hats and one guy wearing full army camouflage, ready to fight all of Italy's wars on his own.

In the middle of the space a handful of officials stand before sets of scales, and their job seems to be weighing and ultimately ratifying purchased truffles – a process possessed of some ceremony.

I'm kind of impressed, and Bethany is clearly on the lookout for a truffle to rival our recent acquisition.[26] Vincent looks more interested in the wine, and it seems all the merchants here know Maurice and they regard him in much the same manner as the waiters at what I presume was one of his restaurants.

'It's more for the tourists,' says Maurice.

'Where's the main game then?' Vincent asks, prompting a nervous peep from Rémy.

Maurice waves off his concern. 'Of course, of course. No secrets.' He leads us out the rear of the hall, back onto the street and down a tight, charming alleyway in the direction of the sunset. The street pitches around me woozily, and I presume that's more the jet lag than by design.

Soon we're standing by the side entrance to a church, more of a chapel really, old and humble, built from thin marl bricks, no taller

---

26   A companion maybe.

than a regular suburban house. There's some glasswork, although nothing ornate, your mandatory set of holy stone statues, and a single wooden crucifix atop the crested roof.

There's a guy smoking a cigarette by the door and he acknowledges Maurice – not in the same reverential way as the rest of the town, more collegial. He obviously knows Rémy too, but regards the rest of us with suspicion, particularly Vincent. Once again Maurice flaps a hand, and the guy shrugs and steps to one side as Rémy opens the door.

Bethany enters first, to a kiss on the hand from the guy finishing his smoke, and I actually see her knees buckle slightly as she moves into the church. Two steps later mine do the same, for we have entered the Cathedral of Truffle.

'Jesus God-worshipping Christ,' says Vincent, filling his lungs.

The aroma is exultant. It's suffocating. It casts a rich, invisible mist above the pews and altar, permeating the entire space, warming it.

There are a dozen people inside, all of them men, some resembling Maurice in attire and girth, others more outwardly rural. They're set up throughout the church, with benches laid in the nave and card tables by the choir stalls. One guy has commandeered the pulpit itself. They have plastic containers for their truffles, like in the market, although they are larger and more ramshackle. No one is wearing gloves.

I'm drawn down the central aisle to a guy near the front sitting in one of the pews. He doesn't seem to have a display case at all, but as I draw nearer I see he's holding a large glass jar, the kind of thing you'd see housing lollies in old-fashioned sweetshops, and inside is a truffle maybe three times the size of our Il Principe.

Its owner stands upon my approach and, with a twist, removes the lid from the jar, liberating a scent that is distinct from the prevailing olfactory haze, but undeniably sympathetic. A kind of muscular overlay to a harmony that is already soaring.

'Jude!' Maurice calls out. 'This is the first truffle you address?'

'Wasn't entirely voluntary if I'm honest, Maurice.'

'You climbed to the top. It's the best find of the season so far. Not the biggest, true, but clearly the best. A good sign for your nose!'

I'm trying to get my head around how this thing isn't the largest truffle presently in circulation[27] when I notice Bethany over the other side of the church in the midst of an experience that seems spiritual in nature. She's sitting at one of the pews, head bowed, with a scarf draped, habit-like, around her head. While not perceptibly at prayer, she has adopted the posture of the saint or martyr, the Christ even, as though in submission to something greater.

The men have mostly let her be. I don't know whether this is because women are frequent visitors or, more likely, because they are awed by the novelty.

I head back over to where Vincent is nattering with Maurice and Rémy. As a man with a keen appreciation for quirky, highly specialised spaces,[28] I expect Vincent to be a pig in shit in this setting. Sure enough, he's grinning like a kid with a cinema ice cream, thumping Maurice jovially on the back, and it occurs to me that his excitement will be as much about the commerce here as the sensory experience.

We are standing, after all, in an illegal truffle market. Even now, Rémy reaches into the breast pocket of his jacket and pulls out a tightly folded wad of five-hundred-euro notes that is as thick as a house brick.

So what's that, a hundred thousand euros? Looking around the room with fresh eyes it's plain that every man present has hand in pocket, clutching a similar wad. A million euros, cash, in a tiny

---

27 It's patently bigger than photos I've seen on the internet purporting to show the 'world's biggest ever truffle'.

28 Specifically, his anechoic chamber.

chapel off the main drag in Alba, and maybe five times that value in ready raw truffle.

Rémy departs to join Beth in aromatic communion and I hear Vincent say, 'What's the deal, Maurie? Didn't all just fall off the back of a truck, surely?'

Maurice grapples with the idiom for a moment before getting enough of a handle on it to respond. 'It's the earth, Vincent,' directing a pious gaze towards the chancel,[29] 'it belongs to God alone.' He grins, then Vincent grins, and Maurice says, 'Let's say that as with The Big Boy, provenance can be dubious.'

What's not in doubt is that these are actual white truffles, whereas The Big Boy is not actual pinot noir from Domaine de la Romanée-Conti, so the term 'provenance' is a slap there from Maurice and it seems to land on my cheek alone.

The newly written-down value of The Big Boy in the context of his function as rent guarantor has yet to be canvassed with Vincent, and I'm not sure if Maurice's 'the rent was to be paid by the thing' defence will pass muster in Vincent's court of law. But he hasn't mentioned it yet, and I'm now in his employ in the truffle, saffron and wine business, so maybe things take care of themselves. Or maybe I'm drunk on truffle fumes in a fucking outlaw bazaar in a chapel in Alba.

Beyond that, it's now clear that Rémy is hitting on Bethany, and how I didn't see that coming I have no idea. She's in one of those moods where everything feels like fairy floss and that means the whole world is sweet.

I'm back sitting with those 'what right do I have to feel sick about this?' sensations and I step away from the other guys to

---

29 I know these churchy terms because all my life I've sung in choirs. The chancel is the space around the altar.

take stock. I'm more or less sober[30] so can run some dispassionate self-analysis[31] but none of that works. At least the jet lag's taken a back seat.

Mid-malaise we start walking to the restaurant, Bethany in deep conversation with Rémy, charmed, while Vincent and Maurice have moved beyond flirtation to a kind of macho petting contest where they slap each other's backs and tug one another's arms. I feel like the kid left against the playground wall after the captains have picked teams. Worse than that I feel like I'd pick Bethany, now more than ever, but why would she want to pick me?

Maurice is well known at Piazza Duomo. 'Decent fucking local, mate,' Vincent says as we're shown in and, mercifully, I'm able to shift gears emotionally. There's no such thing as a bad time to sit down to dinner at a three-Michelin-star restaurant, but it's preferable not to arrive ravaged by pathetic, indefensible jealousy.

A bottle of 2002 Krug arrives, the cork is out of that in a flash, and I'm wondering who makes the toast. Maurice takes the initiative and says, 'To Bruno. For bringing us together. May our ventures thrive in his honour.'

That works, and while sipping I notice Bethany has my truffle resting on her thighs and is stroking the case like it's a lapdog. She's next to me, with Rémy on her other side, and Maurice and Vincent completing the amply-spaced circle.

'Should we send Il Principe to the kitchen?' Beth asks.

---

30   There is no wine in here, no smoking (of course), and the atmosphere really is one of cautious congeniality, the kind of vibe you might find in a gymnasium locker room where everyone's taking steroids and they know it's illegal but, hey, we're all having a good time and don't the results speak for themselves?

31   Along the lines of: i) why would I want to control her, even if I could?; ii) she is the opposite of something I could 'possess' and that's one of the reasons I like her so much; and iii) even if she does hook up with him it's 'only sex', and no different from me hooking up with someone myself.

Maurice smiles. 'My dear, no need to fear for a lack of truffle this evening. We have close relations with this place. It's taken care of.'

Both Vincent and Maurice say 'it's taken care of' quite a lot, and I wonder what it must be like to arrive at a point in your life where you're able to saunter around the place taking care of things. I guess I can take care of the wine at a dinner party, or the washing up, but I feel weak in the company of these men and maybe that's my vulnerability taking up arms against the jealousy, in a pitched battle for the state of my mind.

Wine helps. Krug in particular. And by way of further distraction we have been presented with menus,[32] more as a formality, it seems, as Maurice has already taken care of what we'll be eating.

'It's difficult to go past the truffle menu at this time of year,' he says.

You pay a hundred and fifty euros for those six courses, the truffle levied separately by the gram. Maurice has brought his own, and when the scallops are presented a short time later the fine flakes of white delight are as broad as the shells themselves.

I wouldn't expect to get near the wine list with either Vincent or Maurice present, and with both at the table I surrender to a tour of their reckoning, confident it will comprise massive high-alcohol reds.

It's something of a shock, then, when Maurice takes the book, reassuringly gigantic in girth, and hands it across the table to Bethany. 'Maybe you can take care of ordering the wine tonight?'

So now Bethany's taking care of something, and that will mean another bottle of champagne before the resumption of our troubled romance with Italian white wine.[33]

'What tends to be your poison, Vincent?' Rémy asks.

'I'm a bit of a patriot. Love the Aussie stuff, shiraz in particular.'

---

32   At this time of year there is a dedicated truffle menu in addition to the pair of degustation offerings and a full à la carte selection.

33   They've just never really appealed.

'Not so much French wine in your cellar?' from Maurice.

'Bit of champagne, bit of d'Yquem, maybe a few hundred bottles of bordeaux. Not much of a pinot drinker if I'm honest.'

'And what of Italy?' Maurice asks. 'Maybe you've been tickled by a nebbiolo or two?'

'Kicked in the dick more like it, Maurie,' says Vincent, to laughter from everyone but mostly Beth.

'And, Jude, how's it going with your restaurant?'

'Learning on the job,' I say. 'Getting help from people who know what they're doing.'

'It's the only way,' and then, smiling, 'not that Bruno ever listened to another soul about anything.'

'I want to know how you and Bruno met,' from Bethany.

'I owe him a lot,' says Maurice. 'I was living in Paris and came here to Alba as – maybe you would say a vagabond? – really with nothing, and I stumbled into the truffle business. With my first find, a good one, the size of a woman's fist, I return to Paris on the train. No restaurant would touch it. They had their regular suppliers – the business is very incestuous, you know. But Bruno offered me one thousand francs[34] and, more than that, a meal and a bottle of wine. Later he introduced me to some of his friends, people who had small places like Batard Rouge, and from there I built some trust and soon could start selling to the one-star restaurants. And so it continued.'

'Would love to have met him,' says Vincent.

Being given carriage of a wine list for an evening presents a number of challenges, especially when you've only just met some members of your party and you're pretty sure you won't be picking up the bill come night's end. You want to be able express yourself, to expose something of your own wine sensibilities, but avoid obvious 'show-off' wines and those at the very pointy end of the price list.

---

34   Around one hundred and fifty euros.

Bethany circumvents that convention by ordering a Costa Russi Langhe-Barbaresco, from Gaja, at seven hundred euros a bottle.

'Well, why not?' says Maurice, and Vincent deploys both hands to form a kind of protective shield around his genitalia, presumably in deference to the dick-kicking pronouncement from earlier.

And now we are eating venison, served not just with truffle but with foie gras,[35] and the very young barbaresco forms a sheer mesh around my palate, waiting for a fatty breach. It comes, mostly from the sauce, and what's left at the end of that coalescence is just joy. Then you realise you have fresh truffles in your mouth as well.

We're all silent, on similar trips, and I look across to Bethany and she's looking at me too and I think maybe I make this a moment.

---

35   More like a foie gras sauce if we're splitting hairs.

Four days later

That Bethany is still muling Il Principe around Europe is one thing, the fact that she now carries what is left of him wrapped in tissue in her bra, as in directly between her breasts, brings a novel gravitas to his dénouement. If she and I hadn't tumbled into our own moment earlier this week I would probably feel slighted by the affection afforded him.

We are now in Paris. 'Don't write me any poems,' Bethany said in bed last night after dinner at Histoires,[1] and I appreciated the note.

I don't know how to act. The whole show is different once physical intimacy takes the stage. I want to seem strong, tough even, but I'm still just me... only now sometimes naked.

It was only when it happened that I realised how much she was already a part of me. Not her brain, or the way she felt, but her skin. We didn't connect so much as soak, and in that rush I felt her meeting something she'd left. Some confluence of energy. Some kind of homecoming.

When the last drops of her barbaresco were poured at Piazza Duomo she had pointed at the decanter and called for a second bottle.[2] Her presence at that table was such that I thought she must have been given a taller chair than the rest of us, that the pedestal wasn't metaphorical.

Then she started talking me up, telling the guys what a great singer I was, telling them how I'd designed the bag and how I was building the restaurant. Rémy clocked what was going on and slotted graciously into a wingman role.[3]

---

1   The Mathieu Pacaud restaurant.
2   Such a Bethany move.
3   When I thanked him later he looked at me strangely and asked for a translation. Apparently there's not an equivalent term in French.

Around the first dessert it became clear that I didn't love her anymore. That ship sailed. Now I was in love with her.

It was Vincent who slipped me the half-bottle of Taylor's Vintage Port as we were leaving, purchased on the sly as he and Maurice were jostling to pay the bill. Didn't say anything, just snuck it into my jacket pocket.

Everything went perfectly after that. It was cold walking back to the car so I gave Bethany my jacket and the first thing she did was feel out the bottle. Mystery bottles tend to pique her curiosity, but this one stayed in situ without further interrogation.

'I'll leave you to your nightcap,' Vincent said when we made it to the hotel, and then she was in my room and it was like we were on that couch in Adelaide again.

By that point I was submerged, a one-note instrument pitched just for her. Playing underwater. Yet even then, even when it was clear she was holding her breath down there with me, I still thought about putting it off. Delaying it a day, wondering if I could make it more perfect.

She took off her dress. I woke in the morning with unopened wine.

Now we are cosied up at Batard Rouge, Antoine walks in, and either he clocks us holding hands under the table or he can smell Il Principe on Beth, or very possibly both. This elicits an impromptu slapstick routine complete with jaw-drop and double-take. I admire him for resisting the urge to gawk at the truffle down Bethany's top.

'It happened,' I say to him.

'I can see.' He takes a seat beside me, grinning like someone's ordered Cristal.

'Nothing changes,' Bethany says.

Everything has changed. The world looks different, has a different hue, and the overall pace of life has altered, although not in a strictly linear way.[4] Certain moments thicken and persist, while others, whole hours even, dissipate in a flicker.

Batard Rouge looks different too, and when I mention it Antoine says, 'She cleaned the place up.'

He's right. There are fewer boxes of wine stacked around the walls, meaning another table or two can be accommodated, several of the more garish pictures have been taken down, and someone seems to have moved about the place with a dusting implement.

In short, it looks better, as do the plates of food arriving at neighbouring tables. Very much the same menu, only less rustic and more attentively presented. I'm even seeing the occasional garnish which, if we discount shaved truffle, Bruno would never have sanctioned.

I am down to the equivalent of one meal per day, which is standard for me in the fortnight after falling in or out of love. I don't think it's anxiety, although those embers do flare occasionally. Certainly I'm nervous about meeting Annette.

Paris is the worst place in the world to be off your food, especially during white truffle season, but I have been pulling my weight in relation to Il Principe's dignified annihilation. Bethany is eating as much as ever.

I am interrogating the menu when a woman walks in the front door of the restaurant bearing a slender tan leather attaché case and leading, well, an attaché of some kind.

'Fuck, it's a lawyer,' says Antoine through clasped lips, as he stands to greet Annette.

'How can you tell?' asks Bethany.

'Just take a look at the bastard.'

All this necessitates an awkward shuffle to a larger table, and this clumsy dance plays out while introductions are made in

---

4   It's not like time seems to pass faster or slower.

two languages with the lawyer gazing curiously and lengthily at Bethany's cleavage.

He's a ramshackle kind of fellow, with black brogues brought to a high shine, trousers falling someway short of the task typically assigned them and a jacket with room to accommodate an additional human. He carries a scuffed black briefcase, and his tie is so thick it would not look out of place if rolled as a napkin. No business card is proffered, but Annette introduces him as Pedro, a spectacularly odd name for a Frenchman but appropriate for the man now sitting opposite.

It is the first time I have met Annette. She is younger than I expected, perhaps in her late fifties, and wears a shapely, almost structural linen dress of the kind favoured by French women of around that age.

We sit down and Madame produces a single typed page from her case which she hands to Pedro. He looks it over, as though conducting a final review, then places it directly before me.

Bethany leans back in her chair and folds her arms to get a better view of the drama unfolding, and I'm reminded yet again that she's a junkie for excitement.

The document – a letter – is written in French and addressed to me. I scan it before sliding it over to Antoine who mulls over the thing for a full minute.

Annette and Pedro sit in silence, Pedro taking time out to wind the sapphire-encrusted dial of his oversized watch, and I've been transported back to the annual trophy night at high school, where the headmaster used to read out the list of prizes by year level and I tended to be in with a chance when the music awards came around.

Eventually Antoine speaks. 'This says you are free to use the name "Batard Rouge" for your restaurant, you are free to use the recipes and any additional intellectual property associated with the business.'

A pause, prompting Beth to lean in.

'The cheque, however, has been cancelled. Madame regrets that Bruno's estate cannot invest in your restaurant, and she hereby returns any shareholding or equity that may have been assigned to her husband, either legally or constructively. She wishes you all the best in this venture.'

No award for me this year, then, and suddenly I'm in a kind of fright, still and silent and disassociated from what's around me.

I feel like I'm standing on a traffic island, cars rushing everywhere, dozens of lanes crossing and intersecting, and I step out to try to corral it, to slow it down, but it doesn't stop, it speeds up.

'Jude, it's okay.' Bethany places one hand on my forearm and rests the other on my cheek, reminding me gently to breathe.

Oxygen helps, and seconds later I'm back in my body and back in the room. Annette seems concerned and reaches over to fill my water glass.

'Sorry, Jude,' she says. 'It's just too much for me.'

I come to see her properly for the first time. She looks tired. Worn. Yet possessed of a marked and possibly recent resilience. A strength, if not quite an energy.

'Madame,' Bethany begins warmly, 'we shared a lot with your husband. He helped show us how to live. This restaurant is one of the most special places in the world for me and my friends, and we'll honour it in Melbourne. Thank you for that opportunity.'

Then she stands, followed by Antoine, which brings Pedro to his feet, and soon we're smiling and shaking hands, and I put the letter in my jacket pocket, and Antoine says something in French to Annette that is met by a series of earnest nods, and in short order we're out the door of her restaurant.

'Shall we go back in and eat?' Beth asks once Annette and Pedro have disappeared into the lunchtime crowd on rue de Richelieu.

'You guys go,' I say. 'I need to walk for a bit.'

I don't know what I'm going to do. Bruno's money was basically spent, I owe Vincent for all the work on the fit-out, and my credit cards are already presenting symptoms of significant trauma.

I focus on forward motion for now, and for some reason hook left onto rue de Rivoli, the very last Parisian street on which anyone should attempt to calm themselves. It's mostly a rammed thoroughfare chocked with tourists pushing at one another to buy trinkets and postcards, and I'm part of that bustle now, at least until I can cross the Seine.

My first thought is to call Vincent to tell him the news and ask him, I don't know, whether he's happy to keep me as a charity case for another nine months.

I have my phone in my hand, scrolling for his number, when it starts ringing and it's Rob calling me from his office.

'Hey,' I say, now halfway across the Pont Neuf.

'Jude, mate, how's the trip?'

'Highs and lows, Rob, if I'm honest. How are you?'

'Ah, much the same here. Look something's come up that's pretty material and I thought better to let you know right away.'

Rob has his lawyer voice on, always a harbinger of serious news, and I make physiological preparations for a second panic attack, putting some distance between myself and the low stone wall running along the side of the bridge.

'I've got Terry here with me,' Rob says.

It takes me a second to scan through my mind's shuffled deck of names and faces to produce the card bearing the snow-white smile of the improbably tall, impeccably dressed Terry Lee: he of the Bowen Estate Cabernet and million-euro escrow.

'Hey Jude.' Terry's voice through the speakerphone, and I swear I hear wine being poured in the background.

'Are you guys drinking?'

'We're a bottle in, Jude,' Rob says. 'Evening over here,' and then, 'How's Bethany?'

'In love with a truffle,' I say, 'but seriously what the fuck's going on?'

A pause. I can tell they're looking at one another across Rob's desk, maybe even playing rock paper scissors to determine who will announce the next fresh disaster.

'Right.' It's Rob. 'First things first, Terry confirmed this afternoon that the acquirer of your bag design was, indeed, a multinational. In fact, it was the largest luxury goods brands in the world. Moët Hennessy Louis Vuitton.'

'Cool,' is all I can muster.

'Absolutely,' Rob continues, 'but the thing is –'

Terry jumps in here. 'Jude, in the course of shoring up our ownership of the intellectual property we discovered that a functionally identical bag design has been under copyright in Italy for more than ten years. During that time bags have been produced in small quantities, but more or less continuously, by a fellow living in Argentina.'

'Guys, I had no idea…'

'Jude, no one's accusing you of ripping it off,' says Terry. 'It's just a horribly unfortunate coincidence.'

'So… what does it mean?'

'At the end of the day it's not good,' Rob says.

'Jude, we've had to challenge your registration here in Australia on the basis that it's not original and we've succeeded in having it declared null and void. Meanwhile we've acquired the rights from the producer in Italy.'

Best to sit down at this point, I reason, so I pull up a piece of slate at the side of the bridge and press my back and shoulders to the wall, knees curled to my chest.

'Jude, we could fight them on this,' Rob says, 'but I've seen the design and Terry's brought in one of the bags made five years ago and the thing's near-as-dammit identical.'

'So, it's over?'

'We're in breach of contract, Jude. A pretty fundamental breach if I'm honest.'

I didn't even read the contract but it's clear I'm beaten, crushed into composite, and how did I not contemplate this possibility?

'Jude, we don't feel great about this.' It's Terry again. 'We know it's going to sting. And it's not a million euros, but we've arranged something for you – kind of a consolation prize. You're in Paris, I believe?'

'Crying on a bridge.'

'Do you think you can travel to one of our estates in Champagne?'

'Sure.'

'Terrific. Get yourself to Moët in Épernay. Someone will be there to meet you.'

The adults going by are too busy taking photos and pointing at monuments to notice me slumped against the curved stone recess of the bridge. They've seen it all before anyway. Had some version of this themselves at one time or another. It's the children who look. Quick stares through worried eyes. Two boys who look like twins are peeking through identical ice-cream cones, pulled along by hurried parents. I see my brother in their faces, or the brother I know from photographs. I don't feel anything but I want to smile, to let them know it's okay. Only now they're gone, and I can't move the muscles in my face.

The next day

I'm driving to Champagne, alone and hungover.

From the bridge I'd walked for three hours, past Sainte-Chapelle – where you once had to charm a guard to enter but now the queues form at daybreak – across Pont Saint-Michel, in the direction of the Sorbonne.

I was tracking towards the Luxembourg Gardens, beloved from my first trip to Paris yet rarely revisited. I took a photograph back then and pinned it to my desk wall at home. I'd arrived with a baguette and some supermarket cheese and sat on my backside soaking in sunshine. It was August and the sky seemed a special shade of blue. Different from Australia, a deeper hue. I remember the contrast in colour between the flowers in the garden beds. The reds were most vivid. Seeping almost, both the poppies and the peonies. The climbing roses, in many tones, were art on the run. It was a form of incursion, as though my brain had been called on to recalibrate its colour memory.

Or maybe it's the photograph I remember, rather than the potted moment. Like a wine label snapped at the end of dinner and stored on a phone. The image becomes the thing.

But yesterday the sky was grey and I decided to skip the gardens, buy more booze, and head back to Batard Rouge for dinner.

I was around the corner and so ended up digging around for a bottle at La Dernière Goutte in the 6th. Browsing for wine is among the least destructive of my soothing strategies.

I'm also a sucker for symbolism, and today is very likely the end of something, so what better than the Petit Chablis Franc de Pied L'Inextinct, from Louis and Catherine Poitout.

It's a crazy old wine. One of the few[1] in France drawn from pre-phylloxera vines. The block is only half a hectare in size, and apparently the vines survived by virtue of their high water content and sheer glorious enormity. Only about a thousand bottles are made each year, and I trudged down rue Bonaparte clutching one of them.

Batard Rouge is not technically a BYO establishment[2] but by the time I arrived news of Annette's decision to *annuler mon chéque* had clearly been disseminated and I was met with sympathy, a deft hand and a corkscrew. I was hungry by then, so settled on steak tartare followed by an actual steak.

I was there, but not really, as the food arrived, trying to focus on the glass in front of me to combat my tumble into this new abyss.

I'd never tried anything from the Poitouts before, nor been known to sing the praises of petit chablis while hanging from chandeliers of significant size.

It smelled bright. In fact, its brightness was ridiculous, almost comical. Add to that an extraordinarily pleasing colour, a comforting colour, and early impressions were heartening. Even initially it was a wine in two parts. Fresh and radiant, for sure, but with something lurking beneath or behind. A kind of weight, but one that rises in the mouth.

Not long after my first refill I decided to introduce another variable by taking myself and my glass into the Paris night to smoke a cigarette.

Nicotine is brutal on wine. Its effect on our senses is a standalone reason not to smoke at all (if additions to that long list are necessary), and the mild disorientation[3] experienced by occasional

---

1   Others include Bollinger's Vieilles Vignes Françaises and Henry Marionnet's Provignage Romorantin.

2   It is actually not at all a BYO establishment.

3   Head spins.

smokers surely fouls our neural pathways as well. It is actually horrific. Yet also sometimes necessary.

I don't know if it was the smoking that did it,[4] but the wine grew gentler and I convinced myself that what remained would benefit from some time in a decanter.

Music was playing at Batard Rouge, and I didn't remember hearing that before. It's low and ambient, piano, probably Bach, and surely this is something introduced post Bruno's death.

The wine continued to shift in the decanter, softening, moderating. A blending of layers and a redistribution of weight. Dimensions merging.

I don't know if the decision to self-destruct is ever taken consciously, but a third of the way into my second bottle[5] I was on that trajectory. Only I wasn't capable of conscious movement, not even downward. I felt like one of those walls Hayden and I had been hoofing our boots into back in Melbourne.

Bruno's cheque. The Big Boy. The bag money. A trinity of fortune gone. Annulled, counterfeit, and non-existent. What in the fuck? It was easy to turn to wine and, having turned, to slip and, having slipped, to slide, down, down, down. To wreck things. On my way I remembered Bethany, and in a more sober moment may have reasoned that she alone ought to square the ledger. That the rest didn't matter. But when you're falling, when material is being smashed, you tell yourself you don't deserve any of it. Not even those things you've tried to hide away. You convince yourself that at some point you will break them too. Because that's what you do.

---

4   I would describe the L'Inextinct as a high- performing 'cigarette wine'.
5   A châteauneuf-du-pape from Clos des Papes.

I ended up at Nico's chatting with a girl from Barcelona, and I'm pretty sure I tried to kiss her after I walked her to a taxi on what I guess was rue Saint-Honoré.

Then I couldn't figure out how to open the hotel room door, and Bethany had to get up to let me in, and it was 6am and she was naked and went to hug me, and over the stench of cigarettes and self-hatred came the smell of the Spanish girl's perfume.

I tried on some excuse, and it's not like she was angry, but I saw that look, even through her early-morning fog. It was shock more than disappointment, like 'why would he do that now?' then she turned around and was back in bed by the time I'd kicked off my shoes.

Four hours later I woke to sunshine and a hangover of exquisite brutality. I remembered something about needing to go to Champagne. Bethany was gone. Not 'gone, gone', just gone out. Leaving a note that read 'I'm here.'

Now I am driving through Reims, where I know they have a grand cathedral almost as famous as the one I have never visited in Cologne. I've spent a lot of the drive on the phone, talking to the Crew back in Melbourne and picking through the rubble of the past couple of weeks. It's been masochistic.

Erica called, having spoken with Adrian, and she knows more about the bag thing than me, having seen pictures of what we might now call the original.

'It's hilarious in a way, Jude,' she said. 'It really is close to identical. Someone had the exact same idea. I'm surprised they don't think you ripped it off.'

'Erica…'

'No one actually thinks that, babe. Just a bitch of a coincidence.'

I called Heidi after that and she listened as I told the story, made a series of noises, all of them supportive, then asked about Bethany.

'That part's real.'

'Not the worst year ever, then.'

'No.'

Hayden hadn't heard any news and launched into a monologue on restaurant progress before I could edge in and tell him we were fucked.

'Don't pay anyone,' I said, 'and see if you can return those dining chairs.'

'We're almost ready over here – I just painted the dunnies. By the way, how's Beth?'

'Let me call you later. I need champagne.'

The gates out the front of Moët & Chandon don't look like the kind that are always left open, and there are no other cars in the driveway. This would ordinarily see me park in the street, but I'm in no mood for pleasantries so I tuck the rented Peugeot by a flowerbed, just metres from the door.

I have my bag with me, and I wrap the strap over my shoulders in defiant ceremony. There's a woman wearing a suit standing at the entrance. Perhaps it's the hangover, or that I'm staring into the sun to meet her gaze, but she looks like a Gallic hybrid of my mother and my high school music teacher, which is not entirely disagreeable.

'Jude,' she says, offering her hand. 'Je suis Camille. Please, come in.'

I've had neither the emotional energy nor the time to properly prepare for my first visit to Champagne. Standing here now I don't even recall much of the drive over, but as pilgrimages go it's significant, and following Camille into the building I am smacked by the history of the place. By its hum. I almost want to sing a note in accompaniment.

Camille, meanwhile, has the aura of a woman with a knack for delivering bad news, and I wonder if she's the one they send to growers to tell them their crop hasn't made the cut that year.

'I know some of the story,' she says. 'I was told a few of the particulars.'

'It's been an adventure.'

'It brought you here.'

'I would have come anyway, in time. I'd hoped the occasion would be more celebratory.'

'Champagne isn't just for celebrating.' She smiles. 'We never made a heavy investment in that concept around here.'

'Is it all you drink?'

'A wine from Burgundy occasionally, rarely a red. Champagne is enough.'

She stops in an archway and now the vibrations come heavier still.

'I'll take you down to our cave,' says Camille, and I'm thinking there's probably a case of Dom in this for me, but hardly worth the drive, what with everything smouldering.

I am in Champagne, though, on something resembling a private tour of the Moët & Chandon cellar, and that really should feel more like things coming together than falling apart. I resolve to steel myself towards gratitude over contempt, at least in the presence of my French mother/teacher, who is clearly doing all she can, knowing only some of the story.

'That's the bag?' Camille asks, both of us in the archway, facing one another. It's calm and noiseless but for the pulses and throbs thrown by the bones of this place, of this business that's spent close to three centuries making the same thing over and over, doing a damn decent job of perfecting it.

I hand the bag to her, heavy with the weight of my stuff. She turns it over, inspects the stitching, opens the clasp, looks inside.

'It's nice, Jude. A compartment for everything.'

'That was my thinking.'

'Might have been strange if we made ten thousand of these, no? Tourists lining up for them at Louis Vuitton on the Champs-Élysées?'

'I had imagined it.'

'Now it's just for you.' Then, handing it back to me, 'Do you know what bags symbolise in dreams? Responsibility. Your burden. The things you carry.' Then, nothing. Just silence, her gaze. Smiling, but only with her eyes. 'Also, Jude, you need to brush your teeth. And from someone working in a winery this is serious advice.' Now she smiles with the rest of her face, and she's short some enamel like all of them but a long way from dissolved.

Down the stairs now, Camille leading the way, and soon we're in the tunnels, nearly thirty kilometres of them in total if I remember correctly. Camille tells me the oldest dates back to 1743. This one is impeccably lit, the racks bathed in half-light from below, the domed white chalkstone roof glowing rough atop flawless walls of bottles.

'I wonder what you're expecting?' says Camille.

I take a moment to situate the question. 'From this walk through your cellar?'

'Yes.' She grins. 'Your gift.'

She stops at a stout wrought-iron door. The room inside is darkened and full of wooden boxes. Camille unlocks the door and says, 'It's in there.'

'Where in there?'

'Everything in there, Jude. That's your wine.'

Now she turns on the light and there are boxes everywhere, many of them old, and all bearing the insignia of Moët, Dom Pérignon, Ruinart and Veuve Clicquot.

I pick an older-looking box and open it, and there's wood shavings protecting six immaculate bottles of Ruinart Prestige Cuvée 1979.

'Picked for you this morning,' says Camille. 'None of them have ever left this cellar.'

I'm stroking the boxes, patting them, taking it in.

'I've not seen anything like it,' she says. 'I guess they felt pretty bad.'

I open another box and it's 1990 Dom Pérignon.

'Are they all aged?' I ask.

'A mix of everything. Old and new, from all our houses. Fifty dozen bottles in total.'

Being close to so much champagne is exhilarating. And different from the walk through the tunnels in that the wine there seemed oceanlike. An impossible, undrinkable sea. The wine in this room is different. It is to be consumed. Not hurriedly, but fondly. Over many years.

I want to open all the boxes, which Camille can sense, and maybe she's concerned for her afternoon, schedule-wise, so she hands me a hefty sealed envelope and says, 'I've written everything down for you here.'

I take it from her, touch a box or two more, souveniring a handful of wood shavings from the open Ruinart crate before joining Camille back in the corridor.

'We'll courier them. Anywhere in the world. But perhaps you'll take one bottle for now?'

In the cave she selects a single wooden box and hands it to me. It is Krug, from the year of my birth.

Camille doesn't bother to lock the door as we set off back through the tunnel, and her stride is brisker than before. My steps are slower; I touch a bottle or two, inhabiting the space. She's maybe five metres in front of me when I stop and ask her who chose the bottles for me.

'I wonder why you ask?'

'What an assignment. To pick from all your reserves, and seemingly with few limitations.'

'Since you bring it up, Jude, I chose them myself.' She sets off again, slower this time. 'They're the ones that are special to me.'

The next evening

Bethany didn't ask about the champagne, on account of her being pissed with me, so I didn't volunteer it. Vincent may not even have noticed I'd taken off for the day as he had pulled an all-nighter with Maurice and Rémy that, while not running to fifty cases of champagne, sounded like a *Boys' Own* adventure on a rich man's dime.

'Mate, we did some damage. Mostly pinot but serious gear.'

We are flying back to Melbourne. Vincent told us in the taxi to the airport that he'd used airline points to get me and Beth upgraded to business class. I was in bad shape, that much was obvious, and Bethany had said little since my return to the hotel.

She did tell me she was angry and hurt, that she couldn't care less about the Spanish girl, but that she'd thought we were in this together now, and why did I habitually meltdown in these kinds of moments? And anyway wasn't life mostly still fairly rosy, and why the fuck do I seem to sabotage the things I love? Actually, she'd said a few things.

'Not sure I can do it,' says Vincent now as the flight attendant offers him a glass of champagne. He does, though, and so do me and Bethany. I'm seated between them, wondering how long it'll be until Beth raises her privacy screen.

This is the first glass of champagne I've had since being in France and I guess it's non-vintage Clicquot or similar, so nothing of any rare distinction, but it is unnervingly cold and smacked with a sweetness that I attribute less to the wine and more to my palate and brain craving calorie nutrients. No one suggests a toast.

Vincent will say something eventually, I figure, but when I turn to him his eyes are already closed and his enormous fingers clasp his glass at the summit of his gut. He is gone, and you have to admire the man. To push yourself to the point where your literal last effort is exhausted by a solitary sip of champagne, then to collapse into the long ride home.

'How's Il Principe?' I ask Bethany.

'Let's not talk about bullshit, Jude. If you want to say something, say it.'

'I went on a bender. I'm sorry.'

'Stop saying sorry. Stop vandalising things and then apologising.'

'I'm –'

'You're what? What are you, Jude?'

'A bit broken.'

'Do you know what you actually are?'

'An idiot?'

'No,' then a softening of voice. 'You're not an idiot.'

'What, then?'

'I want you to see it for yourself. To see that you're enough.'

'Enough of what?'

'You're enough, Jude. You. Are. Enough. I'm enough. This is all we get.'

'I'm not, though.'

'You say that because you think feeling weak means something's missing. So you try to fill it in like a trench at the end of a war. Or worse, you just deny it. Or you take the things you love and turn them into lists.'

'How are you supposed to choose wine without a list?'

Sometimes conversations end unexpectedly, and this is one of those times.

We're up in the air, the plane thrumming and the windows rattling in a way that only feels normal after maybe a hundred incident-free flights. Vincent is still asleep and they've not bothered to detach his glass, as is surely airline policy, or maybe entreaties were made without success.

There are three cashews to sixteen pretzels in the snack bag I've been given. I make this point to Bethany knowing her anger at this will be greater even than mine, and that this will bring us closer. It works, eliciting a tirade against pretzels, the ferocity of which I was not anticipating.

She wants wine now but doesn't want to look at a list, even the miniature aeroplane one, so just tilts her head back and says the word 'chardonnay'. We are flying with an airline where this call to action is sufficient.

Bethany has stacked her pretzels and wants mine to complete a tower that shows fledgling architectural promise.

'If you could only drink chardonnay from one region for the rest of your life what do you choose?' she asks.

'Australian region, I assume?'

'Ya.'

'Probably Yarra Valley. Give it twenty years and it's Tasmania.'

'Does New Zealand count?'

'Not sure it does, Beth.'

'A lot of good chardys around from small-producing regions. Could absolutely drink a lot of Giaconda. A lot of By Farr.'

'Mornington?'

'Not this duck.'

'Adelaide Hills is on the small side too, in terms of range.'

She's finished her glass, the flight attendant is refilling, and I didn't even notice what she's drinking. She sees me again, though, which is progress.

'I lost a day or two,' I say. 'Did Antoine go back to Spain?'

'He's coming to Melbourne.'

'What?'

'Wants to help with the restaurant.'

'Beth...'

'We all want to.'

'I need to take stock. I don't even know if it's possible anymore.'

'It's a fucking restaurant, Jude, not a skyscraper. It's possible.'

'I was thinking I could sell my wine.'

'You're gonna need to do something.'

Hayden called again this morning to confirm he had ignored my instructions to stop work. Builders were waiting to be paid, light fittings hadn't gone in, there was the matter of connecting with suppliers for produce and the final touches on the wine list. 'Otherwise we're in business,' he'd said.

In addition to Bruno's napkin scrawlings, our operational blueprint comprised two documents delivered by Adrian early in the construction process:

1. A photocopied handwritten to-do list on how to open a restaurant. More than eight pages long, it's been added to and edited many times over the years, presumably coincident to the establishment of each of Adrian's new operations. It's really a series of action items, although possessed of no discernible pattern or order. For example, 'connect electricity' comes in at item number 108, and is entered in different handwriting, suggesting it didn't warrant mention on the original list. Written at the top of the first page is: DO NOT OPEN RESTAURANT UNTIL EVERY GODDAMN ITEM IS TICKED OFF.

2. A spreadsheet, containing a profit and loss statement that Adrian calls a 'business plan'. This is your standard income and expenses breakdown, where you can approximate the latter, but the former is akin to plucking numbers from thin air. No one ever opened a restaurant where the P&L showed a loss, yet the vast majority of restaurants fail, so this thing is presumably massaged habitually.

I'd spent a lot of time tinkering with this plan, wishfully modelling scenarios based on anywhere between twenty and sixty covers per evening. But how much on average will they spend on wine? How much does bread cost? Do we even open for lunch? I had a template from one of Adrian's restaurants he'd deemed similar, but that place only lasted six months.[1]

Beyond that, the spreadsheet was misleading, or at least not entirely fit for purpose, in that my deal with Vincent specified a rent-free period of between three and six years, subject to the manoeuvrings of The Big Boy. That arrangement is now in question, if not shot entirely to pieces. And it showed us making money. Like they all do.

The to-do list was helpful. Hayden and I had taped it to the wall by the entrance to the kitchen and chipped away at the bastard thing, crossing off each item in turn.

Often you'd be drawing a line through one task and then notice another you had already completed. Those 'free lines' were satisfying, although not more than ticking off the genuinely big-ticket items like selecting cutlery and installing wine fridges.

I kept overall carriage of the list but on site it was mostly Hayden wielding the biro. Adrian had come in every few days, usually adding items rather than removing them, and Erica was handling a lot of the wine stuff so that Hayden could work with me and the builders.

Hayden had taken photos of the list and texted them to me before our flight took off. We're down to around twenty things still to cross off, the most annoying ones of course. Sitting here now, though, I'm looking at tasks that between us we could probably knock off in a fortnight. There are still a few slots open on the wine list and a vast array of candidates lying in wait.

I'm contemplating riesling options when Bethany turns her head and says, 'So how much are you in the hole?'

---

1   Maybe there were issues with the electricity.

'What have I spent? Personally?'

'Including the travel and all the other shit.'

'It's credit cards, a loan from Vincent, a little bit of cash I had myself… I owe eighty grand to the builders.'

'So how much in total?'

'Around two twenty.'

'And for that you have a nearly finished restaurant. And some trips to Europe.'

'Super glad I didn't buy that toucan.'

'Toucan ownership is a big responsibility.'

'Turns out they're extremely demanding birds. Anyway, in the end we actually spent less on the fit-out than we planned. Hayden helped. You all helped. I still owe everyone money, though, Beth. And I'm penniless.'

'You have a job at least. Working for your new mates.'

Vincent stirs, his glass of champagne still propped on his stomach. In one motion he wrests it from gut to mouth, draining it like a thimble of water.

'Jesus, I needed that,' he says, either of the drink or the nap. Then, grinning, shaking his head, 'Shit, hey. What a trip.'

Here again he's ambiguous, but it's the first smile I've seen in ages and I'll take it.

'Judey,' Vincent says, 'I was just dreaming about you. Dreaming about the restaurant.'

'Dream is right, tracking towards nightmare.'

'Keep the faith, mate.'

His glass is refilled with champagne, Bethany and I are both now drinking chardonnay, and all three of us are snacking on pretzels in the absence of actual food.

'That reminds me,' says Vincent, reaching into a pocket and pulling out an envelope, 'this is for you.'

He tosses it over, almost knocking the glass out my hand. I open it and it's filled with five-hundred-euro notes.

'What's that?' I ask.

'That's fifty thousand euros. Had a call from Adrian yesterday, said you might be in need of an investor or two given recent events. He walked me through a model he uses for some of his places that have shared ownership. Made sense to me so I mentioned it to Maurice.'

'Maurice?'

'Anyway, he had some cash on him at the time and was happy enough to toss it into the mix.'

'Right.'

'Bit of a joint venture type thing we've got going on now, Jude, if that's okay. Details to be finalised.'

'Fifty grand takes care of a detail or two, no?' says Beth.

'I want this to work, Jude,' says Vincent. 'Want it to be a place I can come myself a few times a week. I like the wine list idea too.'

'And Maurice?'

'Maurice gets it. Maurice was mates with Bruno; he's at Batard Rouge all the time. He won't miss the money.'

Bethany rests her hand on my forearm.

'Just one thing, mate.' Vincent points at the envelope. 'You'll need to carry that into the country. Got myself into a bit of bother in the past with this kind of thing.'

No doubt.

'Also what was that about a toucan? I know a guy.'

Three weeks later

If there's truth in wine it is probably temporal. Wine is about time. Moments and millennia. In the mouth, in the bottle, and in the ground.

At Kay Brothers, in McLaren Vale, they keep a diary describing goings-on in the vineyard and winery. The first entry is from February 1891, when the land was purchased, and a new entry has been made every day since. Another will be made today. Mostly they're about the weather or about new plantings or bottlings, and the thrill of it is turning to some random date, say eighty years ago, and realising things don't change very much. Vines are pruned, there is frost, fences are repaired, budburst begins. A natural cycle. A flow.

It's also true that wine can resonate deeply with place. That's the thing in Burgundy, and when you see that narrow band of gently sloping hillside the correlation makes sense. The diary at Kay's speaks to place as well, but more than anything it speaks to time.

If you read it with a glass of wine in your hand, something else happens. You flick through days and months, while in your mouth there are moments. The wine moving through you and around you comes from that place, out the window, from berries on a vine that has lived in dirt for more than one hundred and thirty years.

It's best to do it with the Block 6 Shiraz, which is a product of their very oldest vines. In its own way it plays tricks with time, revealing itself not so slowly as barolo, but on a track uncommon in Australian wines. Tannins assemble hours after decanting, the framework of the wine forming lushly and late. If you knocked off the bottle in minutes at a dinner party with friends you'd miss almost all of the show.

The temporal mix gets better still when drinking old wine. Then you add time in the bottle. To open a fifty-year-old wine from ancient vines in soil that is itself tens of millions of years old. To smell it, to breathe it, in an exchange that lasts just seconds. To absorb it, fully, over minutes. What a trip.

Hayden called me to say he wanted to be the sommelier at Batard Rouge. The conversation lasted ninety seconds but had been in the bottle for fifteen years. Of course I wanted him to do it. I hadn't asked him because I thought he already had a job and wouldn't want to work with me anyway. Meanwhile, he was thinking I was looking for someone with a stronger résumé.

He said he had twenty grand to chip in for equity and that Heidi had found another twenty and could they pool that together for one unit? This was the first I'd heard of units or any form of share structure but I was nervous and, more than anything, glad he wanted to be the sommelier, so I said, sure let's do it, we can iron out the details later. Then I called Heidi to ask what the fuck was going on and she said, sorry, yes, Adrian had led a discussion the day before where that model had been proposed.

In my experience this sort of thing is best scrutinised over food and wine, and I suggested that to Heidi who said it had already been arranged.

There are only three or four things left on the restaurant's to-do list and one of them is a test run of the full menu in circumstances simulating actual service: orders coming thick and fast, and the kitchen needing to function harmoniously or at least not mess up too obviously.

In the past week I've tried every dish on the menu. Our chef is cocky but can take suggestions and, in some instances, direction. The fact that he's worked previously with most of the kitchen team looks like a significant asset. They all seem to get along back there, obviously relishing the fact that they have their privacy and are not exposed to the dining room, as is commonplace in restaurants right now.

What an act of savagery inflicted upon kitchen staff to have their sanctuary laid bare. Who even knew what a restaurant kitchen looked like until twenty years ago? Maybe in Paris or Lyon you would be invited back for a peek after dinner and they'd stop shouting at each other for long enough to nod in your direction, but even that was a rarity.

Anyway, we couldn't afford to build an open kitchen so the team remain gratefully behind swinging doors and out of earshot, at least when music is playing in the dining room.

It is noiseless now as I clatter in through the rear to find Bethany setting a table for nine.

'Thought you were at your mum's,' I say.

'I got bored. And excited. Wanted to set everything up.'

She uses the strap of my bag to pull me close and kisses me like she's not in a hurry.

The place looks like a proper restaurant, although there are boxes stacked here and there as well as piles of papers related to suppliers, equipment and staff. Most of the paintings we bought have been hung on the whiter-than-white walls, and they're bright and playful and add warmth to a space that needed it.

The lighting isn't perfect. Compromise was necessary, and maybe we can splurge on some table lamps once we start to turn a profit. Perhaps we'll be able to afford fresh flowers occasionally too.

I'm happy with the floorboards. They are oiled rather than polished and seem soft instead of shiny. I'm excited to see what they'll look like when stained with splotches of wine.

There's a small bar in the corner that Hayden and I helped put together and the shelves are mostly stocked, although not quite, and on the main counter I notice The Big Boy himself, perched with immoderate pride, still covered in lipstick marks from his debut in Paris.

'What's that doing here?' I ask.

'Vincent brought him in. Said something about serendipity.'

'Sick bastard.'

'Did you bring a bottle?'

'It's out the back.'

The wine list is lurching towards completion, although the current version is a mess of red pen and there are four or five spots up for grabs. I've chopped and changed maniacally this past week and it's getting settled tonight, I guarantee it.

'Do you still love it?' asks Bethany. 'Your list?'

'Never more. The pain now is a kind of gratification. Tonight I brought nebbiolo, which is controversial.'

'Can't please everyone.'

'It's not even about pleasing people. I want something definite, something with symmetry.'

'Help me set up the stemware?'

Bethany is drinking a beer, and the smell of onions frying in the kitchen moves me to join her.

'You're a double-act with everything now?' It's Rob, pushing open the door with his boot on account of an archive box held in both arms and a bottle of what looks like Tyrrell's Semillon tucked under an armpit.

'We're setting a fucking table together, Rob,' from Beth.

'I was wondering when you'd turn up,' I say to the semillon rather than Rob. 'Are there more bottles in the box?'

'Jude, there are more than five hundred bottles of wine in this building. We're good for wine, for tonight at least. This box is about the future.'

'If it's your last will and testament I want your burgundy,' says Bethany.

'Actually I should write a will,' says Rob.

'It's shareholder stuff?' I ask.

'More than that,' he says haughtily. 'It's everything.'

'All of it?' Beth asks.

'Draft form, for everyone's approval, but you have your company constitution, shareholder's agreement, a series of explanatory spreadsheets and documents pertaining to the overall structure, Jude's share buyback agreement, and a few other bits and pieces that are a little more esoteric. As a package it is a thing of not insignificant legal beauty.'

He starts unpacking, placing bundles of documents between the fork and knife of each setting. A kind of sadist's placemat. Together they sit as thick as a wine cork fallen on its side.

'These explanatory documents...' I say.

'Mate, don't stress. I know it looks like a lot but there's an elegance to it. Even ran it by Terry.'

'Terry?'

'He wanted to come in for ten grand but I told him we were fully subscribed.'

Hayden walks in with Heidi right behind him. Hayden committed to reconditioning his spare room in anticipation of more regular visits, and she'll be staying at his place. Heidi has two bottles wrapped in foil, while Hayden is carrying a Bass Phillip Estate Pinot Noir, which has been near the front of my mind since the beginning. Certainly there needs to be something of the Phillip Jones legacy on this list, although that's a pronouncement I've been making about a lot of producers lately.

Vincent has also arrived, likely through the back door although it wouldn't surprise me if there's some other entrance to this building for which he alone has a key. Possibly subterranean. He sees me looking at his brace of bottles and says, 'One of these is from Maurie.'

'Has Maurice ever even tried an Australian wine?' asks Bethany.

'I asked him that in Paris. He said he once drank a pinot from Washington State on an aeroplane. Said it as though that might almost count.'

Vincent's hands are so huge I can't properly make out what he's holding but it's a reasonable bet it's shiraz. On the plane ride back from Paris, in a drunken attempt at humour, I suggested that he should open his own restaurant, serving only this varietal. The menu would lean towards red meat, not even beer would be available for purchase, and even water consumption would be limited so as not to dilute the potency of the wine. 'I like it,' he said, stroking his chin, 'although you'd have to rip out the cold water taps in the bathrooms. Like they used to do in nightclubs.'

Erica rolls in now, pulling Antoine along, with Adrian clutching bottles at the rear. It is clear by their stagger that they have come from lunch, and it is Friday so that equates to a lunch of some gravity. Antoine in particular looks dazed and wears a curious glow, hopefully a product of jet lag more than alcohol poisoning. Erica wears a faux fur jacket, buttoned up, over pleated high-waist jeans. She looks like a stylist on their night off.

'My absolute loves!' she squeals, and when we are her loves rather than her bitches it's a sign she's yet to hit the calvados (or anything stronger than muscat).

'Where did you get that beer?' asks Adrian.

'I need time to assimilate,' says Antoine. 'And some bread.'

Before that I need to squeeze the man and ask him about his grilling at the hands of his university superiors in Spain.

'It was a skewering,' says Antoine, as I release him from my embrace. 'From the Dean and the executives from Bodegas Torres. Then they patted me on the back and told me not to do it again.'

'And then…' prompts Erica, who has heard the story at lunch.

'Then the wine guys present me with a case of their shittiest fucking wine!'

'It's genius,' says Rob. 'If they give you something decent[1] it's to try to change your mind. Give you something awful and it's so you know your place.'

Hayden and Bethany are seated, looking through Rob's pile of documents. This piques the interest of the rest of the crew who drop into chairs and come to order, most holding cans of lager. Heidi has opened her bottles and pours them side by side.

Tonight isn't meant to resemble a formal tasting – I don't know what it's meant to resemble – but everyone knows the list needs to be locked down and that this is the last opportunity to make a stand for a particular wine.

'We're storytelling again?' asks Adrian.

'Maybe we let wines speak for themselves,' says Heidi.

'Having come this far…' says Rob.

Definitely chardonnay, says everyone, as glasses are raised. Antoine offers 'cool climate' of the first sip and 'yum' of the second. Our curiosity is quickly killed by the revelation that they are Eileen Hardy and Yabby Lake Single Vineyard, respectively.

The Eileen Hardy tastes like a cure. I'm desperate for more Tasmanian representation on the list and this blend is mostly Tassie with a smattering of fruit from the Yarra Valley and possibly elsewhere. Beyond that I'm loving what's in the glass right now, and this is a wine we used to buy at auction for eleven bucks a bottle back when all the fruit was from Padthaway.

The Yabby Lake would need to bump something of consequence off the list to find a place but it's a class act, the price point is sharp,[2] and it would be nice to have something else from the Mornington Peninsula.

Regionality is as much a challenge as juggling varietals. I'm not populating the senate here, nor is this an exercise in affirmative

---

1   For the conglomerate produces many fine wines.
2   Which we badly need.

action, but ground must be given in the name of even-handedness. If the Yabby Lake makes it then Mornington has a chardonnay, and very likely a pinot with the imminent inclusion of the Main Ridge I noticed under Adrian's arm a few minutes earlier. Surely that's about right?[3]

'Wait!' says Antoine urgently. 'I forgot about my blend!'

The crisis is no more desperate than convention around serving order, although I agree that by rights he might have pulled the cork out of his Sorrenberg first. He is drunk, however, and in no position to focus on much other than the act of extraction itself.

The Crew are doing me a lot of favours here, recognising holes or discrepancies on the list and advocating wines to fix my failings. The Sorrenberg Semillon Sauvignon Blanc ticks around five boxes, one of which is marked biodynamic. It's also the only white blend in consideration.[4]

Adrian is running plates tonight, unprompted, as although we are putting the kitchen through their paces we didn't think to ask any front-of-house staff in to assist.

First course is our take on foie gras, although I'm not sure we should call it that given the whole 'tubes stuck down the necks of geese' imagery it tends to illicit. Pâté sounds a bit 1970s swingers party, even if that's what we mostly call it in Australia. As at Batard Rouge Paris we are serving it in a slab, accompanied by toast and a few greens, and I'm thinking about adding a piece of fig when they're in season.

Foie gras works best for me as a standalone brunch, accompanied by a bottle of sauternes,[5] on the kind of day in Paris where you're

---

3 As surely as many will argue that the Yarra Valley is over-represented at the Peninsula's expense.

4 Which we absolutely need given our tendency in Australia to vinously mix and match.

5 Possibly a throwback to the Grosset botrytised dessert wine and bacon and eggs of Clare Valley Gourmet Weekends past.

likely to skip lunch on account of a serious dinner reservation later on. I've never had the mettle to order sauternes with an entrée, so have usually reverted to champagne as an accompaniment. The Sorrenberg is a fine match, though, with enough acid to chisel a trough in the fat and enough fruit to fill it. Antoine thinks it's a winner too and uses the word 'dimensionality', which I'll allow, with a warning.

'It really does taste like sauvignon blanc,' says Erica.

'Had a good run there for a while as a varietal,' says Rob.[6]

While the sauvignon blanc traits come through in an initial burst, over time the semillon cavalry rolls in. It's a remarkable transformation, and Hayden says he'll ask punters what they're looking for in the wine and if they say semillon he'll decant it.

No one has said anything about Rob's mounds of documents, although they have been rearranged to accommodate plates and additional stemware for what looks like a Cullen Kevin John Chardonnay.[7]

'Can we run through the thrust of this paperwork?' I ask, and it's Adrian who answers.

'Jude, we want this to work. And with your recent change in fortunes we're offering to make Batard Rouge Melbourne a partnership.'

'Guys, that's great but what's lost here is that I don't have any money, like none at all – I'm actually a couple of hundred grand in the hole.'

'We figured on that, mate.' Vincent now. 'You'll need to clear your debts, but under Adrian's plan you'll be a shareholder here without needing to stump up any cash.'

'Where's the money coming from then?'

---

6   The guy who averaged a carton of Cloudy Bay Sauvignon Blanc per month for three summers straight.

7   Being opened and poured by Bethany.

'From us,' says Heidi.

I shake my head.

'Jude, if you turn to page three of the explanatory memorandum…'
Rob holds up a document and we shuffle our papers.[8]

'Nothing for free here, Jude,' from Adrian. 'Cash is cash in this
game and to get your shares you'll be sacrificing salary.'

Dinner has gone from raucous to congressional in the space of a
scallop. It is a lot to take in, and I don't know what I was expecting.
A job maybe, at best? Working for a wage? To be somehow bailed
out and for the show to go on, but for Vincent and Maurice to
end up owning the thing? Speaking of which, Rob mentioned an
employment contract, so I fish that out of the pile. It's double-
stapled in deference to its weight.

The money is fine,[9] and turning to the 'list of responsibilities'
section I note I'm to spend half my time on the restaurant floor and
half on administrative stuff for an overall forty-hour working week.
Written in there is a 'release' permitting me to work another twenty
hours for Maurice and Vincent. Adrian clocks my baffled evaluation
of the sum of these numbers, puts an arm around my shoulder in an
avuncular way and says, 'That's hospitality, mate.'

The food now is a medley of the menu, starting with the
entrées. Around the table is steak tartare, our scallop dish,[10] plates
of asparagus served with sous vide eggs, and two serves of French
onion soup. Forks are flying, snatching for this and that.

I had wanted rudely yellow yolks for the top of our tartare,
but I'm yet to find the eggs for the job. They have them in Japan,
probably a product of what they feed their chickens, and maybe I
can convince Vincent and Maurice that shipping in Japanese farm

---

8   See Appendix 2.
9   More than I have earned for any job, in fact, though we remain at village
     level gazing longingly at 1er Cru.
10   Poached in white wine then placed in their shell atop a mushroom purée.

eggs to supplement their product line-up makes sense beyond the aesthetic qualities of my steak tartare. The yolk in front of me now is deep lemon in colour, straw almost, and I hold up my glass of Kevin John to find their hues nearly identical.

I'm half a glass in before I realise that Cullen, too, grow biody-namically. It's unusual to have two Australian wines in a row born of that same philosophy. The Kevin John is an expensive wine, and would sit at the top end of a chardonnay list that I know will be criticised for being overly safe. But it's just like the Moss Wood Cabernet. You never regret buying it and it's impossible to recall a bottle that wasn't a pleasure.

'Jude?' Rob taps his glass. 'You with us buddy?'

'Hey, yeah. The eggs –'

'Bethany just described you as a functional romantic,' says Erica. 'Let's work on the functional part?'

'I'm good,' I reply, looking over at Beth who tilts her chin towards me and grins. 'So. We own it together?'

'We own it together,' says Rob, 'with an enterprise value of four hundred thousand dollars; all the set-up expenses covered; enough cash in the bank for a year's worth of working capital; and a three-year lease signed on favourable terms.'

'Opened that door for me at least,' I say to The Big Boy, roosting on the bar. 'Even if you're just a doorstop now.'

'That's enough cash?' asks Hayden.

'Gets us to the gate,' says Adrian. 'There are easier ways to make money than running restaurants.'

Vincent now, grinning, 'Always said I needed to lose a bit of coin in the restaurant game before losing serious money in a winery.'

'Back to our glasses,' says Rob, which by now are filled with Tyrrell's Vat 1 Semillon.

'Icon,' says Heidi.

'Never really understood it,' from Beth.

'Jude, is Rockford Semillon locked in?' asks Hayden.

'The Rockford isn't going anywhere.'

'Two wines from the same winery' – Erica now – 'on a list that's only a page long and that you want to be definitive?'

She's referring to the non-negotiable inclusion of the Basket Press Shiraz.

'Rockford's my favourite winery. Besides, the Basket Press doesn't even really count.'

'There's the small matter of supply,' says Erica. 'Each of us here only gets six bottles a year – we'll be doing well to get a few cases in total for the restaurant.'

'When it's gone, it's gone,' I say. 'Needs to be on the list.'

'Back to the Vat 1 then?' suggests Antoine.

'Honestly, how do you fit two semillons on a one-page list?' Adrian now.

'Has to be two,' says Hayden, 'and I'll be pushing hard for the Sorrenberg blend as well. Varietal semillon is one of our only truly original contributions to the world of wine, and Vat 1 is the shining star. Should be a lock.'

'Needs to be served less cold than this,' says Antoine. Probably all the wines tonight have been on the chilly side, which is a challenge for restaurants generally.[11]

The Vat 1 in my glass now looks fifty parts water, one part olive oil, and smells like it's hiding behind something. A perfect lemon maybe. Depending on when you try it and what you're eating, it becomes either more water or more wine-oil. It is reminiscent of swallowing honeysuckle as a kid.

'Is it wetter than most wines?' asks Rob.

'Yes,' says Antoine.

This goes unchallenged.

---

11   A sommelier once offered to position a bottle of white wine 'nearby' an ice
      bucket, after I was overly prescriptive about temperature.

Adrian and Hayden have conspired to pour their pinot noirs. The Main Ridge is from 2015 and so was made by the winery's founder Nat White prior to handing over the operation to new custodians. Maybe a decade ago we were tasting at their cellar door and Adrian's then-wife fell in love with the place. 'Fine,' he'd said to her. 'One day we'll buy it.'

When it came on the market years later, and with his marriage hanging by a stem, he asked his still-just wife if she wanted it. She didn't. He pushed on unperturbed and tried to organise a syndicate to make an offer.

On the 'standing on the terrace in the late afternoon with a glass of wine' scale, I rate Main Ridge second only to Coriole, with Samuel's Gorge mounting a strong case in third.

'Crunchy,' says Antoine,[12] who is sliding over the edge.

I've moved to the Bass Phillip as plates of food accumulate, and it is the duck that's hit hardest in the early onslaught for reasons obvious to those with pinot in their glasses.

We're going to do different things with vegetables here, keeping them simple and seasonal and offering them as substantial sides rather than wannabe mains. Adrian is against it – 'You can't charge seventeen bucks for a bowl of fucking beans'– but I'm determined to have a go at doing precisely that. French-style, always fresh, always changing, usually with a shit-ton of butter.

A couple of years ago Hayden called me excitedly mid-week to say there was a 1996 vs 1999 DRC dinner that night, that two spots had come up at half price, and that he in turn would pay for half my ticket. Only five hundred dollars, then, but a bargain in the end.

Daryl Somers was there, with a budget that extended well and truly to the part of Burgundy where the rubber hits the asphalt, and so was Phillip Jones.[13] I sat next to him and spent much of the night

---

12   Of the Main Ridge.
13   Of Bass Phillip.

looking at his tasting notes. It was disheartening in a lot of ways, like hearing one of the greats sing your part in the Requiem. By the time the marron came out, I realised that I would never possess anything approaching that level of knowledge. Worse still, I would never possess the sensory skills, the instinct, the romance, the zealous and authentic vocabulary. The overall sense of really getting it.

When faced with an existential crisis of this magnitude it is helpful to have a ready crutch, and thankfully at that moment I had six generous glasses of DRC.[14]

Now I am eating steak and there are two new glasses in front of me, one hosting my Jasper Hill Nebbiolo and the other a Mount Mary Quintet Cabernet Blend. Another pricey wine, the Quintet, especially with the Moss Wood already locked in, and it's a good thing the Bowen Estate is there at the top of the cabernet list for those who thought they'd walked into a bistro rather than a rich guy's cellar.

There will be a place for Yarra Yering on this list and there needs to be a place for Mount Mary as well. I had the Triolet[15] shortlisted, but Antoine's Sorrenberg fills that slot ably, leaving me well placed to add the red blend.

'Gorgeous with food,' says Rob of the Quintet.

It's a wine I've tried only a handful of times, usually with some formality, either at a tasting or earnestly beside another cabernet. Certainly never with steak frites and mushrooms. Too often, revered wines are put on a pedestal rather than a dinner table.

---

14   The only thing that cast a shadow was the revelation late in the evening that the hosts had mixed bottles of the same wine into a decanter prior to serving. So both bottles of '99 Échézeaux lumped together in a magnum decanter and served 'so everybody gets the same wine'. Many months on, I was yet to make peace with that. I should have asked Phillip what he thought.

15   A Bordeaux-inspired white blend of sauvignon blanc, semillon and muscadelle.

Meanwhile, everybody loves Jasper Hill but there's no consensus on which cuvee should make the list, or indeed on whether a nebbiolo should feature at all. Beyond that there are strong views on other Australian nebs that may lay claim to inclusion.

'You put Steve Pannell's on there and you win twice,' says Antoine. 'You get your nebbiolo, and a winemaker that needs to be represented.'

'Then what from Jasper Hill?'

'Shiraz or semillon,' Adrian answers.

'Fiano,' says Antoine.

'Don't get me started on fucking Fiano…'

'Strange to have a fiano and not a nebbiolo,' says Heidi.

'Stranger still to have Jasper Hill's fiano and not their nebbiolo.'

This isn't getting any easier, and around the room I see that acknowledged. Everyone is looking at me.

'So, Jude. Do you want this?' Bethany now.

'I'm putting it to the group,' I reply, 'I know I want the Jasper Hill to –'

'Not the nebbiolo,' she says softly. 'This. That we do this together.'

'With you at the helm,' says Heidi.

'Well…'

'It's not a trick question, Jude. And it's not a trap.' Heidi again.

'Or a charity,' adds Erica.

'I wanted to make the list,' I say. 'And to do something with Bruno.'

'Been a wilder ride than that,' says Rob.

'It's been… unexpected. Like a tasting where every bottle's corked but you leave drunk anyway, wondering what the fuck happened.'

'Yet here we are,' says Adrian. 'Ready for the next bottle.'

'Let's open it,' I say.

'Let's open two,' says Vincent.

Antoine stands and raises a glass, then we all do. Rob's documents are suitably wine-stained by now, marking our consent to the arrangement.

I'm pretty sure Vincent understood the symbolism behind the whole 'opening a bottle' thing, but he has opened two and one of them isn't straight varietal shiraz. To be fair The Signature by Yalumba does contain shiraz, but it is predominantly cabernet sauvignon and entirely worthy of inclusion in any conversation about great and iconic Australian wines.

'Gotta have a claret on your list,' says Vincent.[16]

'How are we only realising this now?' asks Erica.

'Another blend,' says Hayden.

'It's important,' says Antoine.

'Geez, it tastes like cabernet,' I say to Vincent. 'Are you coping?'

'Brick red to look at,' he says, holding his glass to the tablecloth. 'Almost thick.'

Australian cabernet can have a lifted quality, seeming to permeate unfamiliar parts of the nose. Maybe it's those menthol or eucalypt traits, maybe it really does waft or draw in a manner that's almost gaseous. Either way it is intoxicating, and despite the steadying presence of shiraz, The Signature is potent and exhilarating.

'Old-school,' says Vincent.

I'm eating duck confit now, and with food the Yalumba blend develops a certain hotness, probably from the alcohol. Vincent's second bottle is Luke Lambert Syrah. Another entry from the Yarra Valley, but I could do with more cool climate offerings, and this is seriously cool booze.

Antoine is brooding over his glass in a manner that is sullen even by his standards. Is it disappointment? What does that even

---

16   Even though the term more accurately refers to bordeaux varietals alone, we
      have adopted it in Australia to describe our, well, signature blend of shiraz
      and cabernet sauvignon.

mean in the context of wine? I throw a cork at him and he actually catches it, then says, 'We're approaching the end.'

'Dessert will follow.'

'The list.'

'Yeah, thank Christ.'

'That's not what I mean. For you it's a love letter. For me it's more like saying goodbye.'

'What, to us?' My voice rises and cracks. 'Antoine's breaking up with us!'

'No, no… this crew I'll love forever.'

'What then?'

'To old-fashioned wine. And it's not about what we've drunk tonight. It's just… me.'

'You think you can get by on natural wine alone?' Rob.

'You're fucking crazy.' Adrian.

'I'd describe at least two of the wines we've had tonight as natural.' Hayden.

'Guys, let's not even start this.'

'I'll always reminisce,' Antoine says, 'and often revisit. Wine is not like cake – we don't run out of slices. Our choices can be fluid.'

'And you're choosing differently?'

'More and more.'

'Maybe we let him BYO?' Hayden suggests.

'As long as it's Australian,' says Rob.

'Agreed,' I say. 'In fact, let's toast it.'

'Got any champagne, Beth?' giggles Erica, now nursing her coat and sporting a linen shirt that is somehow vastly whiter than the tablecloth and napkins.

She's told them. Or at least one of them. It's just the lunch crowd grinning, and they look at me now like something has changed. They are warm looks, though. Reassuring.

Some of the others glance up from their plates for a moment before returning to their conversations. Antoine looks happy to have the heat taken off him for a while.

Last week I gave all my champagne to Bethany. It's still on the water, but I took the birth-year Krug from Camille around to her place and we drank that, then I handed her the list of all the bottles I'd been given and told her I loved her and that I wanted her to have them.

As we drank the Krug, I tried to explain the gesture and how it would help me make sense of things. Beth said she'd love to make a ritual out of drinking champagne together, and toasted us.

'To be enjoyed in a series of moments,' she said.

'To sparkling.'

The Krug was as crowded and complex as you would hope. A hundred things happening at once.

The table now is a mess of plates and leftovers and glasses more full than empty. It's raucous. Everyone bubbling in the froth of the now. Heidi is chatting with Erica and I know from their gestures, from the way their eyes meet, that they're talking about something other than wine.

Bethany gets up and goes behind the bar. I've been floating from one conversation to the next and no one's paying attention to either of us. She takes The Big Boy by the neck and shoots me a look that's serious and piercing. The kind you'd expect during sex, not fondling counterfeit wine. I smile, laugh even. Her eyes widen, like it's a game. I'm fixed in her gaze.

Fuck. She's opening it. The bottle's mostly out of sight but I can see the capsule in her hand and a corkscrew at work. Now it really feels like sex or, more specifically, sex in public. It turns. It's released. She takes it in her hand.

Never has a jeroboam labelled DRC been opened in full view with fewer people giving less of a fuck. It's a lesson in perception and in how things change. When he was real everyone cared. Bethany opening that bottle would have been grand ceremony. Now she's just a drunk girl pouring bin juice in a corner by herself.

I love that it's our joke to share, and to add to the ceremony I get a tray of fresh glasses. Bethany's pouring some of the wine into a decanter, holding The Big Boy in both hands. She stops at what looks like a bottle's worth, enough for everyone to try. What's her next move here? Present it as a mystery wine or make it known we're off to the races with The Big Boy?

She takes the cork back to the table, and it's huge as you would expect – even from here I can see the name of the domaine printed towards the top. She hands it to Adrian on her left. He takes delivery like they're passing drugs in a nightclub, fiddles with it for a while, curiosity aroused, then places it on the table in front of him.

Erica notices next, which makes four of us now not speaking, then Heidi, and in seconds those over the other side of the table stand and stare. Vincent looks the most shocked,[17] and then everyone clocks the fresh stems in front of them.

'We drink it?' asks Adrian.

'Fuck all to lose at this point,' says Vincent.

'It's going to suck balls,' says Hayden. 'Do we know when it was made?'

'The domaine reckons recently.' Vince says. 'Last fifteen years or so is when most forgeries happened. Cork looks in suspiciously good nick too.'

Bethany is filling glasses from the decanter, we're all gawking at the wine, and the look on Antoine's face reminds me of the time we had dinner at the restaurant Bones in Paris and they served us pork cutlet cooked rare.

'What do we think it's going to taste like?' asks Heidi.

---

17   Wearing an expression that might translate as 'that's my fucking bottle of wine'.

'Let's hope the forger knew what they were doing,' Vincent says, 'and that they took their time.'

'Let's drink it,' says Hayden.

'Wait,' says Bethany, as hands reach for stems, 'I want to toast Jude.'

'We could toast him with something better than this, Beth…'

'No. The journey's in the glass. No matter what it tastes like. Here's to you, Jude.'

'Something smells funny,' says Antoine.

'Dude, we're having a moment.' Hayden clips him on the shoulder.

'Wait!' Antoine's on his feet, grave and sober. A cowboy ready at dawn. 'Please. Nobody taste this yet. Something's happening.'

'Is it poisoned?' asks Rob.

'Shut your mouth, Robert. This aroma… Bethany, the bottle was opened when?'

'Ahhh, five minutes ago.'

'Vincent, how sure are we this bottle is fake?'

'Absolutely, unequivocally one hundred per cent sure.'

'Based on your conversation with Aubert de Villaine?'

'Based on a bit more than that.'

'I must know because what I'm smelling here… at this point I don't have words.'

'Yeah, I wasn't going to mention it, but I sent The Big Boy off to Switzerland for caesium-137 benchmarking.'

'You fucking what?'

'Bit complicated to explain,' says Vincent, 'especially right now.'

'You're gonna need to.'

'Basically there's this isotope that wasn't in nature until the Yanks dropped those bombs in World War II. So if there's no caesium-137 in a wine you can be sure it was made prior to 1945.'

'Not to state the obvious, Vincent,' says Adrian, 'but this is meant to be from 1978.'

'Turns out there have been a couple of other events that made a mark. One in particular in Chernobyl in 1986.'

'I'm calling bullshit,' says Erica.

'Deadset. They got The Big Boy into the lab and checked him for it.'

'What, they opened him?'

'Nah, they can figure it out through the glass. Pretty crazy actually. Anyhow at least some of what's in there is post-Chernobyl. So it's utterly, completely counterfeit. Not even up for discussion.'

'Then what's going on here?' I ask.

'And when can we taste it?'

'I just did,' says Antoine, 'and I want to propose another toast. To Bruno, and to all you beautiful bastards.' Is he crying? 'To whatever's in my glass. To adventures in wine.'

I feel like I'm hallucinating. The others sip, but I want to take a moment with the aroma and try to find a foothold. This is fake wine. That ought to be the foothold. A microclimate has settled around this table, though, and it is very real. Isolated, but multisensory. Freakish weather conditions.

There's a vaporous aura surrounding the blast zone of this wine, maybe inspired by Vincent's talk of isotopes. It's like a glowing halo. Like the yellow hue that rings the apostles in oil-renderings of Christ's Last Supper. All from a wine that is bloodier in its redness than any I have seen before.

What's crazy is that right now the nose seems dark and closed. In the olfactory haze that's seen Antoine depart earth for realms more celestial, the fact is this wine has yet to open up.

I realise now I've drunk some. Not consciously, not deliberately, but sure enough it's happened. And what it feels like is reverberation.

The moment after the clash of cymbals. But it's not an echo. That resonance is what it is.

It starts again, arcing and probing. The length of this wine, the persistence. Meat and mineral. Every kind of berry. There's a clarity, though, a precision that is utterly counterintuitive. It's like being able to see through clouds.

'So what's happening here?' Rob says. 'Someone invented a chemical that emulates perfection in wine?'

'It just can't be,' Antoine says to nobody.

'It's everything,' says Heidi.

'Whatever it is, it's in its window,' says Vincent, and most of us laugh.

It does have an apex quality, though. Surely it could never be more than this? Surely it can only descend, gently, from this summit.

For now it lasts and it changes. And it has joined us at the table. We're coming to the end of our glasses and we're drunk. But not as though consummating a night of serious drinking. More like babies on their mother's breast.

Bethany
Earlier that day[1]

I got a croissant at Loafer in Fitzroy North and thought I may as well walk to Matteo's[2], where Vincent was meeting me for lunch. Probably didn't need the croissant. Just hard to walk past knowing it's sitting right there. I'm in shoes that are sensible to the point of sporty, and I took the longer route through the gardens because it's Friday and the sum of my non-sex exercise so far this week is zero.

Some of the others were going to Scopri for lunch[3] but I excused myself. More important business to attend to, kicking off with Vincent at the restaurant. Walking in, I was surprised to see him drinking a glass of wine that wasn't red in colour.

'Someone play a trick on you?'

'G'day Beth. Nah, Matteo sent it out. Ice-cold Leo Buring Leonay Riesling. Pretty fucking decent actually.'

As instructed, Vince had brought along The Big Boy on the premise that he should serve as the mascot for tonight's dinner. Jesus, this bottle... you could put it in a gallery. If we could convince some hot modern artist to say it was their creation[4] we could probably get rich selling it.

That's a scam for a different day, though, and I signalled for a glass of riesling myself before going through a motion or two with Vincent, stuff about the restaurant and the documents Rob had

---

1   At which time Bethany lets the cork out of the bottle.
2   Much loved Fitzroy North restaurant.
3   Not Jude unfortunately. I'd tried to sell him on it to give me a longer window at the restaurant, but he was too stressed.
4   Forged wine and all.

drafted, possible learnings from past hospitality operations, all that kind of bullshit.

Even the smartest of men, the straightest of straight shooters, can be led gently down the path of one's choosing by nothing more that the attentive cultivation of their ego. No manipulative intention on my part, at least not in this instance, just a desire to be done with lunch and into the serious work of the day.

I had insisted that Vincent not bring a bottle,[5] telling him I'd grab something from my own collection and that I'd need to get back to work afterwards. Jude is the only one who knows I quit my job on Wednesday. I'll tell the others when I'm ready.

'What are we drinking, Beth?' he asked, as we made easy work of the riesling.

'A li'l something I've wanted to share with you since we met.'

We were sitting at the front of the restaurant, by the window, and they have a ledge there which is perfect for bottles and decanters. Nowadays it's used for mobile phones, and in Vincent's case keys, wallet, sunglasses, one of those pens where you can click to choose between four colours of ink, and a set of old-school headphones.[6]

Anyway, our waiter brought the wine over in a decanter and had the good grace to bring the bottle as well so Vincent could see it was Noon Eclipse.[7] This elicited a low frown and a pursing of lips – a 'well, fuck me' kind of look.

'That's actually a bit of a coincidence,' he said.

'What do you mean?'

'Ah, doesn't matter. It's a wine I serve to guests from time to time. I'll show you some day.'

---

5   Other than The Big Boy.

6   Maybe it's the restaurant setting, but they're like two soup bowls resting on threadbare cushions, joined by a bent barbell. They could fit around my waist and preserve modesty in the process.

7   Mostly grenache, with a little bit of shiraz and graciano.

We drank it, and at eight years old it was in exactly the right zone. Still all muscles and grip but with its jagged edges mostly mellowed. 'Frank Bruno, late career,' Vincent said. 'The boxer.'

'How long does it take the average male to acquire a working knowledge of all the world's sports and pastimes?' I asked, more out of curiosity than irony.

'That stuff's mostly in the bank by the time you're twelve or thirteen,' he said. 'Probably earlier now with the internet and cable TV. You never stop learning, though. I had the guys from my band over to watch the curling last night.'

I went with two entrées, in deference to tonight's dinner, and had begun on my veal when Vincent said, 'I heard you came into some champagne recently.'

'In a manner of speaking, Vincent.'

'He's a funny bugger. Gives away the only thing he's left with.'

'He'll be alright.'

'How do you reckon he's going to go with all of us climbing on board?'

'He'll see it as a favour.' I'm timing my responses to fit between mouthfuls.

'I'm worried it's a hijacking.'

'He's different to you, Vince. You see dots to be joined and you join them. It's instinct. It's how you measure success. Jude, he just... he sees dots. He might reach out and grab one occasionally or step back and admire them, but no one gave him that pen. It's actually quite beautiful.'

'He's gonna see some penmanship tonight... more than two hundred pages.'

'Just one page he cares about, though.'

Vincent swung back on his seat, making a tour of the restaurant with his huge hazelnut eyes. 'You know, the day I met Jude I invested thirty million in a property development deal in West Melbourne.

Worked out recently that since then I've spent around thirty hours on that and more than five hundred hours on this restaurant.'

'Wait till you compare the returns, though.'

Laughter from Vincent. 'You're funny fucks, the lot of you.'

'We do okay.'

'Yeah, you do. I sometimes wonder if anything bad ever happened to any of you.'

'All of us carry our shit. We're just not very good at talking about it.'

After lunch, it was briefly back to my place to collect supplies and then to Batard Rouge, with a full two hours up my sleeve before Jude or any of the kitchen staff were likely to appear to start prepping for dinner.

At the restaurant, behind the bar, I laid everything out:

1. The Big Boy.
2. An assortment of corkscrews, a butler's friend,[8] and a Swiss Army knife.
3. Two Riedel magnum decanters.
4. An empty and thoroughly cleaned double magnum of 1990 Yalumba Menzies Cabernet Sauvignon.[9]
5. A steel wine funnel and strainer.
6. Several long-handled brushes, one retractable.

---

8   A kind of corkscrew with two thin prongs that slide down the neck of the bottle allowing the cork to be extracted without damage, also known as an Ah-So.

9   From an earlier dinner.

7. Three used jeroboam corks from burgundy bottles in reasonable condition, painstakingly procured.
8. Maybe thirty pieces of capsule,[10] in various states of decay and in various shades of red.
9. A soldering iron.
10. An actual regular-sized 750 ml bottle of 1978 Domaine de la Romanée-Conti, Romanée-Conti.

We buy most of our French stuff from either Jeremy and Heidi at d'Or to Door in the Barossa Valley or Darren at Grand Millesime in Yarraville. Jeremy was the one who came through with the DRC. Specifics were not discussed, but the provenance was assured. He was willing to trade it for something like a third of the champagne gifted to me by Jude.

When we were drinking the Krug the other night, Jude told me about the woman from Moët who presented him with all the wine. As I agitate the capsule off the neck of The Big Boy I wonder what she'd make of all of this. Or Isabelle and Nadya. I reckon they'd be into it.

This capsule has come off without a fight, so no need for items seven through nine on the inventory. Through the neck I can see the cork looks in good condition too. Let's get that bastard out then. Might as well try the butler's friend first.

Once again it's a breeze, practically gliding out. I guess that's what you get when you buy fake wine. Holding the cork up to the light it makes the best possible impression of being genuine. Maybe the cork and the bottle are real? Anyway, for present purposes this guy can go straight back in once the rest of my business has been attended to.

Okay, let's liberate some juice... Out it flows, into one decanter then the next, pouring ruby red, looking bright under the light and

---

10   The protective foil sleeve on the neck of the bottle.

smelling like fruit, even from here. The Big Boy is heavy, even more to hold and pour than to lug around, and I splash a bit on the bench in the process.

The bottle is a bit of a worry. It's way more transparent than I was expecting, and I'm wondering how I'll be able to disguise that given it'll be sitting on the bar three-quarters empty for most of the night.

But when you've seen a thing a hundred times and you've no reason to believe it'll be any different the hundred and first time, how closely do you look at it anyway? Also, the bottle is pretty much covered in lipstick and glitter and other crap, and you'd need to be right next to it to find a space to see through. I'll keep the bar lighting low and use my powers of misdirection.

I've spent a good part of the day thinking about the right moment to taste the counterfeit wine myself. I'd settled on waiting until the end of dinner and trying it with everyone else[11] but I'm half-dregging right now so I pull a stem from the rack and pour myself a decent-sized glass from one of the decanters.

Actually, I don't mind it. Definitely pinot and absolutely the bastard child of something. Sign of a good forgery, I guess.

Think about how most counterfeit bottles are opened... you've got this thing notionally worth thousands of dollars and a bunch of rich dudes all sweating on whether or not it's going to be fucked. Everyone wants to believe it's good, that it's worth the money or worthy of the occasion. That it's not a failure and that they're not diminished by having served it.

So if you're a forger you make something that toes that line. Give it a bit of the old Burgundy barnyard but also some freshness, and these guys think they've hit the jackpot and found a perfectly preserved bottle.

---

11   My plan being to pour it at some point; I mean, why not?

I'm reaching for a second glass when I realise I'm not yet half done here. Head back in the game. I pour the counterfeit wine from the decanters into the empty Menzies bottle. Might as well use one of these spare corks even though I reckon this wine would probably benefit from a few hours getting to know itself. I stash it under the bar out of sight. Right. Time to clean the interior of The Big Boy. There's a decent amount of jootz[12] and crud resting around the base of the bottle. I bring a kettle almost to the boil and pour in a litre or so of water to see how far that gets us.

Most of the way it turns out, and with a few careful turns of a cleaning brush the inside of The Big Boy is sparkling and practically sterilised. While he drains and dries, I turn my attention to what is by far the trickiest task.

It only occurred to me this morning that the legitimate bottle of DRC could itself be shot and actually worse than the forgery.

Let's open it and see. The bottle itself looks its age; the fill is around the shoulder as you'd expect. I cut the capsule and inspect the top of the cork. No ullage, everything looks in good shape. I'm drawn to my favourite corkscrew to get this next job done.

I guess I've been drunk during the act of opening most of the wine bottles I have attended to in my life, but I have always been good at it. Most of the Crew will hand difficult-looking bottles to me,[13] especially late in the evening.

Jude is surprisingly shit at it, although he is the best at salvaging corks that are dead to rights, like when someone has yanked half of it out with a waiter's friend, and the rest is hanging by a sodden thread, millimetres from sliding into the body of the bottle. He has a variety of tools in his arsenal, some unconventional.

He also taught me that old hospo trick of holding a just-opened bottle with bits of cork floating in it over a sink and tapping it

---

12   What we call the sediment at the bottom of old bottles of wine.
13   Or Antoine, it's true.

aggressively on its neck. You lose a tiny quantity of wine but usually those cork fragments fly out with it.

Oh, I've just pulled it instinctively. And there she is: a perfectly extracted DRC cork propped on my corkscrew, its base moist and crimson and its sides firm. Huh. Reflex memory. Anyway, it's out! Now let's have a tiny taste.

Bringing it to my nose is an affirmation. Not just of the quality of the wine, but of the inherent goodness in all things in the universe. It's flowers, but they're pressed. Hmmm, not pressed so much as stepped on, barefoot. Stems soon to stretch straight, petals to turn again towards the sun.

I'm not even going to try it. I'll take my share tonight with everyone else, knowing that I'll very likely get my tits blown off. I feel like it needs some time to open up, but it would be a travesty to see it edge over the cliff. I'll stick to my original plan and decant it now into the newly cleaned Big Boy.

There's a tiny amount of sediment, but not so much, as the wine has been travelling and only standing up at my place for a couple of days. Plus, it's Romanée-Conti sediment. Maybe I'll have it on toast in the morning.

The cork needs some gentle persuasion but soon sits snugly enough. I cut away a small section of the capsule before sliding it back over the neck. That's definitely fake. It's been scuffed up a bit to give the impression of age but the foil is in far too good a state. I give it a cursory solder in the end, if only because I had to line up at a hardware store to buy that thing.

I put The Big Boy up on the bar and take a few steps back into the dining room to see how the level looks. It's not great. But having him on display is a part of the ruse and everyone will be drinking or drunk and anyway what am I going to do at this point?

Wine wankers would hate the idea of drinking a bottle like this so late in the evening, but I think it's perfect. It has to come at the end. When the busy work is done and when we've toasted the restaurant and drunk to its success.

Do I tell them what they're drinking? Not right away. Not until they're under its spell and fussing and pontificating and roaring and in raptures. Not until it's in their mouths and through their bodies and with some amount still in their glasses. Not until then.

Appendix 1. Bag Design Diagrammatic

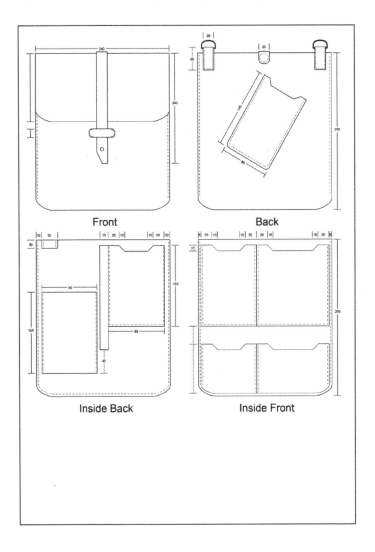

Front

Back

Inside Back

Inside Front

Appendix 2. Batard Rouge Melbourne Shareholding and Structure (Overview)

Table of Shareholders

Name	Amount	Shares	Comment
Vincent	(120,000)	3,000	In lieu of two years' market rent
Maurice	80,000	2,000	Cash (50K euros)
Hayden	20,000	500	Cash
Heidi	20,000	500	Cash
Adrian	(5,000)	125	In kind. Consultant.
Rob	(5,000)	125	In kind. Consultant and all legal.
Erica	(5,000)	125	In kind. Consultant, accounting services, and board member.
Antoine	40,000	1,000	Cash
Bethany	25,000	625	Cash
Jude	(80,000)	2,000	Carry / In kind / Earn out
	(310,000)	(10,000)	

Notes
- Proprietary Limited company with 10,000 shares.
- For voting purposes, 1000 shares equal one unit. Bethany, Adrian, Erica and Rob combine for a unit. Antoine has one unit. (Mechanics are spelled out in the Shareholders' Agreement.)
- Board comprises four directors: Jude, Vincent, Heidi and Erica.
- Jude's employment agreement outlines the decisions he can take himself, as General Manager, as well as the other elements of his package.
- Jude receives carry for sweat equity and for brokering the concept (per Shareholders' Agreement). Needs to 'earn out' the rest of his shares.
- Rob, Adrian and Erica receive their shareholding in lieu of in-kind contributions: Rob and Adrian handle legal and accounting work; Erica sits on the board and assists with suppliers.

Appendix 3
Batard Rouge Melbourne Wine List

House of Arras Grand Vintage
Domaine Chandon Blanc de Blancs
Primo Estate JOSEPH Sparkling Red

Grosset Polish Hill Riesling
Leo Buring Leonay Riesling

Mayer Chardonnay
Hardys Eileen Hardy Chardonnay
Yabby Lake Single Vineyard Chardonnay
Cullen Kevin John Chardonnay

Tscharke Girl Talk Savagnin
Sorrenberg Semillon Sauvignon Blanc
Rockford Semillon
Tyrrell's Vat 1 Semillon

Coriole Sangiovese Rosé
Ochota Barrels The Price of Silence Gamay

Mac Forbes Yarra Valley Pinot Noir
Ashton Hills Estate Pinot Noir
Main Ridge Estate The Acre Pinot Noir
Bass Phillip Premium Pinot Noir

Bowen Estate Cabernet Sauvignon
Moss Wood Cabernet Sauvignon
Mount Mary Quintet

Luke Lambert Syrah
Clonakilla Shiraz Viognier
Mount Langi Ghiran Shiraz
Rockford Basket Press Shiraz
Kay Brothers Block 6 Shiraz
Penfolds Grange

Wirra Wirra Church Block Cabernet Shiraz Merlot
Yalumba The Signature Cabernet Shiraz
Samuel's Gorge Grenache
Noon Eclipse Grenache Shiraz
Jasper Hill Nebbiolo
Charles Melton Nine Popes Grenache Shiraz Mourvédre (Magnum)

De Bortoli Noble One Botrytis Semillon

Yarra Yering Potsorts

Index